THE CASE OF THE ELUSIVE
BOMBAY DUCK

Also by Tarquin Hall

The Vish Puri mysteries

THE CASE OF THE MISSING SERVANT
THE CASE OF THE MAN WHO DIED LAUGHING
THE CASE OF THE DEADLY BUTTER CHICKEN
THE CASE OF THE LOVE COMMANDOS
THE DELHI DETECTIVE'S HANDBOOK:
VISH PURI'S GUIDE TO OPERATING AS A PRIVATE
INVESTIGATOR IN INDIA
THE CASE OF THE REINCARNATED CLIENT *

* available from Severn House

THE CASE
OF THE ELUSIVE
BOMBAY DUCK

Tarquin Hall

**SEVERN
HOUSE**

First world edition published in Great Britain and the USA in 2025
by Severn House, an imprint of Canongate Books Ltd,
14 High Street, Edinburgh EH1 1TE.

severnhouse.com

British Library Cataloguing-in-Publication Data
A CIP catalogue record for this title is available from the British Library.

ISBN-13: 978-0-7278-8922-5 (cased)
ISBN-13: 978-1-4483-0820-0 (e-book)

All Severn House titles are printed on acid-free paper.

Typeset by Palimpsest Book Production Ltd.,
Falkirk, Stirlingshire, Scotland.
Printed and bound in Great Britain by TJ Books,
Padstow, Cornwall.

Praise for the Vish Puri mysteries

"These books are little gems. They are beautifully written, amusing, and intensely readable"
Alexander McCall Smith

"Hilarious . . . Filled with engaging twists"
Booklist Starred Review of
The Case of the Reincarnated Client

"Lively, amusing . . . Hall creates delightful characters and provides illuminating glimpses of contemporary Indian life"
Publishers Weekly on *The Case of the Reincarnated Client*

"Humor is mixed with skilful plotting"
Booklist Starred Review of *The Case of the Love Commandos*

"Thought-provoking and charming"
Publishers Weekly Starred Review of
The Case of the Love Commandos

"Thoroughly engaging"
Booklist Starred Review of
The Case of the Deadly Butter Chicken

"Will appeal to all mystery lovers, particularly fans of Michael Stanley, Alexander McCall Smith and Colin Cotterill"
Library Journal Starred Review of
The Case of the Deadly Butter Chicken

"Outstanding"
Publishers Weekly Starred Review of
The Case of the Deadly Butter Chicken

About the author

Tarquin Hall started travelling when he was eighteen and worked as a cowboy in Texas. When lassoing cattle proved to be a skill that eluded him, he drifted into journalism, cutting his teeth in Afghanistan, and then East Africa and Turkey. A subsequent career in TV news took him to many other countries. While based in India, where he spent ten years, he married broadcaster and children's author, Anu Anand. They are now raising two children in Bath.

www.tarquinhall.com

ONE

'Without doubt, this is the best day of my life!' declared Vish Puri to his executive secretary, Elizabeth Rani, as he sat beaming with pride behind his desk in his Khan Market office in New Delhi.

Never mind that in Puri's fifty-nine years a number of other days had already won that same distinction. There was his wedding day for one; the births of his three daughters; and one or two landmark events in his professional career – his unmasking of the Butcher of Bangalore, for example.

There had also been that one perfect day in Kashmir in the late Nineties when he and Rumpi had watched the sunset over Dal Lake and been rowed back from the Shalimar Gardens to their luxury houseboat by the light of a full moon – and then been served the richest, most succulent rogan josh he had ever tasted.[1]

'I must say, Madam Rani, just now I'm feeling as light as a feather,' said Puri, though the manner in which his considerable weight crushed the leather upholstery of his office chair suggested otherwise.

'Yes, sir. And again my congratulations, it is well deserved.'

Elizabeth Rani's words were perfunctory, but then the news that Puri was to be crowned the 2021 Private Detective of the Year by the International Federation of Private Detectives (IFPD) had reached them over two hours ago, and this was her third visit to his office since then.

'In my profession, nothing tops it, actually,' Puri went on. 'As you well know, when the nominations were announced two months back, I did not allow my hopes to get up. Twice before I've been shortlisted, and my hopes were dashed upon the rocks. Thank the God on both occasions I was not available to travel to London for the award ceremony, owing to various

---

[1] Author's note: a full glossary of Indian words and terms that may be unfamiliar to some readers can be found at the back of the book.

commitments and all. As such I saved both time and money, not to mention the humiliation of playing second fiddle. But now the IFPD has been good enough to inform me I am confirmed as this year's winner, it will be my pleasure to clear the decks so to speak.'

'Yes, sir,' said Elizabeth Rani, who stood with notebook and pen in hand, eager to move on to more pressing business. 'With regard to travel dates, I checked with the agent and there are seats available this coming Monday.'

'And the gala award dinner, that is next Friday, I believe?'

'Yes, sir. So you'll have time to recover from your jet lag and enjoy the sights. I should warn you flights are quite costly, owing to the booking being last minute.'

'Money is no object, believe me, Madam Rani!' declared Puri, expansively. 'Kindly book extra baggage allowance, also. It is my understanding the trophy is a large one. For that matter some space will be required here in my office amongst my many previous prizes and accolades.'

'Understood sir. Now should I bring Mrs Sethia to you?'

Puri gave a start at the mention of his client's name. 'By God, in all the excitement I'd forgotten about her appointment, actually,' he said.

Elizabeth Rani started towards the door. 'I should warn you, sir, she's looking very anxious. Seems to believe her husband has been cheating on her.'

'He has not in fact. But that being said, it is not as if he has been spending his spare time at the library, either.' Puri reached for the Sethia file. 'Kindly be good enough to keep her occupied for three, four minutes, Madam Rani. Some preparation is required on my part.'

Puri spent the time reminding himself of the advice he had been given on how to handle a distressed woman. His best strategy, he decided, would be to emphasize the positive and avoid at all costs sharing the whole truth, though without flat out lying to her. Hopefully, she would be so relieved that her husband was not playing around that she would leave satisfied.

And if not? He placed within reach his faux silver filigree tissue box with a scented Presto! tissue peeking out of the top, and then turned to his crib sheet entitled 'Dealing with Distressed

Females'. This comprised some helpful sentences Rumpi had suggested he use during uncomfortable situations with women clients who turned emotional.

Puri read the first line out loud: '*I cannot imagine the pain you're suffering. My heart goes out to you.*'

He perused the notes he'd scrawled in the margin as well. *Don't be stiff! Try to show some heart! Smile!*

He was practising a smile when the door opened and his client entered in silence.

Mrs Sethia radiated anxiety, her head bowed like a frightened child. He wondered if this was not this prim, pious woman's natural state.

'Most good of you to come, madam, please make yourself comfortable,' he said, motioning her into one of the chairs in front of his desk. 'Hearty apologies for the wait, some other pressing work was there.'

Puri dispensed with the customary offer of chai or coffee and biscuits, owing to the extreme form of vegetarianism practised by Mrs Sethia and her family and the minefield of dietary restrictions he would inevitably find himself negotiating.

'With your permission and no fanfare, madam, I will get straight down to business,' he said.

'Kindly do so,' said Mrs Sethia, her voice scratchy and uneven, like the recording of an old LP. 'I am prepared for the worst.'

'It is nothing like that, I can assure you,' said Puri, managing to pull a half-smile. 'I've good news, in fact. Your concerns have proven unfounded, we can say.'

Mrs Sethia contemplated this news for a moment with a dubious frown. '*Unfounded?*' she repeated, her thin fingers fiddling with the strap of her handbag. 'You mean misguided? That can't be the case, surely?'

'Madam, allow me to assure you, categorically, one hundred per cent – one hundred and fifty per cent, in fact! – no hanky-panky has been taking place on your husband's part.'

'But he is seeing someone, some . . . *floozy.*'

'That is what I'm telling you, madam: no floozy is there. Rest assured Mr Sethia is not carrying off an affair.'

It had been overcast until now, but with what could easily have been misconstrued as a heavenly benediction, the sun broke suddenly through the clouds and great beams burst into the room. Mrs Sethia's tired, worried eyes blinked repeatedly as they adjusted to the light.

'Then how can you explain all the strange behaviour on his part, all the secrecy?' she said, still unbelieving.

'Madam, we have carried out surveillance of your husband for the past week, round the clock, 24/7. Not once was he out of our sight. What is more, using latest state-of-the-art technology, we monitored all calls made on the home phone, office phone and his portable. Naturally, we checked phone records, bank statements and credit card transactions for any untoward activity, also. No stone went unturned. Had Mr Babulal Sethia so much as clipped his toenails, we would have observed him doing so.'

'But the late nights, that musty smell on his shirts—'

'Your husband is a good and decent, hard-working individual,' said Puri, encouragingly. 'That is something to be grateful for, no? Your worst fears have come to nothing.'

Still, Mrs Sethia looked as forlorn as ever. 'I don't know what to say,' she murmured.

'My advice to you, madam, is return home in the knowledge your worries are over and enjoy life,' said Puri. 'Make the most of the time you have together. New chapter.'

His words were punctuated by the buzz of the intercom. He reached over his desk and pressed the talk button. 'Yes, Madam Rani, just we're concluding our business. Mrs Sethia will be with you momentarily.'

But Puri's secretary had an urgent call to put through. 'Sir, it is Ravi Scindia from Action News! calling.' She sounded starstruck. 'He wants you to appear on his show, *Mission Truth*, tonight. An exclusive interview.'

'Regarding?' asked Puri, loftily.

She whispered: 'The International Detective of the Year Award, sir.'

'How this producer came to know about that, exactly?' Puri asked with some dismay.

'I didn't think to ask. Should I do so?'

Puri took a moment to answer. In his mind he was piecing together the probable chain of events that would have led to Ravi Scindia calling. First, Mr Charles Harding, the IFPD president, had called from London shortly after one o'clock. He'd specified that news of the award 'be kept under wraps', and so Puri had assured him using one of his favourite maxims that 'confidentiality is my watchword'. Straight after the call, however, Puri had called Rumpi to let her know they would be travelling to London. Though he had insisted she tell no one, least of all his mother, he should have anticipated that his wife would have done the exact opposite. Bad news and dark secrets can be kept under wraps effectively in an Indian household, but never good news. It would have taken Rumpi twenty minutes at the most to call her three daughters and then her best friend, Poonam. 'Don't tell a soul. Chubby will kill me if he finds out!' he could hear her saying. But no doubt Poonam was playing bridge in the Willingdon Room at the Gymkhana, surrounded by the great and the good: politicians, senior bureaucrats, the odd general and perhaps a retired, senior journalist, all with little enough going on in their lives.

In short, all of Delhi knew by now.

'Tell Ravi Scindia he is very much mistaken, the winner has not been made public as of yet,' Puri instructed Elizabeth Rani. 'It is fake news.'

Turning his attention back to Mrs Sethia, he could see from her doubtful expression that the interruption had not played in his favour.

'Mr Puri, something does not add up,' she said. 'Last Wednesday, my husband returned home well past nine in the night, claiming he'd remained at the office. However my sister reported seeing him near Jangpura at seven forty-five.'

'Could be he was at a business meeting,' suggested Puri.

He registered the sound of several phone lines ringing unanswered in reception.

'But you told me you could account for every minute of my husband's time,' objected Mrs Sethia. In both demeanour and attitude, she seemed to be growing bolder and less inclined to accept his word.

'Madam, you retained my services to ascertain whether your husband was conducting an affair and I have dutifully fulfilled my commission to the utmost,' he said just as the intercom buzzed again.

This time Puri welcomed the interruption.

'Sir, a call from the additional secretary, Ministry of Finance,' said Elizabeth Rani. 'He's requesting a meeting tomorrow morning at ten o'clock at the Gymkhana Club.'

Puri didn't know this particular additional secretary, but the position was about as senior as it got in the machinery of the government of India – and this was as good as a summons.

'He explained what all it's about?'

'Concerning your upcoming visit to London, sir.'

'Please confirm the same,' sighed Puri. 'You've taken some other calls meantime, sounds like?'

Elizabeth Rani read off a list: 'Rohan Thukral, the president of the Indian Confederation of Detectives, called to congratulate you. Jagdish Uncle called from Jalandhar, requesting you bring back a dialysis machine from the UK for his brother. Also, Sushil Jaitley says he'll be dropping off some barfi for his sister living in *Brom-lee*.'

By now, Mrs Sethia's arms were crossed and her eyes were tightly narrowed. 'I'm starting to wonder if you're trying to hide something from me,' she said when he rejoined the conversation. 'I wonder: has my husband paid you off?'

Puri felt a rush of anger at the suggestion, but remained calm.

'Madam,' he said. 'Not once have I taken one single payoff in my entire life and believe me I'm not about to start here and now. If you will excuse me, I believe our business has been concluded in a satisfactory manner.'

His mobile phone was ringing and the screen displayed his mother's ID. He considered ignoring the call, but knew there was no point. She would just keep calling.

He reached for the handset and answered: 'Mummy-ji, I'm with a client, actually, I would need to revert,' he said.

'One minute is required, na,' she replied, an undertow of indignation in her voice. 'I came to know you received the big international award, from Preeti Paswan no less.'

Mention of Preeti's name made Puri cringe. Of all people, the news had to come from her: Mummy's arch nemesis, at least in Punjabi Bagh circles.

'The award is not official as of yet, but somehow there has been some leakage,' he said, trying to placate her. 'I had planned to come round this evening to tell you in person, actually.'

'No need, na, I am just calling to pass on my congratulations,' she said. 'Your father would be so proud, Chubby. Now tell me one thing: you'll be flying to London on which day?'

'On Monday itself.'

'What time exactly?'

Puri hesitated, ever cautious about sharing more information than was necessary with his mother. 'I believe it should be in the afternoon or thereabouts,' he said, vaguely.

'In which case you will pick me up at ten sharp.'

'Why would I do that?'

'Naturally, I'll be accompanying you to London, na,' she said as if he should already have known as much.

Puri lowered his voice and, turning away from Mrs Sethia and cupping the phone in one hand, told his mother that there was no way she could come to London.

'Why?'

'Mummy-ji, we will discuss the matter later.'

'Nothing to discuss, it is decided. Just I spoke with Rumpi five minutes back, and she's in total agreement. No tension, I'll purchase my own ticket.'

The line went dead and Puri turned back to his desk, alarmed by what his mother had just sprung on him. Suddenly his patience for Mrs Sethia was exhausted. He had done all he could to protect her husband, in part because he sympathized with the poor man just wanting to enjoy a little, innocent fun, but enough was enough.

'Madam, I have gone out of my way to avoid causing you distress,' he said. 'In my opinion you would be better off not knowing the whole truth. But given your insistence, it seems I've no choice but to reveal all the intelligence we gathered.'

He opened the Sethia file and took out a grainy photograph of Babulal Sethia standing in a galli behind his office with a colleague. The two of them were puffing on cigarettes. In passing this to his client, Puri provoked a horrified gasp.

'Smoking! But it's forbidden!' Mrs Sethia's voice was shrill.

'Your husband smokes at most four or five cigarettes a day,' said Puri, though he knew it was closer to a pack.

'He's an addict? Is that what you're telling me?'

Without further comment, he passed her a picture snapped

in a bar where Mr Sethia had enjoyed a cold beer with a friend.

'*Drinking, also!*'

Tears pooled in her eyes as she stared in disbelief at the images. 'How could he?'

'Madam,' said Puri, in what he regarded as a soothing tone but might have been considered by others as a work in progress, 'I myself enjoy the odd peg or two and no harm has come to me, let me assure you.'

'He is polluting himself – and our home!' Mrs Sethia sobbed. 'It would be better if he was having an affair. That, at least, I could live with.'

Puri reached for the faux silver filigree tissue box and handed it to her.

Trying to recall the words on his crib sheet, he said, 'I cannot imagine what all you're suffering. My heart pains for you.'

Mrs Sethia tugged out a wad of tissues and wiped her face.

'Next you'll be telling me he's eating meat!' she said.

'No, no, nothing like that,' said Puri and, without her noticing, managed to slide the next photo – of Babulal Sethia biting into a thick, juicy chicken burger – safely beneath another file.

TWO

The best day of Puri's life – or at least this latest one – did not end on a positive note. It was marred by a petty quarrel with Rumpi, which predictably centred around Mummy and her plan to accompany them to London.

It ended with his wife going up to bed in a huff and Puri calling to her from the bottom of the stairs.

'Mummy-ji does not have so much as a passport let alone the required visa, and we leave in three days, only, meaning this discussion is so much of wastage!'

To this Rumpi replied over her shoulder in an almost pitying tone, 'Oh, Chubby! What are you thinking? Are you really that naive?'

She went to sleep in the spare bedroom while Puri headed up to the roof to tend to his prize chilli plants.

As he applied diluted neem oil to the emerald-green leaves of his Jwalas, he endeavoured to reflect on other matters, but Rumpi's words kept coming back to him. They seemed to imply that she knew something he didn't.

Surely, though, there was no way Mummy could get a passport in a couple of days? The wait was at least three months. And securing a UK tourist visa these days was near on impossible at short notice. Letters of guarantee were required, along with deposits of substantial sums. Candidates also had to undergo at least one interview. At a minimum, the process took a month, which was why Puri had played it safe and secured his and Rumpi's visas three months ago after IFPD published the shortlist of nominees for the award.

Not even Mummy could overcome that level of bureaucracy.

'Case closed,' he assured his chilli plants. And having harvested a few of his fiery Ghost Peppers, returned downstairs to end the day by cracking open a bottle of Johnnie Walker Blue Label, a gift from a wealthy and extremely grateful client, which he'd been saving for a special occasion.

Puri poured himself a peg and soda and eased back on to the comfortable leather couch in the living room, toasting himself and his success.

He was savouring the solitude and quiet when his phone rang.

Having spent most of the afternoon and evening taking congratulatory calls from family, friends, well-wishers, and various toadies (including a number of junior private detectives), he picked up the device and interrogated the screen with diffidence.

It was Rinku, his incorrigible childhood friend.

He knew instantly that he had no choice but to answer: to ignore the call would be to invite complaint and ridicule no matter what excuse he gave.

'Oi, saale! Long time, yaar!' Rinku's slurred words boomed into his ear. Evidently he'd been drinking.

'Likewise, you bugger,' said Puri, his voice taut, a product of the apprehension he always felt these days when, on rare occasions, the two childhood friends spoke. 'Sab changa?'

'I came to know congratulations are very much in order! All that time spent spying on frustrated housewives has paid off finally!'

'I've not been sitting idle,' answered Puri, awkwardly.

'Who'd have thought it, ha? One of the Yo-Yo Gang a bloody international celebrity!'

'Hardly a celebrity.'

'Don't try putting on modesty with me, Chubby. I know you. Right now, you're feeling prouder than a peacock. Don't deny it. And that is how it should be. You're being honoured at the international level. I'm bloody proud of you. Now where's my invitation, yaar? I'm checking my inbox and *noth-ing.*'

'Invitation to what exactly?'

'Arrey! Your bloody award ceremony, what the hell else?' said Rinku, his voice thick with sarcasm.'

'You wish to attend?' asked Puri, taken aback.

'Yes I *wish to attend,*' said Rinku, mocking Puri's formal tone. 'That comes as a surprise to you somehow?'

'I think some confusion is there,' said Puri. 'The event is to be held in London – in the UK,' explained Puri.

'You don't think I know where London is or what?'

'Nothing like that. But it is not an *auto* ride, that is the point.'

'Listen, these days I'm back and forth from UK every other week. I've some investments here and there.'

Puri shuddered to think what these might be. As far as he knew, Rinku had gotten into road construction and still operated a gambling syndicate and a car breaking operation. The prospect of him turning up at the event in his cowboy boots, gold chains and a loud shirt, and fraternizing with the world's most accomplished private detectives and law enforcement dignitaries, caused Puri's mouth to go suddenly dry. He took another gulp of Scotch and said, sounding apologetic, 'I would need to check in with the organizers on numbers. There is limited capacity.'

'You're the bloody award winner, Chubby. Tell them you want an extra chair. Better make that two. I'll be bringing a friend.'

'Meaning a lady friend?' He pictured an escort in a bandage dress.

'Not to worry, yaar, I won't embarrass you,' he said, snidely. 'She'll either be a nun or a save-the-tiger volunteer. Now tell me: where you're putting up in London?'

'At Rumpi's cousin's place. The area is named the East of Ham.'

'Sweet, yaar, that's not far from my pad. I'll take you to this club nearby. Chubby, you won't believe the place. The dance floor is like a forest of long legs as far as the eye can see. Easy to get lost in.'

Puri could never tell whether his old friend was serious about taking him to such places, or it was a rhetorical suggestion.

'I've committed to Rumpi to visit all the sights, actually,' he said.

'Same old Chubby, ha?' chuckled Rinku. 'Always letting your hair down. What's the dress code, by the way?'

'Meaning the gala award dinner? Strictly black tie.'

'Like a penguin suit? No problem, I've got a leather one,' said Rinku and hung up.

In Puri's dreams, the gala award dinner turned to disaster. The IFPD president, Mr Charles Harding, stood on a stage, opened the envelope containing the identity of the winner, and announced Mummy's name instead of his. His mother then went up on stage and, having accepted the trophy, proceeded to tell the audience about all the embarrassing moments from his childhood, including the time he ate a piping hot gulam jaman and got a burned fat lip. Rinku was there, too, relaxing in a big jacuzzi filled with bikini-clad prostitutes. And Mrs Sethia – somehow she was the talking monkey from *Chhota Bheem*, Jaggu – swung from the chandeliers above, throwing bread rolls at him.

Still tired and trying to shake off the residual horror of this nightmare, Puri rose at almost half past eight.

By the time he'd washed and spent the requisite time needed for the meticulous grooming of his moustache, there was no time for breakfast – perhaps a blessing as he seemed to be still in Rumpi's bad books.

By nine, he was on his way into south Delhi, his driver, Handbrake, at the wheel of his old Ambassador. It was a bright November morning, the sky as clear as ever it looked in the capital these days. Like the underlay of a scrape painting, the promise of deep blue could be glimpsed through the dusty pall that hung over the city. The commute at this hour was a battle of steel and horn through seething traffic, and Puri spent a good deal of the time on the phone, finding out what he could about Dilip Shrivastava, the senior bureaucrat who had summoned him for a meeting.

'Madhya Pradesh cadre topper, 1986-batch IAS,' a contact told him.

Translation: Dilip Shrivastava, who hailed from the central state of Madhya Pradesh, had scored amongst the highest few per cent of those applicants who sat the National Civil Services 1986 examination (competing with around half a million others from across India) and entered the elite Indian Administrative Service. Shrivastava had moved quickly up the ranks. After serving as a district collector, he'd been appointed principal secretary for finance in the Madhya Pradesh state government; there he built himself a reputation as a crusader, uncovering a number of major scams involving local politicians and big business. For the past year, he'd held the additional secretary post at the Ministry of Finance, a job that came with colossal amounts of responsibility, only a few rungs down from the top. By Puri's estimate, he must be in his mid-fifties.

The fact that such a senior neta had asked to meet at the Gym meant it must be either a hush-hush official matter or a personal one.

Either way, he did not want to be late and, once the Ambassador was free of the gridlock on the Gurugram Expressway,[2] and reached the shaded, sun-dappled avenues of south Delhi, he instructed Handbrake to get them to the club by ten o'clock, 'latest'. This was a nod to ignore the usual mandate of keeping as close to the rules as could be achieved on the capital's roads and drive like everyone else. As such, over the course of the next fifteen minutes, the driver gladly committed multiple traffic offences, including speeding to overtake, blocking oncoming traffic on a roundabout, running a red light, and taking a shortcut down a one-way lane. Handbrake sounded the horn every ten seconds or so, and showed no mercy to small fare like tempos and auto-rickshaws, bullying them out of the way like a lion scattering deer at a watering hole. Only when Handbrake turned into the pillared entrance to the Gymkhana Club – even in making that turn he callously blocked oncoming traffic, causing it to brake hard – did he return to Responsible Mode and proceeded sedately up to the whitewashed, colonial clubhouse at ten on the dot.

At the front desk, the in-charge informed Puri that Shri Dilip Shrivastava was waiting for him in Viceroy's Corner. He proceeded into the heart of the building, blissfully aware that the club director's wife, Mrs Col. P. V. S. Gill (Retd.), had recently undergone a hip replacement operation and would be out of commission for a week at least. As such, the squeaking of his rubber-soled, orthopaedic shoes on the hardwood floors failed to draw the old harridan out of her office and earn him a ticking off about the noise and whatever else she saw fit to pull him up on.

Around the first corner, however, he ran into Retired Brigadier Manpreet Kanwal.

'Ah, the conquering hero of the hour!' he bellowed. 'My dear fellow, you're a credit to this institution and the nation! Allow me to shake your hand.'

He encountered Mrs Vinita Ahluwalia next, coming out of the Blue Room and a meeting of the Compliance Committee.

'You must be tickled pink, Mr Puri!'

But the most challenging member to shake off (at the best

---

[2] Gurgaon, Puri's home, was renamed Gurugram in 2016 by the state government.

of times) proved to be Mr Nikesh Sardesai, known to everyone as 'Bubbles'.

'When you return from London we would be honoured if you would address the South Delhi Optometrists Association,' he said, taking Puri by the hand and not letting go. 'I've recently taken over as president and we have a very active membership.'

By the time the detective managed to extricate himself from Bubbles' clutches – 'Don't forget Bingo and Biryani Night on Sunday!' – he was almost ten minutes late, and reached Viceroy's Corner vexed and apologetic.

Dilip Shrivastava gave no indication that he was put out by Puri's tardiness. Yet he was clearly a man who valued meticulousness; and his well-groomed head of salt-and-pepper hair, bespoke Nehru jacket and straight-backed deportment completed an impression of calm confidence. By comparison, dressed as he was in his so-called safari suit and favourite Sandown cap, which was beginning to fray, the detective felt positively slovenly.

'I was just reading about you in the *Express*,'[3] said Shrivastava. 'I take it you've seen the piece?'

Puri's expression indicated that he hadn't – the bureaucrat passed him the paper.

'TOP DELHI SLEUTH BAGS INTERNATIONAL AWARD' blared a headline on page one.

'India's very own Sherlock Holmes, Vish Puri, head of Most Private Investigators Ltd., Delhi, who made headlines after collaborating with a reincarnated witness to solve a sensational murder committed in 1984, has been named Private Detective of the Year by the International Federation of Private Detectives. The much-coveted award is considered the Nobel Prize for worldwide investigators.'

'You look far from pleased,' observed Shrivastava, noting Puri's frown as he read the article.

'Sir, I'm not at all fond of the comparison with that Sherlock Holmes fellow,' he explained. 'He was fiction, whereas I am fact.'

'Surely Sherlock Holmes's powers of observation are something all you detectives seek to emulate?' said Shrivastava.

---

[3] The *Indian Express*, generally abbreviated to just the *Express*.

'With respect, sir, Sherlock Holmes is a Johnny-come-lately we can say,' said Puri. 'The techniques of deduction he laid claim to were employed in India when Britishers were living in caves, painting themselves blue and all.'

He also felt compelled to point out that the story included, 'So many of inaccuracies.'

'But you *are* travelling to London to collect the award?' Shrivastava sought to clarify with a look of concern.

'Unofficially, yes, sir, that is correct,' Puri explained, to the other's relief. 'I gave my word to the IFPD president, Mr Charles Harding, that the news would remain top secret, so to speak, but thereafter made the mistake of informing my dear wife. As it turns out, this act was as good as issuing a press release.'

'Delhi is like a village,' observed Shrivastava with a small smile.

'A village populated by so many of washerwomen,' said Puri with well-fed prejudice.

A waiter approached.

Though famished, the detective decided it would be better not to order his usual chilli cheese toast, a messy affair, and stuck to chai and some of his favourite Marie Gold biscuits. The two men then spent five minutes engaged in small chat, establishing various professional and social connections. By the time their refreshments arrived, Puri was developing a more refined impression of Shrivastava. Beneath the affability and suave exterior, he sensed steely drive and determination – and possibly ruthlessness.

'You've been following the Dr Bhatt case, no doubt?' asked the bureaucrat, finally getting down to business.

Who had not? The story had dominated the headlines for the past four months. Dr Harilal Bhatt, from Mumbai (previously Bombay), founder and former CEO of the Indian pharmaceutical company, Bio Solutions – for years one of the poster boys of modernizing India – had fled the country in early July.

A self-made entrepreneur who built his company from scratch, Dr Bhatt had made a fortune in manufacturing cheap, generic drugs for India and the world. His star had reached its zenith with the release last year of a ground-breaking drug. 'Dia-Beat' was touted as a cure for diabetes that promised help for millions. Bio Solutions was suddenly a world player.

But in the months following the so-called miracle drug's release, many patients developed side effects. A number died – the Ministry of Health estimated at least three hundred across India. And, subsequently, internal emails leaked by a Bio Solutions whistle-blower revealed that Dr Bhatt and his team were aware of the risks. Amidst the scandal, the company's share price dropped through the floor; and soon it emerged that Dr Bhatt had bet the company's future on the drug, having secured hundreds of millions of dollars in loans from various Indian state banks to fund his research. Hours before the Central Bureau of Investigation (CBI) was due to arrest him on charges ranging from culpable homicide to fraud, Dr Bhatt had boarded a private jet.

'We're sure he's in London,' said Shrivastava. 'But in four months, Scotland Yard has failed to locate him. What is one more missing foreign billionaire hiding out in London to the British? They've got their hands full chasing after all their home-grown jihadis and looking after their royal family. That's why we need you, Mr Puri. You're the best. And we want you to locate Dr Bhatt. Find whatever hole he's hiding in and we'll handle the rest.'

Ordinarily Puri would have jumped at such an assignment. But he was planning to spend just a week in London and had promised Rumpi he would take a break from work. She had always wanted to visit London and was looking forward to seeing all the sights and catching up with a number of relatives.

'Sir, with respect, while I am honoured by your request and the offer is a tempting one, regretfully and with apologies, I must decline,' he said. 'I'm not the man for the job, actually. You would be better off retaining a professional in the UK.'

'Out of the question,' said Shrivastava, dismissively. He turned his right foot a few degrees clockwise and then back again with a controlled intensity that somehow denoted displeasure. 'You're a patriot and we can trust you to act in India's interest.'

'Sir, kindly understand, I would be very much a fish out of water,' Puri tried again. 'London is a city of millions with a large population drawn from across South Asia. So many desis are there. That poses a considerable advantage for any Indian wanting to go to ground.'

'All the more reason why we need you – not some gora police officer who doesn't know his dosa from his dhokla.'

'Sir, with respect, I would not be so hasty in writing off the Scotland Yard,' said Puri. 'Over the years, I've had cause to collaborate with a number of their senior officers and found them most capable in every which way.'

Shrivastava sank his voice. 'The minister himself has asked for you,' he said, playing his trump card. 'He has the utmost confidence in your talents, experience and ingenuity, and knows you can be trusted to rise to the challenge.'

Puri could practically feel the walls of the corner he had been backed into closing in around him. This was not a request; he was being ordered to take on the case. And if he refused? Before long, he could expect a visit from the Income Tax Department. The Ministry of Labour and Employment might come knocking as well. And though they would fail to identify any out-and-out illegal activity on his part, they would tie him up with paperwork.

On balance, letting down Rumpi was not so daunting a prospect. Still, Puri was not confident of success.

'Sir, kindly understand a week is too short a time for completion of such a manhunt,' he protested. 'I would be working solo, without the assistance of my team members.'

'You're aware, there is a substantial reward on offer for Dr Bhatt's capture?' asked Shrivastava, ignoring his concern. 'The Bank of Hind is offering ten lakh for anyone providing information that leads the authorities to his whereabouts.'

'Yes, sir, I'm aware,' said Puri with little enthusiasm. 'Frankly speaking in my experience such rewards are rarely honoured.'

'Believe me Mr Puri, I'm in a position to ensure the Bank makes good on its commitments,' said Shrivastava, making it sound like the matter was settled. 'Now, I'm sure I don't need to spell out for you the sensitivity of the situation and the necessity, until such time as you locate Dr Bhatt, for absolute secrecy regarding your involvement. Our arrangement must be an informal one, you'll be acting as a private citizen. Otherwise, protocol would demand we inform External Affairs and they in turn the High Commission in London and we'll have a jurisdiction nightmare on our hands.'

'Sir, you yourself must be aware that locating Dr Bhatt is one

thing, while extraditing him from the UK is another matter altogether,' said Puri. 'With Kingfisher's Vijay Mallya, he has not
been returned to India to face justice despite every which effort.'[4]

'Dr Bhatt is in a different category to Mallya; the man is
responsible for dozens of deaths.' This was said with sudden
intensity, and Shrivastava had to check himself. He paused for a
moment, then added, 'Forgive me, but it galls me to think about
all the innocent lives this man has ruined and the possibility he
might escape justice.

Shrivastava checked his watch and stood. 'Now, I've a meeting
at Racecourse Road. The best of luck in your search, Mr Puri.
The country is counting on you,' he said and promptly left.

Never mind that Puri had not actually accepted the job, let
alone had a chance to discuss his fee.

Puri ate a plate of rumble tumble eggs and toast which he washed
down with a couple of cups of strong sugary chai before covering
the short distance to Khan Market.

He found the waiting area outside his office filled with bouquets
of flowers and boxes of Indian sweets. There were also several
soft toys, including one enormous teddy bear wearing a T-shirt
that read 'YOU'RE MY HERO!' – this from the All-India Chilli
Growers' Association, South Delhi Chapter.

The messages were also piling up.

'The managing director of Raja's Mouche Wax wants you to
appear in an advertisement,' Elizabeth Rani told him. 'And you've
been invited to give the graduation speech at the School of
Military Intelligence passing-out ceremony in Pune.'

Puri reminded Elizabeth Rani that the winner of the award was
yet to be officially announced and she should continue to commu-
nicate this to any well-wishers or media persons who called.
As for all the gifts, he suggested they be divided between the
staff or given away – all apart from a box of fruit mithai from
Bengali Sweet House which he took into his office.

He proceeded to devour these one by one as he went through a

---

[4] Once known as the 'King of Good Times', Mallya, the former head of
    United Spirits, left India for the UK in 2016. Subsequently he was
    charged with bank fraud to the tune of $1.1 billion.

dossier that Shrivastava had left him. It contained a general profile of Dr Bhatt, most of it familiar to Puri: the son of an army officer, he was an Indian Institute of Technology Delhi topper; studied medicine at Harvard; founded Bio Solutions in 1989; had been lauded by politicians; hobnobbed with Bill Gates; holidayed on Richard Branson's private island; written the best-selling, *The Indian Century*, advocating a blend of Indian-style capitalism that embraced many of India's time-honoured, traditional values. Dr Bhatt himself exemplified this philosophy, remaining good to his Brahmanical Gujarati roots and faith. The one concession to this was the divorce from his first wife and his second marriage to a glamorous Delhi-born fashion model and socialite ten years his junior, Shweta Kamra.

The dossier also included a report by the Banking Section, Ministry of Finance, which broke fresh ground. The loans Dr Bhatt had secured for his Dia-Beat research – with a value of nearly a billion dollars – had all been arranged without the usual, requisite formalities through local branches in rural areas. In other words, he'd used local political connections to secure the money, Puri surmised. There would have been kickbacks for all involved, including bank managers, regional managers and local state politicians.

The report also stated that up to seventy million dollars had been plundered from the Bio Solutions pension fund. This had gone into propping up the company following the news of Dia-Beat's potentially life-threatening side effects. There was no evidence to suggest that Dr Bhatt had diverted money to his own personal accounts in India or offshore. Though he retained considerable wealth, it had all been frozen, and the investigators had concluded that he fled the country with, at most, 300,000 dollars in cash.

'From all I've read, we can conclude the following,' Puri told his senior operative, Tubelight, who had joined him in the office and who was helping himself to the last of the mithai. 'Certain elements within The Nexus would not want to see Dr Bhatt extradited from UK.[5] This man could make life uncomfortable

---

5   The Nexus is Puri's term for the loose alliance of politicians, busi-
      nessmen, organized crime and some bureaucrats, judges and law
      enforcement officers, who he identifies as conspiring to protect their
      own interests and collaborating in corrupt practises, thereby undermining
      the rule of law and sapping India of its true potential.

for a good many individuals were he to end up testifying in the court.'

'That would explain why the CBI has made zero progress on the case,' suggested Tubelight. 'They've been instructed to go slow.'

'No such instructions were necessary, agent Avinash Sharma was handed the case,' laughed Puri. 'Believe me, that one could not detect so much as a ladoo in Chawri bazaar.'

He went on: 'Joking apart, we can be sure certain parties would like to silence Dr Bhatt permanently. Knowing this, he will take every precaution to ensure his whereabouts remain top secret.'

'There won't be many he can trust,' observed Tubelight.

'They say he's extremely devoted to his wife. What do you know of her?'

Puri's operative gave a shrug. 'She's become a recluse, hardly leaves her Delhi residence,' he said. 'Word is she took it hard when he absconded. On top of that her father died six months back. She was very close to him.'

The dossier contained a photograph of Dr Bhatt and Shweta Bhatt at a function in Delhi in happier days. He was a good foot or so shorter than her, with thinning hair and prominent jowls; she was looking ravishing in a sculpted designer dress, a large diamond necklace setting off her long, statuesque neck.

'She is not exactly lacking in good looks, we can say,' said Puri with masterful understatement. 'Assuming she has remained loyal and devoted, Dr Bhatt would surely wish to find a way for her to join him whenever possible.'

'Makes sense, Boss. You want surveillance on her place?'

Puri slipped the photograph back into the dossier. 'Night and day, round the clock, 24/7,' he said. 'She is our best shot. Also, I'll want full background checking on Dr Bhatt himself. Should he have any connection whatsoever in the UK, I would want to know. No stone to go unturned. Meantime I've come to know that Inspector Si-maan Brom-ley of Scotland Yard was assigned the case.'

'The gora sahib who sweated a lot – on the museum artefacts smuggling case?'

Bromley had been in Delhi in June four years ago when the heat had peaked at 45°C, and he had indeed perspired a good deal.

'That is the one,' smiled Puri. 'And as you will remember all too well, he is very much in my debt.'

THREE

Puri visited the temple on Sunday evening and made an offering ahead of his flight to London. But it made no difference: he hated flying, was terrified of it, and woke on Monday morning with anxiety gnawing at the pit of his stomach.

His first words to Rumpi were: 'I dreamt the plane fell from the sky and exploded and my body could not be so much as identified, though somehow my Sandown cap survived intact.'

But soon after drinking the cup of bed tea she prepared and brought to him – Rumpi sat with him while he drained the contents – a miraculous change came over Puri. Coming down to breakfast, he felt relaxed and 'quite jolly'. This he attributed to having taken a wash and a shave, and applying a splash of his Sexy Men aftershave.

A second cup of chai improved his spirits still further. So much so that during the drive to the airport, he kept his wife and their two housemaids (neither of whom had visited an airport before and were thrilled at the prospect of their employers flying) entertained with a repertoire of his best sardaar-ji jokes (though it's true he laughed the hardest).

His mood was not in the least affected by a pushy, unlicensed tout who insisted on taking the Puris' bags. Handbrake tried to see him off with little more compassion than he would have shown a feral street dog. But to the driver's surprise, Puri engaged the man and, once they reached the entrance of the terminal, paid him the princely sum of fifty rupees.

The detective also bantered jovially with the hapless Border Security Force sepoy charged with the thankless task of checking passengers' passports at the entrance to the departures terminal, despite the soldier barring the housemaids from entering the building (they were disappointed, though the ride on the moving gangway from the car park had proved a hit).

And when Puri found Mummy at check-in, he joined Rumpi in making his mother feel welcome – 'Quite right, my dear, a family holiday together has been long overdue!' – and marvelled good humouredly at how she had managed to secure both a passport and visa at such short notice.

'No doubt with Mummy's connections, we'll be having tea and crumpets with her Majesty the Queen, yaar!' he exclaimed.

Puri was also charm personified with the young check-in woman and turned giddy to an almost embarrassing degree when she explained that she had been instructed by the airline's management to upgrade him and 'ma'am' to Business Class.

'Our way of saying congratulations on your award, sir,' she explained.

Puri would not hear of his mother travelling in economy unaccompanied, however, and graciously offered her his upgraded seat. She in turn would have none of it: 'I've simple tastes, na,' she said. 'No need for such luxury things. Just you enjoy, Chubby.'

Rumpi agreed with her – in fact she insisted that she and Puri should remain seated together. And before long, they were comfortably ensconced in spacious business-class seats, making the most of the reclining features and perusing the library of Bollywood classics offered on the in-flight entertainment system.

Hot towels were soon brought, followed by flutes of champagne and canapés and, having slipped off their shoes in exchange for the complimentary slippers, they toasted one another.

'Beenu was telling me that when we go to the Houses of Parliament, we must also visit Westminster Abbey,' said Rumpi. 'Several famous poets are buried there and it's where they filmed the Harry Potter movies.'

'Yes, my dear,' said Puri, who even in his present, happy state wanted to temper her expectations of his stamina for seeing all the sights of London. In truth, he hated the prospect of playing tourist. Given a choice he would stick to a few of the main sights like Buckingham Palace and Big Ben, and possibly the Inns of Court where Gandhi studied, and content himself with a few photographs to show everyone back home. More than anything, perhaps, he was looking forward to going to Bates, Gentlemen's Hatters of Piccadilly, where he planned to buy himself a couple of new Sandown caps. And at some point he would try the famous fish and chips at a traditional English pub.

Besides, he now had the Dr Bhatt case to worry about.

He had considered coming clean with Rumpi and explaining the circumstances, but subterfuge seemed the better option.

'Day after we arrive I will be visiting the Scotland Yard for a tour,' Puri told her, laying the groundwork.

'Yes, Chubby, this is the third time you've told me,' replied Rumpi. 'As it happens, Nina has organized some function for myself and Mummy to attend, so we'll plan to meet you after.'

She sat back in her seat and smiled indulgently to herself. 'I can't believe we're actually on our way! I haven't been this excited in years!' She reached out and placed a hand on his. 'I'm so glad we're going to be able to spend some time together. No interruptions. No murders or people shooting at you. Just the two of us. One evening I would love to go to the theatre. Do you think that might be possible?'

'That much I can promise,' said Puri – and in this he was sincere, knowing that there was a limit to how much he was prepared to put into the case at the risk of disappointing her. 'Now I don't know about you, but personally I am ready for a refill.'

They drank another glass of champagne each, and then Puri a third, before the captain came over the announcement system with news of a mechanical issue.

Twenty minutes into the delay, Puri began to show signs of agitation.

'I would imagine we would be taking off soon,' he commented, fiddling with his wedding ring. 'The plane will then reach a cruising altitude of some 35,000 feet or so give or take. That is 35,000 feet high above sea level. Meaning some six miles above the earth.'

'It shouldn't be too much longer now,' said Rumpi, trying to reassure him. 'The captain said it wasn't anything to worry about.'

'My dear, I'll have you know that prior to the Concorde catching fire and crashing in a fiery ball, killing all passengers and crew, the captain said precisely the same.'

'Why don't you watch a movie?' suggested Rumpi. 'They have some of your favourites. *Chori Mera Kaam* is playing.[6] You know how much it makes you laugh.'

---

[6]   The 1975 film stars Ashok Kumar, Shashi Kapoor and Zeenat Aman.

Puri chose to look out the window instead – a couple of mechanics had pulled back a panel on one of the engines and were rooting around inside with their spanners.

'It's a lot safer up here than on the roads, especially our Indian ones,' said Rumpi.

'Personally, my dear, I would prefer to take my chance with a Bedford Truck on the GT Road,' he said as a bead of sweat trickled down the side of his face.

His fingers were beginning to press hard into the armrest, and his knuckles were turning white.

Noticing this, Rumpi told him that she needed the bathroom and went in search of a stewardess.

Soon, she returned with a cup of tea.

Puri refused to touch it, fussy as ever about how his chai was prepared, but she insisted he drain every last drop.

By the time the plane finally pulled away from the gate fifteen minutes later, he was once again feeling pleasantly relaxed.

As the plane reached the runway, Puri started to yawn. His eyelids grew heavy. And by the time they reached cruising altitude, his chin had sunk down on to his chest and he was fast asleep.

Mummy, who had an aisle seat on the left of the aircraft, was not blessed with the most sociable of neighbours. To her left sat a young, non-resident Indian who, after saying a weary hello, wrapped herself in a blanket and went to sleep. The passenger across the aisle was an octogenarian with cataracts and, judging by the manner in which his son bellowed in his ear, stone deaf.

She passed the time before take-off reading her pocket-size Gita, which she always carried in her handbag and, once they were up in the air, took out a ball of yarn and her knitting needles, which she'd managed to get through security. Soon, she was working on her latest creation, a red winter cap for her seventh grandchild, born just a few months earlier to Puri's youngest daughter.

Mummy had long found knitting the perfect activity to undertake while out and about. It was not overtly anti-social like reading. It was a good icebreaker and often a nice topic of conversation: fellow knitters shared a common language, and it was rare to meet a young woman who either didn't know how to knit or wasn't keen to learn. Children were always intrigued to watch how it was done and often wanted to have a go. There was a certain meditative quality to the hobby as well. And though knitting took skill and concentration, it allowed the practitioner to observe their surroundings without appearing too nosy.

Soon Mummy had conducted a comprehensive survey of the immediate human landscape around her. Judging by their accents, the young Punjabi family one row in front and to the right hailed from Ludhiana. While in Delhi before catching the flight, they'd stayed with family in Rohini – how else to explain the plastic bag of barfi they were carrying from Punjab Sweets near Japanese Gardens? The couple in the seats directly in front of her were newlyweds on their honeymoon, both from small-town India, judging by their unworldly demeanours and knockoff designer clothing.

Of far more interest by far, however, was the Indian male occupying the corresponding seat to hers on the other side of the aircraft. He had been the last to board, arriving at his seat hot and sweaty; and shortly after take-off had walked up and down the Economy section before visiting Business Class. He had then called for a stewardess and demanded to be upgraded. When told this would not be possible, he had said something unpleasant, clearly upsetting the young woman.

He was trouble; it was just a question of what variety. 'Hairy One' Mummy had dubbed him for his stubble, heavy thickset black eyebrows and the veritable rug pushing out through the top of his white linen shirt, none of which leant him a cuddly look.

As of now, he was sitting with his chair tipped back above the objection of the feeding mother with a toddler behind him, downing his second Scotch with ice, laughing raucously at some asinine comedy, and shelling the pistachios he'd brought onboard, spilling the shells on to the floor of the plane.

Mummy wondered, as she finished knitting a section of her cap, if he had not been looking for someone when he went through the aircraft.

Her suspicion was further aroused when, soon, Rumpi appeared through the curtain that divided Economy from Business Class.

Hairy One's reaction was unmistakable – his cold gaze fixed
on her like a hunter sighting his prey as she progressed down
the aisle.

'I thought I'd check up on you, make sure you're comfortable,'
said Rumpi when she found Mummy.

'Teek hoon,' she responded, though her thoughts dwelt on
what business Hairy One could have with her – or, more likely,
her son. 'You managed Chubby somehow, is it?'

'Eventually,' sighed Rumpi. 'The happy pills started to wear
off before take-off, so I had to give him some sleeping tablets.
He'll be out for hours. He's so paranoid, started imagining the
plane was going to crash. What a fuss he makes. I don't like to
drug him, but what's a wife to do?'

'When Chubby was a mere boy, an astrologer foretold he
would die in a plane crash,' said Mummy. 'That is where the
fear of flying comes from, na.'

'It was *your* astrologer, Mummy-ji. You're the one who put
this thing in his head.'

'He was not my astrologer, but belonged to Nitu auntie. Same
one who informed me I'd win the lottery – yet till date, nothing.'

Rumpi had to step aside for another passenger coming down
the aisle.

Mummy caught a glimpse of Hairy One watching them before
he looked away.

'Can I fetch you anything, Mummy-ji? Some pani, chai
maybe?' asked Rumpi.

'Nothing is required. I've my knitting.'

'Did they show you how the screen works? There's a library
of golden oldies available.'

'For now, I'm happy doing timepass and getting to know my
neighbours,' she said.

'One of these days you'll have to tell me how you managed to
get a British visa so quickly,' said Rumpi. 'Chubby is completely
baffled. Says it's absolutely impossible to get it fast-tracked, that
they don't bend the rules for anyone.'

'It's a trade secret, na,' said Mummy with a grin, giving nothing
away.

* * *

At around the time the plane entered Iranian airspace, Tubelight turned his auto down a leafy residential street in the wealthy south Delhi colony of Shanti Niketan.

He pulled up behind an old Bajaj tempo parked next to a dumpster. The vehicle was dented and rusted. A sign on the back read, 'DANGER! BIO WASTE!'

This warning was not altogether unwarranted for, in opening the door, Tubelight exposed himself to the stench of body odour and ponging feet mixed with the reek of sour milk.

He held the door open for a minute to let in some fresh air (even Delhi's pollution was preferable) before entering. Stooping down to avoid banging his head on the rusting metal roof, he advanced inside with crab-like motions.

Each step was marked by a crunching noise as discarded pizza crusts and the odd cheese puff disintegrated beneath the soles of his leather chappals.

'The pigs in our colony live cleaner than you,' Tubelight observed.

He sat down next to his young colleague and fellow operative, Flush, the tech whizz. A sticky, empty mustard sachet was stuck fast to the bottom of one of his sandals and he removed it with a curse.

'When are you going to let me find you a good woman?' he added. 'Or at least a maid?'

Flush, who was wearing a crumpled kurta over a pair of faded jeans, gave a dismissive snort. 'Quit cribbing, there's a clear warning on the door,' he said.

He was seated before a high-tech console and, fixed to the wall of the tempo, an array of screens and monitors and a pair of speakers.

As code poured down the main, central monitor like digital rain, Flush's fingers danced gingerly across a keyboard. A screen to the left showed live video of the three-storey luxury villa across the road, courtesy of a hidden camera on the roof. This was Shweta Bhatt's residence.

'We're not the only ones monitoring her calls,' he said. 'There's another tap on the landline.'

'You're surprised?' asked Tubelight. 'Half the world's after her husband. Interpol, Scotland Yard, one or two angry bankers who want their millions back. Plus the entire Indian press corps.'

'I've detected jammers as well,' reported Flush. 'She must have had in one of our competitors, the gear's state-of-the art.'

This meant that Flush's usual bag of homemade electronic tricks, like his remote-control spy geckos, would be of no use.

Tubelight didn't seem that surprised by this revelation, either. In fact he was encouraged: if Shweta Bhatt was going to such lengths to guard her privacy, there was every chance she was in close touch with Dr Bhatt.

'Have you figured out how she's keeping in touch with him yet?' he asked.

'I've only been here since yesterday. What do you take me for, a miracle worker?'

'After you pulled off the North Korean job, yes. Now tell me what you've found out so far.'

Flush gave him the lowdown on all the communications devices he had detected inside the house. Madam used a smartphone. The maid, the cook and the driver all had ordinary, 'dumb' devices. There was a mali who came in the morning and he also used an old, outdated handset.

'I've downloaded the call records for all the accounts and there've been no international calls made in the past four months,' said Flush. 'I'm guessing Madam's sticking to encrypted apps, so I've sent her some spam with GIFs attached. If and when she opens one of them, I'll have access to her phone. The other option is to clone her device. But if she doesn't leave the house, that's going to be challenging.'

'You've hacked the Wi-Fi?'

Flush gave a sarcastic 'tut', as if to say, 'Of course.'

'You mentioned a landline?'

'It's only used by the cook to call the kirana store to place orders.'

'How about Madam? Have you clapped eyes on her yet?'

By way of an answer, Flush's fingers danced across the keyboard, causing one of the blank monitors to flicker into life. Video recorded the previous evening started playing of Shweta Bhatt standing on the balcony on the top floor of the villa. She was leaning on the railing, nervously smoking a cigarette. In a T-shirt and sweatpants, and with no makeup and her hair unkempt, she cut a diminished and lonely figure.

'She's shorter than I imagined,' said Tubelight, noting her trembling fingers.

'Word is she rarely leaves the house, just now and again to walk the dog,' said Flush. 'Her sister visits once in a while.'

'Where are you getting this?'

'Chetu, the delivery boy at the pharmacy.'

'What else did he tell you?'

'The driver had a fling with the maid next door, they used to do it in the back of the boss's car. The dog, Muttu, is taken to a beauty parlour once a week. Dr Bhatt paid for the mali's daughter's wedding. And Shweta Bhatt's on anti-depressives. Chetu delivers her prescription every week.'

Flush had come across an old back issue of Indian *Hello!* featuring a cover story of the Bhatts, and started flicking through it. The main photo showed the couple posing hand-in-hand in front of a large Versailles-style fountain. Inside, Shweta Bhatt spoke of her Italian Renaissance furniture imported from Rome, her love of traditional Himroo textiles and, naturally, her feminist credentials.

'She never missed a Page Three party, was top of the social food chain, attended Ambani weddings, Ashish Reddy's annual Holi party in Goa, was always pictured at fashion shows sitting next to Manish Malhotra types,' said Flush. 'Plus she's a hottie.'

'What are you getting at?' asked Tubelight.

'A woman like that could get herself pretty much any man. You really think she's going to stick by *him*?'

'What can I say? Love's a hard thing to fathom at times.'

'That I wouldn't know,' admitted Flush.

His attention was drawn to the monitor – the gate to the property was opening. A pretty young woman in glasses appeared. She was in her late twenties and wore a simple olive-green cotton kurta with a blue duppatta drawn over her head, and plastic sandals.

'The maid?' guessed Tubelight.

'Savita,' said Flush, his eyes dwelling on her slim frame.

Her intense brown eyes, rimmed with kajal, searched the street as she started off in the direction of the market, a slip of paper clutched in one hand.

'She was hired four months ago. Soon after Dr Bhatt absconded.'

'She's live-in?'

'Her room's in the barsati. The cook stays in the house as well. She's been with the family fourteen years, the driver even longer.'

Tubelight would have expected three times the number of staff in such a wealthy Indian household. The last family they'd watched had employed no less than eleven servants, including four drivers.

'Madam let the other staff go after Dr Bhatt absconded,' explained Flush.

'The delivery boy told you that as well?'

'Right.'

'What else did he have to say about the maid?'

'Her? said Flush, breezily. 'Nothing much. I didn't ask.'

FOUR

Puri felt groggy as he disembarked from the plane. He put this down to the combination of the champagne, which he claimed had been of 'inferior quality', and having slept nine hours straight, which had caused him to go without food. His general disposition did not improve as he, Rumpi and Mummy had to make their way along Heathrow's miles of corridors – incredibly, there were no baggage wallahs in sight and he was left with no choice but to push a trolley loaded with their hand luggage himself.

'They live in what can be called a DIY culture – Do It Yourself. We people are strictly DIFM – Do It For Me.'

These words, spoken by his old friend Dr Subhrojit Ghosh, with whom he'd lunched on Sunday at the Gym – and who had given him a pep talk on what to expect in the UK – rang in his ears.

'In the West there are rules for everything and, believe it or not, it's not like here where people see them as something to be bent or ignored,' Suro had told him. 'In Britain you should expect to queue wherever you go. Believe me, you will never see such orderly queues. If there was a fire in a building, I swear they would form one at the exit.'

Suro's observations were borne out in the immigration hall, where signs posted everywhere warned against smoking, abusing staff, littering, and providing false information on immigration and customs forms. There were warnings of dire consequences for smuggling live animals, weapons, explosives, seeds or even plants. And there were queues. Queues of dizzying length, snaking towards a row of glass cubicles manned by uniformed border officers – and all of them as orderly as routines performed by synchronized swimmers.

Puri was quick to spot a way of getting ahead, however: an empty, wide-open lane on one side of the hall, named, tantalizingly, 'Fast Track'. Evidently this was for important people in a hurry. And ignoring Suro's advice (on the grounds that his friend had always been overly cautious and in his line of work he simply couldn't afford to be), Puri didn't hesitate for a moment in taking it.

He was making good progress, with Rumpi and Mummy close behind and a couple of free immigration booths right up ahead, when a frowning lady officer stepped out in front of him and held out a hand. Trolleys were not permitted in the immigration hall, she said, pointing to the numerous signs that made this particular rule abundantly clear. Furthermore, trolleys were not to be left in the Fast Track lane. Puri's had to be returned to the 'designated area' at the entrance hall.

And no, she was not about to wheel it there for him.

Puri had no choice but to comply with this officious woman's order (the feel of Rumpi's hand squeezing his arm impressed upon him the need to do so). But no sooner had he done so than he tried his luck in the Fast Track lane again.

He was, he explained haughtily when challenged to show his 'upper-class' pass, 'a VIP', invited to the UK to receive 'a top award' from the International Federation of Private Detectives 'at a gala dinner at the world-famous Dorchester Hotel'. But this cut no ice with the lady officer; nor did Mummy's appeal to be permitted to proceed on the grounds that her hips were 'paining'.

The Puris were left with no option but to join the back of the non-EU passport holders' queue, which looked like it stretched all the way to London itself.

Heathrow was not finished heaping indignities upon Delhi's most famous detective, however.

After an hour in the immigration hall, and a further thirty minutes wasted at the luggage carousel where, again, there were no wallahs available and Puri had to load the luggage on to another trolley himself, he was pulled over at customs where his moustache wax was treated with suspicion.

He proceeded into the arrivals hall, vowing to make an official complaint to the British authorities and to pen a letter to the honourable editor of the *Times of India*, describing his experience.

'Anyone's told these Britishers they no longer rule the waves?' he asked Joni, Rumpi's cousin's husband who had come to collect them.

A gentle, understated man, whose accent was as distinctly Delhi as it had been on the day he'd departed India thirty-seven years earlier, Joni tried to make light of Puri's experience. 'News has been slow to catch on,' he said with a calm, welcoming, gap-tooth smile. 'Come.'

He led them to a table in a cafe reserved for customers, and produced a thermos of chai, homemade parathas, a Tupperware container of lemon achaar, another of fresh yoghurt, and a last one packed with sliced guava.

'The drive is a long one, so best to refill now and make use of the facilities,' Joni explained before calling his son, Jagat, better known as 'Jags'.

'He's parked up a few miles down the road,' he explained as the phone rang.

Jags did not answer until the third attempt.

'Were you sleeping?' Joni admonished him, gently. He listened for a moment, then said, 'Yes, yes, everyone is present and correct. We'll be in position presently.'

Joni ended the call and grinned. 'He's a good boy, passed his driver licence some months back.'

He and Puri then engaged in a playful tussle over the luggage trolley (to the detective's relief, Joni won) before the party made their way to the lifts.

They emerged from the terminal on to the drop-off arrivals' concourse. It was a bitingly cold day and the wind whipped around the Brutalist buildings. The three Dilli wallahs, whose coats, scarves and gloves were still packed in their luggage, grimaced at the slate-grey sky, numbed to the bone.

Puri commented that he had only felt this cold when he'd visited Leh high up in the Himalayas. In summer.

By the time the car arrived, his teeth were chattering, Rumpi was complaining she couldn't feel her toes, and Mummy had turned a faint shade of blue.

'This is the famous British weather, is it?' asked Puri once he had thawed out in the car and could enunciate properly again.

'Yeah, it's like being on the Norf Pole, Uncle-gee,' said Jags, grinning into his rear-view mirror. 'You wanna wrap up propa, believe me. Tomorra, the forecast is for like heavy rain and sleet. I've got the heating on full whack.'

In response, Puri gave a vague nod, struggling to decipher the young man's accent and idioms, and wondering how the sweet little boy he'd met on visits to Delhi over the years had mutated into this strange specimen with a spiky hairdo, pierced ears, and jeans that looked like they'd been attacked by wild cats?

'I told you not to skimp on the parking, innit,' Jags was telling his father. 'What were you finking?'

Mummy gave her son a gentle nudge and whispered, 'What's he talking, na? And what is *sleet*?'

Puri said little during the rest of the journey, one that took them two hours along an interminable highway swarming with vehicles travelling at alarmingly fast speeds – the 'London Orbital', according to the big signs – and then through neighbourhoods of narrow streets lined with row after row of identical redbrick houses, bare and lifeless-looking trees, and street lights that cast beams upon drizzle suspended in the gathering dusk.

The white PVC door with the silver Ganesh sticker above the number '72' swung open and the bright, smiling face of Rumpi's maternal aunt's daughter, Nina, appeared. She was wearing a silk sari. Her face shimmered with makeup.

'*Oh – my – Gaaad!*' she squealed, excitedly. 'Kiddan? After *sooo* long! Come, come, get out of the rain. Be warm. Jags, bring their bags!'

Nina was holding a stainless steel aarti tray arranged with a lit diya, bowls of rose petals and uncooked rice, and a small pot of kumkum and musk. She applied some of the paste mixed with rice on the foreheads of Puri and Rumpi, and they in turn passed the palms of their hands over the flame.

Mummy was taking her time exiting the car. She paused by the kerb, complaining about her hips again, and then remembered her handbag on the back seat.

Jags offered to retrieve it while she lingered on the pavement, ignoring Nina's further appeals to hurry in out of the rain, and watching the road in the direction they had come.

'So forgetful I'm getting day by day,' she apologized as, finally, handbag in hand, she stepped over the rangoli pattern on the doorstep and greeted Nina.

Having removed her chappals and added them to the other footwear in the narrow hallway, Mummy then joined the others in the sitting room, gathering around a gas fire roaring beneath a Victorian mantelpiece.

'What a lovely house,' Rumpi complimented Nina when she brought in a tray of more chai and snacks. 'I do so love the leaf design around the edge of the ceilings, very pretty,' she added in reference to the cornice moulding.

'A proper English cottage we can say,' smiled Puri, settling down on the white leather couch. 'It reminds me of Shimla actually. Wonderful old-world charm.'

'But with an Indian touch, na,' added Mummy, indicating the shrine in the corner and the portrait of the guru, Osho, on one of the walls.

'And you are looking well, I must say,' Rumpi told Nina.

'So much weight loss is there, na,' observed Mummy, approvingly.

'Looking quite trim,' agreed Puri.

There came a thud from the hallway – evidently Jags bringing the bags into the house.

'Don't go marking my walls, you!' called out Nina, whose vernacular changed when speaking with her son, her accent more London than Delhi. 'Take Uncle and Auntie's bags up to the front bedroom. Mummy-ji's staying in the guest room.'

She waited for a reply but one wasn't forthcoming.

'You're hearing me?'

'I'm not deaf, yeah!'

The thin walls of the house reverberated, and the little glass effigies of Krishna and Laxmi rattled on the mantelpiece as Jags thudded up the stairs.

Nina rolled her eyes. 'Chubby, while you're here I want you to speak with the boy, try to talk some sense into him,' she said, keeping her voice down. 'You're someone he can look up to and he requires inspiration. What's got into him, I don't know.'

'Always watching Tik and Tok,' said Joni with a smile.

'After passing out of secondary school, he was offered a place at university, but said he wanted this "gap year",' said Nina. 'Fine, I agreed, take some time. But now he's saying he's not interested in continuing his studies.'

Rumpi asked: 'Has he been working?'

'For this *Deliveroo*,' said Nina, disapprovingly. 'My son, the takeaway delivery boy.' She shook her head from side to side. 'Something has to be done.'

'I would say so,' said Puri, embarrassed to learn of Jags stooping to such menial work. 'I'll do what all I can, that is if I can work out anything the fellow is saying.'

'We're not used to his London accent,' Rumpi hastened to add, concerned he had caused offence. 'We'll get used to it in the coming days.'

'Speak to him in Punjabi!' insisted Nina. 'He understands it perfectly. It's all up here.' She tapped her temple with one finger.

'Maybe a little rusty, just in need of lubrication,' said Joni.

The conversation turned to other matters – mainly family gossip. Nina also reflected about Britain, following Puri's experience at Heathrow which had left him wondering if racism was still a problem in the UK.

'Less and less,' said Nina. 'Just look at politics. Rishi Sunak is the current chancellor.'

'A good Hindu boy,' said Joni. 'They're saying he'll be prime minister one day. Just imagine, an Indian in Downing Street.'

By now it was six UK time and Puri was ready for a drink. 'Some thirst is there, actually,' he said. But to his horror, Nina explained that nowadays the house was dry. And worse: the couple had adopted a vegan diet and a good deal of the food Nina prepared was raw. Dinner consisted of moong sprouts and spring onion tikkis, green pea khichdi, a raw cabbage and raisin salad – and worse still – rotis made from oats.

Propriety dictated that Puri had to eat his fill and sound appreciative. He had to play along with Rumpi enthusing about the food, too, and when she suggested they adopt a similar diet, which was sure to help with his blood pressure, he intoned, politely, 'Yes, my dear, why not?'

But the truth was the meal left him feeling unsatisfied and still hungry. Every mouthful tasted bland, even the chillies, and he kept thinking about how, if he was in Delhi, he would find some excuse to nip off to Khan Chachas for a couple of mutton kakori rolls. Perhaps, while he was at it, he would go in for a chicken biryani with a nice butter naan or two as well.

By the time Puri went to bed, he felt positively homesick.

Lying under the weight of thick blankets, he found the pin-drop silence eerie and unnerving. In the absence of the distant hum of traffic and honking from the highway, the barking of street dogs, the tap of the guards' lathis on the road as they made their rounds through the colony, the strains of Lag Jaa Gale coming from the chowkidar's radio, he found it impossible to sleep.

At two in the morning, while Rumpi slept soundly, Puri crept as quietly as he could manage downstairs, though each step on the Victorian floorboards and staircase brought a deafening creak.

In the kitchen, he searched the fridge and cupboards for something substantial to eat. But nothing appealed to him – and he sat down at the breakfast table to read an update from Tubelight on the Shweta Bhatt stakeout.

Puri's back was to the door, and so quietly did his mother enter the room behind him that he gave a start when she rested her hand on his shoulder.

'By God, Mummy-ji!' he exclaimed. 'You're trying to give me a heart attack or what?'

'Chubby, how long I've been telling you to get your hearing tested,' she said. 'Day by day it is getting worse.'

She went to the fridge and took out a bottle of milk.

'Some insomnia is there,' she explained. 'Warm milk with cardamon and a pinch of haldi is required. I'll make you one glass, also.'

Once her concoction was prepared, she joined Puri at the table, passing him a steaming mug.

For a few minutes, they made small chat – and then she asked in a matter-of-fact tone: 'Chubby, tell me, while here in London you've some work, is it?'

'Not at all,' he said, wondering if she'd seen Tubelight's message over his shoulder. 'What gave you such an idea, Mummy-ji?'

'You've plans to visit the Scotland Yard that is all,' she said.

'A social call, only. Inspector Si-maan Brom-ley was kind enough to extend me an invitation. He is proposing a tour of the Scotland Yard, and lunch, also.'

'No doubt you spotted the goonda on the plane? The hairy one.'

'No, Mummy-ji, I did not spot any hairy goonda on the plane,' said Puri with barely restrained patience.

'He was acting suspicious, watching Rumpi when she came to find me.'

'Mummy-ji, perhaps you've forgotten the last time you believed someone was following me? It turned out the individual in question mistook me for Dilip Kumar.'

'He was a stalker all the same.'

'A totally harmless one. He wanted a selfie and my autograph. The poor fellow got quite disappointed when I explained I was not his Bollywood hero.'

'This time is different, na. Hairy One is a professional.'

'A professional what?' Puri's molars had started to grind together involuntarily.

'He was there in the airport, loitering like.'

'A coincidence only.'

'Coincidence, nahi. It is *incidence!*'

The back door to the house swung open and Jags stepped in out of the rain, carrying a Deliveroo bag and a bike helmet.

He looked taken aback to find Puri and Mummy sitting there. 'You two 'aving trouble sleeping, yeah?' he asked.

'Some jet lag is there,' explained Mummy.

'Dad's got somefing to sort it. I can blag you some of his pills,' said Jags.

Mummy blinked back at him. 'Sorry, beta, I'm not following,' she replied and switched to Punjabi.

Despite Nina's assurance that her son understood the language, he seemed to follow very little.

'I'll try to speak a bit slower, like,' he said, reverting to English.

'You need to articulate your words in a proper fashion and use correct vocabulary, not so much of slang,' Puri admonished him. 'Frankly speaking, you're sounding like street trash.'

'Nah, Uncle-gee, you're just not used to like the London accent, thas all.'

'We're used to Queen's English, actually.'

'Yeah, well there's all sorts of English, innit.'

Jags went and fetched some of his father's sleeping tablets, but Mummy refused them.

'Milk with cardamon works better,' she said. 'Now just I'll take sleep.'

'I'll be turning in, also,' said Puri.

They both wished Jags a goodnight and made their way upstairs.

On the landing, Puri whispered, 'Sooner we get that one to India for re-education, the better,' and Mummy nodded in agreement.

FIVE

P uri had experienced his fair share of extreme weather – the relentless monsoon rains of Cherapunjee hammering on the corrugated-iron roofs of Meghalaya's bungalows; severe Himalayan blizzards in Kargil during his army days; heatwaves in Delhi that left air conditioners spluttering. Once, he had been caught in a typhoon off the Bay of Bengal with wind speeds of 120 miles per hour. But never before had the detective contended with the unique meteorological phenomenon of horizontal-falling British rain. It was cold, stinging rain at that, the antithesis of the warm, heavy tropical droplets that were so eagerly anticipated when the clouds rolled over Delhi in late June. And as he and Jags made their way down East Ham high street towards the Underground station, he was forced to keep his head down and fashion his umbrella like the shield of a medieval knight advancing on a position of archers.

Still, the distinct character of Jags's 'manor', as he referred to it, was impossible to miss. Stamped indelibly on to the canvas of tatty, redbrick terraces with their sawtooth rooftops, stretched a long panorama that screamed South Asia, interrupted here and there by a pub or betting shop. Gold bridal chokers and extravagant pearl earrings fit for maharanis dazzled in the windows of jewellery stores. South Asian mannequins with retro Seventies hairstyles and dressed in vivid silk and chiffon saris stared vacantly from the displays of clothing emporiums. Mini markets that would not have looked out of place in bustling Sarojini Nagar offered cauldron-size rice cooking pots and Day-Glo Ganesh idols.

They passed a Hindu temple with an ornate, pink and cream gopuram competing with the rows of Mary Poppins chimney pots, and a good many cheap Indian eateries offering 'pure veg' thali lunch specials and Keralan curries – and for ambience the promise of veneer tables laid with standard stainless-steel drinking cups, waxy napkins and bowls of sonf.

This wasn't London, surely?

'Everyone here is completely desi,' Puri remarked with disapproval to Jags after they stepped into East Ham underground station. He had already caught snatches of Urdu, Hindi, Bangla and Tamil. The employee manning the ticket barriers looked African and sported dreadlocks. 'Where are the proper British people?' he asked.

Jags urged him to keep his voice down. 'Whatch'you getting at, Uncle-gee? You think only white people are British sort of fing?' he asked.

They were standing on the platform now, waiting for a train. A small pool of water had formed around Jags's sneakers. His hoodie was soaked through as well.

'I'm asking you where all the proper, English-speaking white people have got to, exactly?'

There were, in fact, three white men in paint-splattered overalls standing nearby, but they did not fit the bill, at least in Puri's book, as they were speaking in some Eastern European language.

Jags blinked with quiet incredulity in the face of his inverted prejudice. But remembering his mum's advice to make the effort to speak slowly and clearly and pronounce his 'Hs' (never mind that Puri and Mummy spoke in Hinglish, which he struggled with himself!), he tried to bring some clarity to the conversation.

'Basically, Uncle-gee, it's like this,' he said. 'See, most of the old white families, they don't live round 'ere these days. They all moved out to, like, Epping, Chigwell, Essex – basically further east – so what you've got now is a major immigrant population.'

'So segregation is there. East Ham is a ghetto-like-place, in other words.'

'No. No. It ain't like that,' said Jags. 'This isn't South Africa. It's more a sort of result of an economic reality. Plus, desis, yeah – they like to live on top of one another, innit.'

'We are community-orientated people, whereas the Britishers are cold and maintain distance,' stated Puri.

'Yeah, well, I suppose,' said Jags, not at all convinced by Puri's logic. 'Just be careful who you go calling British these days. Look at me, yeah, this is my manor, I've never lived no place else. You can't tell me I'm not British. Same goes for like Idris Elba and Mo Farah.'

Puri had no idea who he was referring to and didn't bother asking.

'Listen, you are Indian, no debate,' he said. 'You cannot pick and choose identity like some fancy dress. It comes from your parents, family. Gotra, also. Without them you are nothing.'

Jags's expression suggested he'd heard this argument before.

'Don't get me wrong, I value my Indian heritage,' he replied, appealing for reason. 'When it comes to cricket I'm like one hundred per cent there for India. But that don't make me Indian.'

Puri, who was on the whole unused to having his view challenged – especially by a younger family member – sought to have the final word by stating definitively, 'What you're talking. Only a half-witted person would say such a thing.'

Jags knew better than to carry on the conversation.

'Whatevs,' he murmured, as a west-bound train pulled up alongside the platform.

The carriage was packed solid – the District Line Morning Mash. Puri was pinned between two builders in overalls discussing the failings of their football team's manager, and a student wearing headphones bleeding thumping music that sounded suitable as a form of torture.

After four stops, the builders were replaced by a thickset gentleman with a tattooed neck; a besuited gentleman with sharp elbows playing Candy Crush on his mobile phone, and a couple of teenagers eating sausage and egg McMuffins.

At Whitechapel, Puri mutinied.

Pushing his way out of the carriage, he staggered onto the platform, tugging open the collar of his Safari suit.

A few minutes later, they were up in the street hailing a black cab.

'The Tube is most disappointing, I must say,' complained Puri once they were on their way again. 'Delhi Metro is better all round. Stations are airier and cleaner and more orderly. The carriages, also.'

Jags, who, now and again, had to contend with visiting Indian relatives who constantly compared everything in London to back home, didn't bother standing up for the Underground. He did warn Puri that black cabs were expensive, but it made no difference.

'For a few pounds more, it is worth the price of admission,' said Puri. 'This is most comfortable – and, see, the driver is proper British!'

The cab passed through the City and along the Embankment, the detective noting approvingly the grand Victorian façade of the Liberal Club and the ornate lampposts with their opaque white globes lining the Thames.

The London Eye and Westminster Bridge pulled into view. A couple of red double-decker buses completed the anticipated scene.

'Now this is the genuine London,' Puri declared, as if Jags had somehow conspired to hide it from him or had never seen it for himself. 'There, also, is the Big Ben!' he exclaimed when the famous clock came into view, adding by way of an admonishment, 'Had we not come by cab, we would have missed it, totally.'

The cab delivered them to the pavement where the iconic New Scotland Yard sign rotated reliably in the drizzle.

'That'll be eighteen pounds, gents,' said the driver as he pulled up to the kerb.

Puri converted the pounds into rupees in his head and his eyes widened when he realized just how right Jags had been. Before the young man had a chance to gloat, however, someone behind them called out Puri's name.

They turned to find a tall, long-necked man approaching. He reminded Jags of a pencil with a rubber on top. This was Inspector Simon Bromley.

'Namast-ay!' he said, pressing the palms of his hands together. 'I must admit I never thought I'd see the day, what with your fear of flying, but here you are: Mr Vish Puri in the flesh. Just goes to show you can teach an old dog new tricks, eh?'

Had anyone else referred Puri as 'an old dog', his response would have been very different, but while assisting Bromley in India on various cases over the years, he had grown more or less accustomed to the eccentric British habit of addressing friends or colleagues with turns of phrase that in some parts of the world would result in spilled blood. The jibe about his fear of flying did not sit so well with him either – and it served as a reminder of the Scotland Yard man's habit of joshing.

'Good to see you looking very much yourself, Inspector-sahib,' he said, determined to give as good as he got. 'Last time we met you were not handling at all well our Indian weather.'

He could picture Bromley with a face the colour of candy floss, his white shirt (did he ever wear any other colour?) soaked through with sweat, looking like he needed to be rushed to A&E.

'Christ, I'll never forget it. Forty-five degrees it was. Felt like I was being cooked in my own skin,' said Bromley, whose natural colour here in his native environment appeared to be pasty, save for his ruddy cheeks and dusky bags beneath his eyes. 'What we do for the job, eh? But that's enough reminiscing. Step this way and we'll get you signed in.'

Jags, who had agreed to bring Puri to Scotland Yard and no further, started to protest that he needed to get home, that he was on shift later. But Puri was having none of it – 'come, this will prove educational' – and before he knew it the young man was being handed a visitor pass.

Bromley took them to the fifth floor and proceeded down a long, silent corridor lined with identical plywood doors – something of an anti-climax for Puri, who had expected holding cells and rooms full of sleep-deprived, coffee-soaked British detectives poring over evidence and mugshots.

The reek of antiseptic cleaning fluid pervaded the place, though in Bromley's uninspiring office this was superseded by the pong of a bacon bap smothered in some kind of brown sauce, which sat half-eaten on his desk.

'Tea, coffee?'

Much to Puri's amazement, Bromley set about preparing the beverages himself. These he served in paper cups.

'No chai wallahs in Scotland Yard, I'm afraid,' said Bromley, guessing Puri's thoughts. 'We have to do for ourselves.'

'I am told yours is a DIY culture,' commented Puri, remembering how his old friend, Suro, had put it back in Delhi.

'Me, I'm a modern liberated man, or so I'm told,' said Bromley. 'Nowadays I even iron my own shirts.'

Puri couldn't tell if this was sarcasm or exaggeration.

'Mrs Lucy is well, I take it?' he asked.

'I believe so, Vish. We're no longer together, if you must know.'

'Is it?' he said, mixing surprise with a touch of disapproval. 'I was very much under the impression yours was a long and happy marriage.'

'I was under a similar impression. Until Lucy went and ran off with her hot yoga instructor. An Indian bloke as it happens. From Tamil Nad-OO.'

'My hearty condolences, Inspector-sahib,' said Puri, gravely, letting Bromley's mispronunciation of the state go uncorrected.

Bromley frowned back at him playfully. 'Well, it's not all bad, Vish. No one died. We still see each other, get together for the kids' birthdays.'

He took to the office chair behind his desk. 'Now let's get on with it, shall we? I got your somewhat cryptic message. First things first, did I hear you right when you called? You're in London for basically a week?'

Puri gave a nod and tried his tea. It was tasteless and he had to force himself to swallow.

'You're a bit ambitious, aren't you?' asked Bromley. 'What makes you think you're going to lay your hands on Bombay Duck in so short a time?'

'Bombay Duck?'

'Our code name for Dr Bhatt.'

'Bombay Duck is a fish,' stated Puri, puzzled.

'Yes, Vish, I'm aware of that.' Bromley's tone was defensive.

'I'm not following. What is the connection exactly between Dr Bhatt and this fish?'

'I'll answer that in a minute,' said Bromley. 'More pressing is what's your part in all this? Are you here in an official capacity?'

'Quasi-official, so to speak.'

Puri went on to explain how the case had come his way, without revealing his client's name.

'Needless to say, my involvement is strictly hush-hush top secret and must remain so,' he continued. 'Our High Commission in London should not be informed under any circumstance.'

'Bit of a leaky ship, is it?'

'Let us say some concern is there regarding bureaucracy getting in the way of progress,' said Puri, diplomatically.

Bromley took a moment to reflect, his forehead corrugated, then said: 'If we're going to do this thing, it's got to be a two-way street, Vish. No secrets.'

'Mutual back-scratching is desirable,' agreed Puri.

'Good, now my guess is you know something I don't, otherwise there's no way you'd take on a case this challenging in London. You're just too cunning an old fox for that.'

Puri wasn't sure how he felt about being compared to a fox, though it was definitely an improvement on a canine. 'Inspector-sahib, believe me, I am totally clueless – of that I can assure you. A few days back, only, I was approached to look into the matter. I've done background reading, that is all.'

'You've *nothing* to go on?' Bromley looked dubious.

'Zero, precisely. Just I was planning on doing piggyback so to speak on your investigation. Tell me some progress is there. You've been chasing Dr Bhatt for four months is it not?'

'Yeah, well, it's not exactly the only case on our books just now, Vish,' said Bromley, guardedly. 'You've no idea how many runaway foreign billionaires there are hiding out in London. From India alone there's – what? – three, including your Vijay Mallya and the jewellery fraudster, what's his name.'

'Nirav Modi,' said Jags. 'That geezer took millions. Goes to ground in London, then turns up shopping on Oxford Street. Well cheeky.'

'Right,' said Bromley. 'My point is you can't swing a stick in London without hitting an on-the-run CEO. We've got Pakistanis, Kenyans, Angolans, Sri Lankans. Don't even get me started on the Russians. All your deposed despots and rebel leaders turn up here, along with runaway princesses from the Emirates, Cypriot hedge-fund managers, Pentagon whistle-blowers. The Met's got to find the resources to deal with all of them. Leaves us spread a bit thin.'

Bromley was starting to look more like he had in the heat in Delhi.

'Anyhow, getting back to Bombay Duck,' he continued. 'It's not as if we haven't made any progress – as a matter of fact, a few weeks back we almost had him. Five more minutes and he'd have been in the bag . . .'

'Tell me.'

Bromley sat back in his chair. 'Just hang on. Now I owe you one, Vish, I haven't forgotten. But before I share, I want your assurance that if you do beat the odds and track down Bombay Duck, you'll inform me immediately. I don't want to be hearing about it on Sky News.'

'One hundred, fifty per cent, Inspector-sahib, no argument from my side.'

'And no funny business.'

'Funny business?'

'Hacking into people's bank accounts, breaking and entering, bugging offices without a warrant, impersonating law-enforcement officers. Or judges. Or four-star army generals, for that matter.'

'You had no complaints about my methods when they got results in India,' said Puri, taking exception to Bromley's admonishment.

'I was hardly in a position to object, was I? But here we have rules, Vish. We have laws. Procedures. Got it?'

'Loud and clear,' said Puri, who was about to relate his experience at customs but realized it was perhaps not the best time to lodge his complaint.

Bromley reached for a file – and spent the next ten minutes explaining how, a month ago, they had tracked Dr Bhatt to a luxury penthouse apartment on Regent's Park.

'When we raided the place, Bombay Duck escaped out the back – and we haven't picked up his trail since.'

Puri asked if he could see the place for himself.

'I figured you'd want to – I've got a car standing by.'

'Very good, Inspector-sahib. But now kindly put me out of my misery. Why Bombay Duck?'

'I came up with it – a bit of a double entendre,' said Bromley, clearly pleased with himself. 'Dr Bhatt's from Bombay and Bombay Duck is actually a fish. Not a lot of people know that. Fish are slippery and this particular type of fish is known to reek.'

'Now I'm following you,' nodded Puri, approvingly. 'Dr Bhatt is a slippery fellow and smells of corruption, also – hence Bombay Duck. Yes, yes, very good, Inspector-sahib.'

He gave a gentle chuckle and then a thought occured to him.

'Another meaning is there, also,' he said. 'Now that we two

are collaborating to solve the case, we can say that Dr Bhatt will not be . . . *ducking* justice for much longer.'

His pun induced a painful groan from Jags – 'Aw, leave it out, Uncle-gee, you're killing me' – and a roll of the eyes from Bromley.

'Comedy never was your strong point, was it, Vish?' he said.

SIX

N
ina took Mummy and Rumpi on a quick tour of East Ham before they reached a terraced street that looked identical to all the others in the neighbourhood. About halfway down, she approached a two-up-two-down that might have been her own, save for the different number on the PVC front door. This was the venue of the 'function' arranged by a cousin on Rumpi's side who had attended a number of big family weddings in Delhi and Punjab over the years.

Mummy was something of a legend amongst this UK branch of the family, owing to her success in recovering a cousin's set of jewellery after it was stolen during one such wedding three years earlier.

Over chai, pakoras and plenty of tangy tamarind chutney, a congregation of close to two dozen local aunties and uncles all pressed into the house, begging Mummy to recount the details of her exploits.

Then it was straight on to Wanstead by taxi for another engagement. This was at the behest of Mummy's close friend, 'Buggi' Bhambri, a widow, whose twenty-four-year-old daughter, Amber, had fallen for a British desi boy called Sanjiv Dhillon. Just a fortnight earlier, he had proposed and, somewhat unconventionally, the two hoped to wed in Delhi in a month's time. Mummy's brief was to meet the family and report back with her impressions, though ostensibly it was just a courtesy call.

The Dhillon family's home turned out to be an imposing, detached redbrick McMansion, with a large front garden paved over to make way for two gleaming BMWs and a MINI Cooper. Blinds masked any sign of activity inside – quite unlike the terraced houses in Nina's neighbourhood where the ground-floor windows were like big fish tanks but with people inside, Mummy reflected.

She noted the CCTV cameras as well. There were three mounted on the outside of the house pointing in different directions. One was aimed down at them as they approached the front door.

Mrs Dhillon answered – forties, all polish and blush and glossy hair, and reeking of expensive perfume. A shimmering gold silk kurta pyjama evinced a tall, shapely figure.

A sudden gust forced her back inside with an 'eek!' and Mummy, Rumpi and Nina, along with a flurry of autumnal leaves, were pushed by the wind unceremoniously into the large entrance hall.

'What crazy weather!' said Mrs Dhillon as she managed to close the door behind them and quickly tend to her hair. 'You poor dears, do come in and we'll get you dry and warm. Ajay, take their coats and scarves. By the looks of it we'll be needing a couple of towels.'

Her husband, a small man with thinning hair in a business suit, dutifully stepped forward and introduced himself.

'The girl will get the leaves,' Mrs Dhillon told him, in case there was any room for doubt. 'Be a dear and tell the caterers we're ready.'

She led the way into a living room decorated in a style befitting the new bijou hotels found in trendy parts of Mumbai and Delhi. Low-set couches, all pastel yellows and pinks, dressed with bright cushions featuring retro images of Hindu deities, sat below big brass lamps that looked like inverted kettle drums. The mauve-coloured walls were adorned with collectable modern Indian art: a large gold-on-black OM and Shiva riding the Milky Way. Somehow it came as no surprise to the visiting trio when their hostess explained that some famous interior designer that none of them had ever heard of had been paid considerable amounts of money to advise on the decor.

'Very bright and eye-catching, na,' said Mummy, charitably.

'And such a lovely garden,' complimented Rumpi, admiring the lawn and beds that lay beyond the French doors.

'I'm not one for gardening but Ajay likes to potter about out there,' she said. 'Ah, here he comes with the towels. Darling, where are the children?'

He explained that they were running late and would join them in ten minutes or so.

'One of the dogs got a thorn in his paw and had to be taken

to the vet,' Mrs Dhillon explained as they all found places on the couches. 'Now then,' she continued, with a practised smile, resting her hands in her lap so that her large diamond wedding ring and perfect nails were on prominent display. 'I understand you're a close friend of Amber's mother, is that right Auntie-ji?'

'I became close to Amber's nani,' clarified Mummy. 'We two met in Jammu, the family's native place. That was a long time back, while we were in our twenties. So we can say that Buggi is like my daughter and Amber my own granddaughter.'

'How nice!' gushed Mrs Dhillon. 'Sanjiv says Amber speaks of you with great fondness.' She glanced over Mummy's shoulder. 'Ah, good, the caterers,' she said, as two liveried young women appeared, one bearing pots of tea, the other a selection of canapés.

'Those are mini idlis served on a spoon filled with sambhar,' Mrs Dhillon explained as the snacks were served. 'And those are tiny paapri chaats. I use a local catering company owned by my girlfriend. I made sure it's all vegan just in case. You can't be too careful these days.'

A discussion about the canapés – 'Innovative, but authentic,' commented Rumpi, approvingly – led to a conversation about the cost of mangoes this season and Mrs Dhillon spoke about her fondness for the Mexican variety, though this seemed like an excuse to speak about the family's summer holiday in Florida. Rumpi spoke of her plans to visit various London sights, to which Mrs Dhillon suggested Madam Tussauds – 'Nowadays they've lots of Bollywood filmi stars. You'll find Shah Rukh, Amitabh, even Aishwarya.'

From waxworks, they moved on to family histories, and Mrs Dhillon explained that she and her husband had grown up neighbours in east London. His parents were from Amritsar, hers originally from Karachi via Jalandhar. The two had been introduced by their families and married in their mid-twenties.

'The first years were a struggle, I don't mind admitting,' Mrs Dhillon explained. 'We started a clothing manufacturing business and in those early years had very little. Our first place had just one room with the kitchen practically in the bedroom! Can you imagine? When Sanjiv was born we brought him home on the bus. Whatever comforts we enjoy today, we have earned through hard work.'

'The company has reached a respectable size and we are expanding day by day,' said Mr Dhillon. 'It may interest you to know, we are planning to open a new factory in India.'

'Now, darling, don't go boring our guests with business talk,' interrupted Mrs Dhillon. 'I'm sure they'd prefer to hear about all your philanthropic work. Ajay is a governor of our local secondary school and supports a charity in Wanstead that rehabilitates rescued animals. Naturally, I do all I can to support the local community through our local Hindu charity, which runs yoga and educational courses.'

'We are a respectable family with strong family values,' Mr Dhillon was at pains to stress. 'Though we have lived in the UK, we have not forgotten our roots.'

Mummy asked to visit the 'WC' and was shown to a bathroom on the ground floor beyond the house's central, sweeping staircase.

She was drying her hands on the monogrammed hand towels when a far-off voice caught her attention. It was a woman's voice, unmistakably Indian, soft and sonorous. Of all things, she was singing a Haryanvi folk song, a sad lament traditionally sung by Muslim women in purdah.

Mummy wondered if it might be a recording, but soon the singing stopped and she could hear the young woman sobbing.

Leaving the bathroom, she traced the sound to the adjacent room, wondering if it belonged to the 'girl' Mrs Dhillon had referred to earlier when she had spoken about cleaning up the leaves that had blown in?

Mummy knocked gently on the door. When no one answered, she tried the handle but found it locked, and decided to rejoin the others.

By now the Dhillon children had returned with the dog from the vet – the teenage daughter, Tanya, and the twenty-six-year-old prodigal son, Sanjiv.

A handsome lad, tall and confident with smart hair, the latter concentrated his charm on Mummy.

'Amber's told me so much about you, Auntie-ji,' he said, and bent down to touch her feet out of respect. 'I'm so pleased to meet you.'

He recounted how he had met Amber on a flight returning from Jammu where she had gone to meet her grandmother.

He hadn't been planning to get married, he said – 'Though Mum and Dad were really on my case!' – but then realized he'd met the girl of his 'dreams'. And he spoke excitedly about plans for the wedding to be held at the Neemrana Fort outside Delhi.

'Moving quite fast, na,' commented Mummy.

'What can I say, Auntie-ji? When I make up my mind, I go for it,' said Sanjiv.

Tanya and Nina, meanwhile, had established a friend in common in East Ham. It just so happened this same friend had been at the morning function and had been telling Tanya only an hour earlier about the exploits of 'some legendary, really canny auntie' who'd caught a jewellery thief in Delhi.

'But that was Mummy-ji,' said Nina.

'No way, I don't believe it!' exclaimed Tanya, and turning to her parents said, excitedly: 'Mum, Dad you've got to hear this story! Auntie-ji is like the Indian version of Nancy Drew. She totally solved a mystery at this Delhi wedding and unmasked the thief. Didn't it turn out to be the bride herself?'

For the second time in a day, Mummy found herself recounting her exploits.

The jewels were stolen during the mehndi, she explained. The cousin in question left them in her suitcase rather than locking them away securely.

'Naturally this invited temptation, na,' said Mummy. 'When the police came they were clueless and immediately arrested the young maid on suspicion.'

'So how did you figure out it was the bride who did it?' asked Tanya.

'From the beginning, Mummy had some suspicions about the young lady and her parents,' explained Rumpi.

'Correct. Both told contradictory information regarding the birthplace of their daughter. I came to suspect they were not her parents, but impostors. I did further investigation and learned they were basically a criminal gang.'

'So the girl was part of this gang?' asked Mrs Dhillon.

'Very much so. I came to know she had duped nine or ten boys in this way. Her profession was Loot and Scoot Bride.'

Tanya smiled at the term. 'Is that a thing, a Loot and Scoot Bride?'

'You hear about them from time to time,' said Rumpi. 'They mislead young men and make off with the wedding gifts.'

'How did you unmask her?' asked Mrs Dhillon.

'The bride drugged the groom and absconded from the bridal suite,' answered Mummy. 'But just I was waiting outside the hotel having anticipated her intention.'

'Wow, you couldn't make it up!' laughed Tanya. 'And from what I heard, that's not the only mystery you've solved, is that right, Auntie-ji?'

'Here and there I've assisted with a few matters,' said Mummy.

'She's being modest,' laughed Rumpi. 'Believe me, Mummy-ji doesn't miss a thing.'

'Is that so?' said Mrs Dhillon with a pinched smile.

The modern apartment block overlooked Regent's Park.

'This area's a popular one with all your on-the-run billionaires, ousted presidents, rebel leaders and what not,' said Bromley as they entered the building, sounding like an estate agent. 'You've got the Oval for the cricket just walking distance, plus the mosque if that's your thing. Lots of private wealth managers and extradition lawyers in the area. And of course there's the park where the nanny can take the overfed kids for ice cream. Edgware Road's not far with all your Middle Eastern restaurants and cafes. Incidentally, that's where we picked up a former Iraqi minister not long back. The man is alleged to have run Saddam Hussein's torture chambers. We found him across from Argos, sitting in the sunshine enjoying a hoo-kah.'

Bromley flashed an ID at the security guard behind the desk in the foyer and called for the lift.

'The building has twenty-four-hour security – another attraction for anyone with a lot to protect or something to hide,' he said as they waited. 'The residents can monitor the security cameras in all the communal areas on their own monitor. That's what saved Bombay Duck's bacon.'

'How so, exactly?' asked Puri, struggling with the mixed metaphors.

'Two of our detectives visited the address, acting on a tipoff that our man had been seen entering the building, and the security guard directed them to the penthouse apartment,' explained

Bromley. 'My guess is Bombay Duck spotted my men on his monitor and scarpered.'

'How'd'e give them the slip then?' asked Jags.

'There's a second, private lift at the back of the building. Goes down into a subterranean parking area.'

They travelled up to the top floor of the building where the doors opened on to a spacious penthouse apartment with wide views over Regent's Park. Leather couches and glass and chrome tables made up the decor.

Jags was much taken with the place, though to Puri his words seemed to contradict his enthusiasm. 'This place is like well shabby, innit,' he enthused. 'Yeah, I could definitely get used to this.'

He came across a master remote control and started pressing random buttons. Automatic blinds hummed down over the windows. The lighting dimmed. A panel on one wall slid back to reveal a huge Samsung TV.

'Never!' Jags exclaimed. 'That's one of them UHD jobs. They come in at like a hundred and fifty grand, easy. It's got 5K and one of them bendy screens.'

He pressed another button on the remote and loud music blasted out of the surround sound.

'Stop doing monkey business!' bawled Puri, shooting him a furious look. 'Return the lighting to normal mode and up the blinds. You're breaking my concentration.'

Jags mumbled an apology and switched off everything while Puri located the second lift at the back of the apartment, and then the monitor that displayed the CCTV feeds from around the building. This he found on the wall next to the main lift.

'Tell me,' he said, turning back into the main room, addressing Bromley, 'you are certain it was Dr Bhatt who occupied this apartment, is it?'

'His fingerprints were all over the place, Vish.'

'Any other fingerprints were there?'

'The cleaning lady's.'

'She met Dr Bhatt in person?'

'She came three times a week but didn't lay eyes on him once. Told us the place was always empty when she turned up and it was always left impeccable.'

'She was retained by who exactly?'

'The building management. They take care of all the cleaners, organize their schedules. Bombay Duck knew exactly when she'd be in and out.'

'You mentioned the apartment is registered to a shell company in Mauritius?'

'"Gladstone Global Holdings Inc." – doesn't get any more generic than that.'

'You've traced the owner so far?'

'We're working on it, lots of hoops to jump through on that one.'

'Leave it with me, Inspector. I've ways and means. Once we conclude our business here, be good enough to forward the details.'

Puri proceeded into the main bedroom where one side of the double bed had been slept in. In a drawer in a side table, he found a bar of unopened Mysore sandalwood soap and a tube of Neem toothpaste. A small puja shrine in an alcove served as further evidence that the occupant of the apartment had been Indian.

Puri moved on to the kitchen next, where he discovered a cabinet stocked with an extensive selection of Indian spices, everything an Indian cook would need to prepare almost any dish. Another contained a large bag of basmati rice and atta.

'He was preparing his own food?' Puri asked out loud, sounding dubious.

'Must have been,' said Bromley. 'But if you look in the recycling bin there's a bunch of containers for microwave ready-made meals as well. All vegetarian.'

Puri examined the containers and in doing so came across a plastic bag from Masala Bazaar Asian Grocery.

'That's one of those international stores, selling all your ethnic spices and unusual, tropical veg,' said Bromley. 'We spoke with the owner. Said he took several orders over the phone and had them delivered downstairs, fruit and veg mostly.'

Puri opened the fridge and found a couple of old aubergines, along with a half-used can of ghee and a small box of mangoes. This contained three remaining fruits, one of which had turned partially black.

'What we have here?' he said, sounding surprised.

'What is it, Vish?' asked Bromley, coming over to the fridge to see for himself. He sounded concerned, no doubt at the prospect of having overlooked something.

'Must be these mangoes were harvested approximately five weeks back,' said Puri, thinking out loud.

'And?'

'They are Vanraj mangoes, only.'

'*And?*'

'They hail from Gujarat.'

'*So?*'

'They were imported.'

'*Vish*,' breathed Bromley, barely containing his frustration, 'mangoes are a tropical fruit. Any found here in the UK would by definition have to be imported.'

'This variety is readily available in London, is it?' Puri's question was directed at Jags who had joined them in the kitchen.

'Couldn't say, Uncle-gee. Round our way, we get mostly Alphonsoes, some Kesar mangoes, and that sweet Pakistani variety.'

'Probably came with the delivery from the specialist Asian food shop, I shouldn't wonder,' said Bromley. 'Why's that one gone partially black do you reckon?'

'I should hazard a guess that some noxious substance was injected into it for nefarious purposes,' said Puri.

'You mean it was poisoned?'

'Most certainly. I would recommend getting a complete laboratory toxicology analysis done without delay.'

'Right you are.'

'But first I should wish to take the other elevator down to the parking area,' said Puri.

In the basement, they found a dozen parking spaces occupied by various sports cars.

'Bombay Duck left on foot, a narrow alley runs behind the building,' explained Bromley.

The Scotland Yard team had failed to keep watch on the back of the building, in other words.

'Must be Dr Bhatt kept his belongings packed and ready to go at a moment's notice should anyone come knocking,' he observed. 'Save for his toothpaste, he left nothing behind. No papers, no ID, laptop – nothing.'

'So who poisoned the mango?' asked Bromley.

'That is the question, no?' said Puri. 'Could be the box was intercepted ahead of the delivery somehow. Or someone gained access to the apartment and did the needful.'

'You can discount the cleaning woman,' said Bromley. 'I spoke to her myself.'

'And the security guards? You interviewed them, also.'

'They're supplied by a company called 365 and the day guards get rotated in and out on a pretty regular basis from other locations,' explained Bromley. 'Only the night guard had been in the building the four months. Name of Rakesh Sharma. I questioned him myself and he seemed as shocked as anyone that the man on the top floor turned out to be Dr Harilal Bhatt. Only laid eyes on him a few times. Said he never went up to the penthouse himself.'

'I should like to speak with this Rakesh Sharma,' said Puri. 'Can you arrange it somehow?'

Bromley had seen no reason to record his details, and when they made their way back down into the lobby, asked the security guard on duty if he knew how to reach him. After learning that Rakesh Sharma was now working day shifts and was on the rota for the following day, Puri suggested that he return in the morning to speak with him.

'Assuming you're right and the mango was poisoned, who – in your view – would have wanted Bombay Duck dead?' asked Bromley once they were outside.

To this Puri gave a light guffaw. 'The list is a long one and includes powerful interests, Inspector-sahib,' he said. 'Millions were issued from public state banks to Bio Solutions in illegal loans, and those responsible would surely stop at nothing to prevent Dr Bhatt from naming them in the court.'

'It's a sure bet that if they traced him here then they'll pick up his trail again, assuming they haven't done so already,' said Bromley. 'But as of now, I've got precisely nothing.'

'Not at all, Inspector-sahib, you have me and, also, now, a poisoned mango,' said Puri. 'That is progress, no?'

SEVEN

At the sound of a polished, Indian male voice – 'Hello, did I wake you, Bebo?' – Flush sat up alert in his chair, crammed a half-eaten slice of Peppy Paneer pizza into his mouth and started recording the call.

'What time is it?' asked Shweta Bhatt, her voice croaky.

'Lunchtime – India time.'

'I was reading. I must have nodded off.' She took a sip of something, most likely water, before asking: 'Are you OK, Gummy Bear? Why are you using this line?'

'I wanted to hear your voice.'

'I'm so glad you called. Are you looking after yourself? Have you been eating properly?'

'I don't want you worrying about me, Bebo.'

'How can I not worry?' She let out a sigh pregnant with despair. 'Every day I watch TV expecting to see you being paraded in front of the cameras like some common criminal, with all those commentators gloating, judging you. God I hate them.'

'That's not going to happen. I told you.'

There was a pause, then Shweta Bhatt said, 'I was hoping you'd call on Sunday. Did you visit the temple again?'

The man cleared his throat with vigour – a reminder to her that they could be certain eavesdroppers were listening in on every word.

'Sorry, Gummy Bear, sometimes I forget the line is . . .'

'It's OK.'

There came a rustling noise, like a pillow being rearranged.

'Just tell me this is going to be over soon,' she said.

'I promised you.'

'I know.'

'And you trust me?'

'Of course. It's just the loneliness is getting to me. Being apart for all this time. I swear I'm starting to hear voices.'

'We need to stay strong for one another, stick to the plan. It shouldn't be long now. Tell me you're not smoking.'

'Same old Gummy Bear: always looking out for me. I'm being good, I promise.'

'I doubt it,' the man said, his tone playful.

He paused, then said: 'I've sent you a new message. It's self-explanatory.'

'I'll take a look.'

'That's one minute twenty seconds. We're out of time.'

'Promise to call again soon?'

'I promise.'

'Love you, Gummy Bear. Stay safe.'

'Love you, too, Bebo.'

The line went dead.

Flush checked the trace program. It identified the call as originating in Botswana. His voice recognition software gave a positive ID on Dr Bhatt.

'He must be using a proxy server,' he reported to Tubelight a few minutes later. 'This time he caught me on the hop. Next time I'll be ready for him.'

Tubelight wondered why Dr Bhatt had called on her mobile line and not used WhatsApp, which was encrypted.

'Maybe he's assuming even her account is compromised so what's the difference? Or he's just messing with us,' said Flush.

'The main thing is they're talking about being together soon,' said Tubelight. 'Keep vigilant.'

Puri and Jags were both famished and were walking down Baker Street in search of something to eat – and they'd started bickering again.

'You've gotta be jesting me, Uncle-gee, my shift starts at four, innit!'

'Family comes first, no exception, final. I require further assistance.'

'But I could lose my job!'

'*Job?* What are you talking? That is not a job? In India delivery boy is for common people, only.'

'Yeah, well, in my book there's nofing wrong with being common. I'm not afraid of getting my hands dirty. That's one difference between India and here, yeah. In Britain, we ain't got servants doing our bidding round the clock.'

Puri walked on in silence, doing his best to avoid the puddles on the pavement. Jags followed a few steps behind.

'I don't know why everyone's getting so worked up about me working for Deliveroo,' he said. 'Mum, Dad – now you. It's just a temporary gig to tide me over sort of fing. The hours are flexible, the money ain't bad. What's the big deal?'

On the other side of the road, a queue snaked up to the door of one of the Georgian townhouses – Japanese tourists mostly. At the sight of it, Jags stopped suddenly and pointed at the building.

'Uncle-gee, you'll never guess what that is,' he said, excitedly. 'That's where Sherlock 'olmes, lived. We should check it out, it's right up your street.'

Puri scowled at the building and the Holmes look-a-like on the doorstep sporting a deerstalker and calabash pipe.

'Nothing would give me less pleasure, beta, I can assure you,' he said. 'Sherlock Holmes was a nothing person.'

'Says who?'

'His methods of deduction were hardly unique let alone original,' said Puri, giving his usual spiel. 'Centuries earlier, they were perfected in India when Britishers were hunting bears and all.'

Jags gave a snort. 'To be honest, Uncle-gee, I don't think Britain ever had a lot of bears.'

'That is not the point – and this is no time for joking, actually. A man's life hangs in the balance and responsibility lies on our heads to ensure justice is done.'

'How do you figure that, then?'

'You imagine the culprit or culprits will leave the matter unresolved? No doubt at this very moment, he, she or they are searching for Dr Bhatt. And no doubt, having fled the apartment in such a way, he's unaware of how close he came to cheating death and will, potentially, be putting his trust in the wrong sort.'

They came across an old-fashioned sandwich bar where Jags said they could be assured of fast service.

While perusing the menu on the wall above the service counter, Puri asked with a scowl, 'What is a "pastey"?'

'It's pronounced "pasty",' said Jags. 'Think of it like a sort of big samosa with a thick crust, and not much flavour.'

'And jacket potato, that is what exactly?'

Jags explained that it was a large aloo baked in an oven and came with a choice of 'toppings': 'There's baked beans and cheese, tuna and sweetcorn. They do it with curry sauce and all.'

Against his better judgement, Puri opted for the latter. It was delivered to their table in a Styrofoam container. He stared at the congealed curry sauce in something approaching horror.

'Now I understand why Gandhi-ji starved in London during his student days,' he said, pushing away his food. 'All that was on offer was bread and butter and boiled cabbage. No wonder you don't find a British restaurant anywhere in the world, whereas our Indian cuisine is enjoyed by all.'

'You'll do all right in East Ham, Uncle-gee, trust me. It's got everything, innit: Hyderabadi biryani, blinding dosa, I know this place that does a mean butter chicken.'

'Where is the time? Rumpi is expecting me for the family function at four.'

Jags bit into his Coronation Chicken sandwich with relish. 'I don't get it, why don't you just level with her, why all this sneaking around?' he asked.

'That should not concern you,' said Puri. 'Now, you're going to help with this thing or not?'

'I don't know, Uncle-gee,' he said, with a weary shrug, 'this just ain't my scene.'

'Which scene you're referring to?'

'This whole detective malarky. It's not what I wanna get mixed up in, if I'm being honest. You've been here in London – what? – twenty-four hours, and already you're dealing with an attempted murder, of like a billionaire fugitive on the run, hiding out in some fancy apartment.'

'Listen, beta, the task at hand is a perfectly straightforward one, actually,' said Puri, calmly. 'No danger is there, let me assure you. Go directly to this Masala Bazaar Asian Grocery and get talking with the employee on duty. Be casual and friendly. You know how. Find out if they delivered a box of Vanraj mangoes to the address, who all was responsible for making the deliveries, if some possibility is there that someone or other interfered with the box.'

Jags mulled over Puri's instructions. 'Get them talking sort of fing . . . Yeah, I guess I could do that.' There was a pause and he breathed a sigh into it. 'Just this one time, Uncle-gee. I mean it, yeah. Tomorrow, you're on your own.'

'That's the spirit, beta. Remember Chanakya's immortal words: "Those who are afraid of failure cannot learn."'

'Chanak who?'

'*Chanakya*, otherwise known as Kautilya.'

Jags's expression was clueless.

'He was one of the greatest Indians of all time,' said Puri. 'Chanakya founded the Maurya Empire.'

'Yeah, Maurya, I've heard of that. It's where the dwarves live in *Lord of the Rings*, innit.'

Puri hoped he might just have time to get something decent to eat in East Ham before getting back to Rumpi. But it was raining again – the horizontal variety had passed and it now hung like a fine, cold mist, the tiny droplets almost suspended in midair – and all the black cabs were occupied.

Standing back from the curb, avoiding the spray thrown up by the wheels of passing double-decker buses, Puri noticed a black Mercedes-Benz with tinted windows parked further up Baker Street, near to the Sherlock Holmes museum.

He thought perhaps that the same car had been parked across the road from the Regent's Park apartment block (though black Mercedes-Benz cars with tinted windows seemed to be in good supply in this part of London) and kept a wary eye on it.

A few more occupied cabs sped past – Puri getting wetter by the moment and the window for a decent lunch ticking painfully by – while the Merc remained stationary, the face of the driver impossible to make out through the mantle of gloom.

When, at long last, a vacant cab finally stopped for the detective, however, the Merc promptly followed on behind.

Puri made a record of the number plate in his notebook and then considered how best to handle the situation. Perhaps he could persuade the cab driver to try to outrun whoever it was that was following him?

'Mr Derek, is it?' he asked, reading the name on the Hackney Carriage licence.

'Derek's my first name,' the driver responded.

'Is it possible for you to drive even a little faster?'

'How do you expect me to do that?' He gestured at the three lanes of traffic ahead of them stopped in front of a red light.

'I'm in something of a hurry, actually.'

'It is what it is, mate.'

'Some space is there,' said Puri, pointing to a gap between the car in front and a couple of vacant parking spaces. 'Beyond, the right lane is free.'

'You're asking me to mount the pavement?'

'If at all possible.'

'There's pedestrians standing there.'

'Honk your horn and they will be sure to make way.'

The driver stared back at him in the mirror. 'You want to get your head examined, mate,' he said.

Puri explained that his head was in good order and that he was a detective from Delhi and was being followed. But still the response was not encouraging: 'Oh, yeah, it's like that, is it?'

The light changed and the cab went two blocks before hitting another red light.

Mr Derek kept eyeing Puri in the mirror.

'What are you then? A sort of Indian Hercule Poirot?' he asked.

Puri bristled at any comparison to Agatha Christie's creation almost as much as he did at any mention of Sherlock Holmes, and didn't respond.

'My wife's read all the Inspector Ghote books,' the driver went on. 'Loves 'em. I've never been to India myself. I'm quite partial to a vindaloo, though, me.'

They were on the move again now and Mr Derek took the next right, watching out for the Merc.

'You're right and all, he's still behind us,' he reported. 'Who's after you, then?'

Puri had to admit that he didn't know, but said he thought it was 'highly probable' he, she or they were bent on locating a certain Indian fugitive whom someone had tried to murder.

'Probably Colonel Mustard with the wrench, I shouldn't wonder,' joked the driver. 'You'll be wanting the nearest police station, then?'

'What is required is a location where I can alight and lose whoever it may be in the crowd,' said Puri.

Mr Derek gave the matter some thought before suggesting John Lewis. 'It's a department store, busy place,' he said. 'I can drop you at the back entrance, then you can walk through the ground floor and out the other side on to Oxford Street. You won't have any trouble picking up another cab there. That should do you. Unless they've got satellite surveillance or put a tracker in your watch or your shoes.'

'You think that is very likely?' asked Puri. This was asked in earnest: for all he knew, this Londoner knew something he didn't.

'Well, you can never be too careful these days, can you?'

Five minutes later, Puri was safely ensconced in another black cab bound for East Ham. Mr Derek's plan had worked perfectly and he had lost his tail (assuming of course no satellites were tracking him).

What a strange, unpredictable lot the British were, the detective reflected. One minute hostile, suspicious, patronizing, absolutely wedded to their rules, the next showing concern and generosity. The driver had even seen fit to waive the fare and wished him the best of luck.

EIGHT

Flush hadn't left his tempo in twenty-four hours and had managed only a few hours' sleep in a hammock suspended between the roof supports of his vehicle.

It was now dark and his replacement, Chetan, would be along in an hour or so, but he needed to stretch his legs and eat something more substantial than pizza or another bag of masala Uncle Chipps.

He exited his tempo, set the alarm, and was locking the back door to his van when the gate to the Bhatt's villa opened ajar and Savita, the pretty maid, slipped nimbly through the gap.

Her demeanour was manifestly shy and, having checked the street in both directions and pulled her yellow chunni over her head, she set off in the direction of the colony market at the end of the road.

Flush followed behind at a safe distance – safe enough not to draw attention to himself, yet close enough to watch the hypnotic rhythm of her long ponytail, which was tied at the end with a bunch of fragrant jasmine blossoms, and swung back and forth above the line of her slim waist.

At the end of the road, she stopped to speak to another female servant working in a neighbouring house with whom she was clearly acquainted. Flush passed the two of them, seeing for the first time Savita's shy yet infectious smile and catching a snatch of her gentle laughter. He reached the market feeling as if his heart was suddenly too large for his chest and started humming to himself, something he wasn't in the habit of doing. The less salubrious aspects of the place, like the dirty public urinals and the spectacle of a parking wallah exchanging expletives with a scooter owner over a matter of five rupees, seemed to fade into the background and his eyes dwelt appreciatively on the flower stand's riot of colour, and the voluptuousness of the pomegranates piled high on one of the phal wallah's barrows.

At the butcher's, where kebabs sizzled on a sigri in front of the shop, Flush ordered a malai chicken roll, and kept an eager eye out for Savita. The market was busy, however – the kirana store was abuzz with shoppers buying everything from boxes of bottled water to packets of ever-popular masala Maggi noodles; at the counter of the 'Government Wine and Beer Shop', rickshaw drivers jostled to exchange grubby ten- and twenty-rupees notes for pocket-sized plastic pouches of rot-gut spirits; servants employed in the homes of the wealthy residents of Shanti Niketan crowded the vegetable stands lining the road, their figures silhouetted against the white-hot light cast by hissing pressure lamps in the gathering dusk – and he didn't spot her again.

Before heading back to the tempo, Flush decided to treat himself to an ice cream and stopped at the Mother Dairy, a cooperative chain selling mostly dairy products along with fruit and vegetables at affordable prices.

From the freezer, he selected a pistachio kulfi and went to pay.

Six or seven other customers stood ahead of him, all pressed in around the counter, each holding up various rupee denominations as they vied for the attention of the lone employee working the till.

Flush stretched out an arm, flourishing a note of his own, and noticed that Savita was at the front of the scrum. Her chunni had slipped back from her head and lay loose upon her shoulders, revealing the long, soft curve of her neck. For all the pushing and jostling around him, he found himself gazing longingly at its graceful elegance.

His reverie was soon shattered, however, when several of the onions Savita was trying to pay for, fell off the counter onto the floor in between the other customers' feet.

Savita stooped down to retrieve them as the other customers pressed forward regardless and, though he risked bringing attention to himself, which was strictly counter to Most Private Investigators Ltd.'s stakeout procedure, Flush didn't hesitate to give her a helping hand, quickly retrieving three of the onions and passing them to her one by one.

Savita took them without acknowledgement – so flustered did she appear that she did not even notice her benefactor – and, having bagged the onions and settled her bill, hurried from the shop.

Flush was left holding her shopping list, which she had also dropped on the floor.

Mummy, Rumpi and Nina sat around the kitchen table drinking chai and munching on onion pakoras and Bombay mix, discussing tea at the Dhillons'.

'For such types, paisa is number one,' said Mummy.

'The family does seem quite money-minded,' agreed Rumpi.

But Nina was more charitable in her opinion. 'Don't you think you're being a little harsh?' she asked. 'Admittedly, they're a little boastful but they seem respectable.'

'The boy is well mannered and polite,' affirmed Rumpi. 'I'll give him that.'

'Handsome, also, na,' said Mummy.

But she was not at all convinced the match was a good one. 'Something does not feel at all right – like so much of indigestion in the stomach,' she added.

'Is it possible you're being too over-protective of Amber?' asked Nina. 'Mrs Dhillon might not be your type. But the boy seems good and it sounds like they're quite the smitten kittens. Or is there something you're not telling us? You went very quiet after meeting the boy.'

'That's true, I noticed the same thing, you seemed distracted all of a sudden,' said Rumpi.

Mummy told them about the sobbing girl. Judging by her accent and the song she'd been singing, she thought her to be a 'domestic help' from Haryana.

'When I knocked on the door, she failed to answer.'

'You're suggesting she was locked in?' asked Nina.

'That I could not tell. But she was in distress, that I know.'

Rumpi could see where this was going and was suddenly concerned. 'Mummy-ji, please tell me you're not thinking of poking around in these people's business?' she said. 'If you've some concern about the welfare of this girl, it's for the proper authorities to investigate.'

'To be honest you'd have to have more to go on if you were going to call the police,' cautioned Nina. 'They're so overstretched, unless it's a knife crime or something serious like that they don't turn up.'

'Calling police or others is out of the question,' said Mummy. 'First we must have the proof.'

'Of course, what was I thinking, how could I have possibly imagined that we could come to London without having to rescue a distressed maid from Haryana?' Rumpi said with brittle irritation, as if appealing to someone beyond the room. 'It was the same in Dharmsala. There I was hoping to have a break from it all, a few days of relaxation, and of course a couple of Israeli backpackers go missing and you and Chubby have to get involved.'

'They were kidnapped, na,' said Mummy, somewhat taken aback by this outburst from her normally unflappable daughter-in-law.

'But that's my point, Mummy-ji, don't you see? Someone is always getting kidnapped. Or murdered. Or blackmailed. It's as if criminals everywhere wait for you and Chubby to arrive and then – and only then – commit their crimes.'

'For me personally, staying idle is not an option,' said Mummy, defensively. 'This girl could be facing some danger. It is my duty to ensure she comes to no harm. One or two hours are required, that is all.'

'There's also Amber to consider,' said Nina. 'I'm sure she'd want to know if her in-laws have a cruel streak.'

Rumpi had folded her arms and was looking down at the floor.

'I'm prepared to help find out if this Haryana girl is in trouble, but after that you have to promise me you'll leave it to others,' she said.

Mummy gave her word – and suggested they return to the Dhillon house the next day and try to meet the maid, who would surely be made to walk the dogs or be sent to the shops.

'I'll go along for a couple of hours; that's my limit,' said Rumpi. 'Have you considered what you're going to tell Buggi and Amber in the meantime?' she wondered.

'The truth,' said Mummy. 'Some question marks remain and we'll revert.'

There came a creak from the floorboards upstairs, and Puri soon appeared in the doorway to the kitchen, bleary-eyed. He had returned to the house some three hours earlier and, after helping entertain Rumpi's cousins, taken a half-hour nap.

Had Jags returned? he wanted to know.

'You two are having quite a bromance,' smiled Nina. 'He tried calling you about a half-hour back, said your phone was in power-off mode and to pass on that he's had some success.'

Rumpi was immediately suspicious. 'What are you two cooking up? You're up to something – I can tell.'

'Not at all, my dear,' said Puri. 'The dress code for the award ceremony gala dinner is black tie and dinner suit. Jags is scouting on my behalf for a rental company.'

'You're planning to hire one?' asked Rumpi with concern. 'Are you sure they'll have your size?'

'I'm not above average for a man my age,' said Puri, indignant.

'Chubby, please, remember what happened with your golfing trousers?' Rumpi turned to Mummy and continued: 'At the first hole, he bent down to place his ball on the thingy and . . .' She made a ripping sound.

Puri ignored their smiles. 'The material was lacking in elasticity, only,' he insisted. 'Now, if you'll excuse me, while snoozing I had three or four missed calls.'

The mobile signal in the house was weak and this provided him with the perfect excuse to speak with Jags in the street.

'Whattup, Uncle-gee?' he asked in answering his phone. 'Yeah, so I went to the shop like you asked and got talking to this guy working there called Pranap. He like manages the place sort of fing. Turns out he's from down Ilford way. Went to school with my mate, Izzy.'

'That is all well and good, beta, but what all he told you, exactly?' asked Puri, impatiently.

'Yeah, well, I was just getting to that, innit,' said Jags, defensively. 'He never laid eyes on Dr Bhatt, but made a bunch of deliveries to the address. Dropped off spices, ghee, rice, karelas – yeah, and before you ask, Vanraj mangoes.'

'Where he delivered them exactly?'

'To the lobby, always in the evening. Then the security guard – the same one your mate Bromley spoke to, Rakesh Sharma – took everything up in the lift to the top floor.'

'Brom-ley told that Sharma claimed he did not venture up into the apartment,' said Puri. 'Tomorrow, only, we'll need to get some answers from him.'

'Yeah, sure, whatever, good luck with that, Uncle-gee. Like I said, I've done all I can.'

But Puri insisted on one final favour. It would not take long, though it would involve a certain amount of discretion and stealth on Jags's part.

'OK, Uncle-gee, I can arrange that,' the young man agreed, reluctantly.

'Be sure to enter through the backside.'

'Yeah, well, I'm not that way inclined, am I?' joked Jags, but his humour was lost on Puri.

Nina had prepared roasted cauliflower curry and tofu bhurji. Puri put on a brave face again, ever careful not to offend, while, worryingly, Rumpi, who genuinely seemed to enjoy the food, asked for the recipes and promised to make them at home.

Afterwards, while he sat in the sitting room with the rest of the family drinking chai, and Rumpi went over plans for the next day, his thoughts were never far from the case and how the mango had been poisoned. Had it been intercepted or had someone else other than the cleaning lady gained access to the apartment? It was imperative he speak with the security guard, Rakesh Sharma – and Jags was going to help him, whether he liked it or not.

'So is that agreed?' he heard Rumpi ask him.

'Is what agreed, my dear?' he asked, realizing that he had been miles away.

'The plan I've just spent the past five minutes outlining for you!'

'Absolutely one hundred per cent, pukka. What time we'll be setting off?'

Rumpi had to go over the plan again. She, Mummy and Nina had a local engagement in the morning and would then set off for central London. First on the agenda was Buckingham Palace, followed by Parliament and Westminster Abbey.

'Very good,' said Puri. 'That would give me the morning to get measured for my dinner suit – and visit Bates, Gentlemen's Hatters, also.'

Nina served more of her terrible soy milk chai and the group played a few hands of satte pe satta.

At ten, they decided to call it a day and put the cards away.

Joni was about to head upstairs when he remembered that an envelope had been delivered for Mummy at lunchtime.

'It was brought by a young man, very handsome, looked like the actor, Hugh Grant. He was driving a posh car,' he said.

The envelope was square, of extremely high-quality paper, and her name was typed neatly on the front.

Mummy took it from Joni and tucked it into her handbag.

'Aren't you going to open it?' asked Nina.

'No need, just it's a formal invitation for lunch for the day after Chubby's award function,' said Mummy.

'Must be from someone very well-to-do,' commented Rumpi.

'An old lady I met in Delhi some forty years back,' said Mummy, before wishing them all goodnight and going up to bed.

Nina, Rumpi and Puri exchanged curious looks.

'What old friend?' mused Rumpi. 'She didn't mention anything about her before.'

'You know Mummy-ji, always full of surprises and secrets,' said Puri.

'Ha, you should talk,' scoffed Rumpi.

An hour later, Puri's phone gave a ping.

Rumpi was already asleep and he was able to put his shoes back on and slip unnoticed out of the bedroom.

He crept downstairs as quietly as he could manage, passed through the kitchen and found Jags at the back door.

Puri followed him down the garden path to the potting shed.

Inside, Jags put on his mobile light and placed it on one of the shelves between a flowerpot and a can of old paint covered in spider webs and dead bugs.

'What took you so much of time?' Puri asked, keeping his voice down.

'You want it or not, Uncle-ji?' asked Jags, dangling a takeaway bag.

Fiendish aromas started to overpower the stink of engine oil and rotting grass cuttings.

'Don't tease, yaar,' said Puri. 'I'm so starved I swear I've been seeing mirages of kharti rolls and chicken frankies.'

Jags opened a takeaway container packed with biryani. Another held tandoori lamb chops. A third green chillies, sliced red onion and lemon quarters.

Puri dug into the biryani, his teeth sinking into succulent chunks of tender, tasty chicken. The chops met with his approval, too – and though the chillies delivered barely a third of the fire of his home-grown Bhut Jolokias, they did not lack flavour.

'Thank the God,' he sighed. 'The situation was getting critical. Come, take.'

'Na, Uncle-gee, I ate already,' said Jags. 'I'm gonna bounce, get into the warm.'

'And leave me unaccompanied?' Puri gestured to the chops. 'Take one, they're juicy.'

'Seriously, I'm stuffed, innit,' said Jags. 'You knock yourself out, Uncle-gee.'

He opened the door to the shed to find Mummy standing on the other side.

She peered over Jag's shoulder at Puri and frowned: 'Chubby, how many times I've told you? Chew slowly to avoid indigestion.'

He quickly swallowed. 'Mummy, what are you doing here?' he asked. 'I've told you before to not go sneaking up on people in this way.'

'Just I spotted the light through the window,' she said eyeing the food containers. 'Naturally I'm investigating.'

Jags looked from one to the other and said, awkwardly, 'OK, so I'll be getting to bed, I reckon,' and headed off down the path to the house, forgetting his phone.

'You're hungry by chance, Mummy-ji?' he asked as if it was perfectly normal to eat dinner in the dark in a potting shed at the back of a garden.

'Nothing, thank you. Just I've something to tell you in private.'

'Concerning the envelope you received?' asked Puri.

'No, Chubby. Just that is an invitation from an old friend.'

'I don't recall you mentioning any such person in London.'

'I met the lady in question in Delhi some forty years back and assisted her with one small matter. Now listen, na, something important is there. When I looked down the street at dinner time, one motorbike was idling not far off.'

'Mummy, please, don't start, I beg of you,' said Puri as he continued to eat.

'When I approached the motorbike, just the driver drove away quickly like. Owing to the raining, I could not get eyeballs on the number plate. But Chubby – I am sure it was the Hairy One from the flight.'

Puri swallowed again. 'That is fine, Mummy-ji, duly noted. I will keep an eye out,' he sighed.

'Chubby, you listen to me, na. I'm telling you, that one is trouble. Do vigilance and don't put Jags in line of danger,' she warned before heading back into the house.

NINE

Flush's mother was sitting at the small table in the kitchen where she and her son ate all their meals, eyes glued to her smartphone. Though the first to champion technology, it had been a mistake giving it to her for her birthday, he realized. Ma was fast becoming an addict, up until all hours of the night on chat rooms and watching TikTok cookery videos.

More worrying still, she had started to scout the internet for potential brides for him.

'Good news!' she declared, as Flush wished her a good morning, hoping for some of her chhole bhature for breakfast. 'You've three matches on Tinder this morning. All local.'

'Ma, I'm not on Tinder,' he replied.

'Your account went live yesterday. Congratulations. See.'

She showed him his profile, complete with photograph. Under 'interests' it read, 'family' and 'computer'. Under 'sexual preferences' she'd put 'no experience'.

Flush's eyes widened with alarm. 'What have you done? How did you even do this? Ma, you have to cancel this account immediately. You can't go around impersonating people!'

'It is for your own good,' his mother insisted. 'Simi is asking for a date.'

'Who's Simi?'

She showed him a portrait of a young woman with a nice smile. 'She is twenty-three. Rajput. Slim, gori girl. Passed out of Delhi University. Family with connections. I told you're available to take her to the movies on Tuesday at seven. Hrithik is starring in a megahit.'

'Ma, I'm not going on a date with Simi. Not next Tuesday. Not ever.'

'If not her, then Priti. She's a good one. Twenty-four, Rajput also. Passed out of Bangalore. Wheatish complexion and homely. Looking for a tall, computer-engineer boy like you. Her skills include ice skating.'

'Ice skating? How is that a skill? And how does that make her suitable?'

'She could teach you ice skating at Ambience Mall. And you can do karaoke.'

'Ma, listen to me, Tinder is a hook-up site. Most subscribers aren't serious about marriage.'

'What is the meaning of "hook-up"?'

'The subscribers are looking for a *casual* relationship.'

'How else will you find a wife? When the pundit came, you rejected every match. Even that nice Bhavna. She was from a status family and Sagittarius!'

Flush's mother served him some chai before frying his bhature, allowing the light leavened bread to puff up in the wok of oil like a blowfish.

'Ma, you're not to put me on any sites,' he reiterated after he had taken a couple of mouthfuls of the spicy chickpeas and fresh coriander. 'Not Tinder. Not Bumble. No dating apps!'

'Then you will meet the pundit again,' his mother insisted, standing over him as he ate. 'He's found another good girl. She is convent-educated.'

Flush sat down at the table. 'Ma, no, I'm not meeting with him again. The fact is: I've met someone.'

'Sorry?' she said, more with scepticism than surprise.

'I've met someone,' Flush repeated.

His mother had to sit down. 'Jai Shri Ram!' she said under her breath. 'Is she Rajput?'

'Of course,' Flush lied.

'What's her name? Where did you meet her? Is her family good?'

'Her name is Savita, I met her at work, and that's all you need to know.'

But the questions did not let up. Where was she born? What was her father's occupation? Was she 'career-minded'? What was her birth date and time of birth? When would she meet her parents?

'I don't want to rush things, I'm waiting for the right moment,' Flush insisted.

But his mother wasn't hearing him. 'To think I'll finally have a daughter-in-law to help around the house and keep me company . . . and grandchildren,' she enthused as she cleared the table. 'So I should tell Simi it is definitely "no"?'

'On Tinder? Yes, it is a definite no,' reiterated Flush, who was already regretting having told his mother anything.

There was plenty for Puri to worry about. Honouring his commitment to Rumpi while continuing the Dr Bhatt investigation was going to prove a headache. Someone was following him – two parties if Mummy was on the money. And uncharacteristically, he didn't feel confident in his own abilities. Outside of India, where at a glance he could place pretty much everyone in society, his powers of observation were blunted. London might be extremely ethnically diverse, but to Puri's eyes everyone looked more or less the same. In their homogenized, American-style cotton clothes, the population presented few distinguishing features, bar the obvious like gender, skin colour, and occasionally a telling accent. Few amongst them wore hats or caps, let alone pagris or topis. There were no tilaks to signal which sects people adhered to. No distinctive footwear, like leather Katki chappals from Odisha. No one wearing Bhujudi shawls from Gujarat. Puri felt like a superhero stripped of his X-ray vision.

It was not worry that kept him from getting to sleep, however: he was used to pressure and he'd faced more than his share of danger.

Rather, it was the deafening sound of silence.

At midnight, at one and again at two, he found himself standing at the bedroom window, staring out at the rows of jagged rooftops and chimney pots set against the glow of the London sky, grappling with the unnatural still of this vast, capital city.

Only the occasional fizz of a car's wheels passing down the road in the rain reminded him that the world had not stopped turning and that he had not been left in suspended, British purgatory.

Some time after three, tiredness finally trumped the silence, though it was but an hour later that he was woken again, this time by the trilling of a lone blackbird in the tree in front of the house – and pulling a pillow tight over his head, Puri regretted not having his pistol to hand.

Then suddenly it was nine o'clock, and Jags was standing in

the bedroom door, explaining that Nina, Mummy and Rumpi had gone out and he'd been charged with rousing him.

'Who is to make my tea?' Puri asked, groggily.

'Chill, Uncle-gee, I've got it sorted, no issues,' said Jags. 'I don't make a bad cuppa myself.'

So began a day full of surprises – the first being that Jags was indeed capable of making decent masala tea, having first fetched some real milk from the corner store.

His chilli omelette, made with eggs that he bought specially as well, did not prove at all bad either.

Puri was just polishing off a second plate with some buttered double roti when Bromley called.

The results were back from the lab: the mango had been poisoned with aconite.

'Approximately two millilitres was injected into the fruit, using a syringe. One bite and it would have been lights out for Bombay Duck,' said the inspector.

'Must be the toxicity level was high?' probed Puri.

'The pathologist's exact words were, "it buries the needle". He hasn't ever come across aconite with that level of toxicity before.'

'Meaning we can be certain it originated in India. A hybrid of Aconitum is grown in one valley at high altitude in Sikkim. When the root is processed in a certain way, and the extract distilled in the laboratory, it is rendered extremely potent. The manufacture and sale of such a deadly substance is banned by government of India. But naturally it can be procured on the black market, though the tiniest amount even is extremely costly.'

'So our suspect is Indian, then.'

'It would seem so, Inspector-sahib.'

'Any progress with finding out who owns Gladstone Global Holdings?' asked Bromley, referring to the shell company registered in Mauritius that owned the apartment.

Overnight, Puri had contacted another capable private detective in Port Louis who was looking into it.

'Rest assured, you will be the first to know,' said Puri, before dropping into the conversation that he had been followed from the apartment the day before.

'Followed?' responded Bromley, sounding alarmed. 'Who was following you?'

'So many possibilities are there, Inspector-sahib. Could be some interested party came to know of Dr Bhatt's previous location following your raid and is hoping he returns.'

'The information didn't come from us, I can tell you that,' said Bromley, sounding defensive again. 'Give me the registration and I'll do what I can.'

Once Puri had ended the call, Jags asked about what had happened the day before after he'd left him in the sandwich bar. 'You said you was followed?'

The detective explained how he had given the Merc the slip, thanks to a helpful cab driver.

'Is it like normal for people to be tailing you, Uncle-gee? Don't it worry you?'

'How worrying will help?' asked Puri. 'In my line of work some risk is there always.'

'So what's your next move?'

Puri reiterated that his priority was to speak with the security guard, Rakesh Sharma.

'It is my experience that such types don't speak plainly and honestly when questioned by police,' he said.

'What do you mean "types", Uncle-gee – you can't just go round generalizing about people.'

'Generalizations are not fixed hard and fast, but people are people and are somewhat predictable,' said Puri. 'Point is, this Rakesh Sharma told Inspector Brom-ley he did not enter the penthouse apartment, when in fact he delivered the groceries to the top floor. Also, it is odd – no? – that Sharma, a desi, interacted with Dr Bhatt in the flesh, so to speak, but claimed he had not recognized him in all that time?'

'So you're heading back to Regent's Park, yeah?' asked Jags.

'I would prefer your company, beta, what with someone-or-other on my trail, but no pressure is there,' said Puri.

Jags looked conflicted. 'I promised to help my mate, Shiv, move out of his place this morning,' he said, hesitantly. 'And later, I've got Deliveroo, innit.'

Flush was back in the tempo, getting a quick briefing on movements and activities over the past twelve hours from Chetan, who was a few years younger than him and owned an even larger

collection of Marvel comics. There had been no more international phone calls in or out. No visitors to the house. One food
delivery had been made the night before from Colonel Kebabs.
Shweta Bhatt had appeared again on the balcony, smoking a
couple of cigarettes. But she had not been tempted by Flush's
phishing emails, and her WhatsApp account remained secure.

'How about the maid Savita's movements?' Flush asked as
casually as he could manage.

'She fetched some milk, took the dog for a walk,' reported
Chetan. 'I overheard the security guards talking; they were saying
she's leaving for her village.'

'Leaving?' asked Flush, barely managing to hide his surprise.

'Sounds like she's getting married.'

'Married? Who to?'

'Why, are you falling for her?'

'She's not my type.'

'You mean a total babe?'

'When did you overhear the guards talking about her?

'Around eight this morning?'

After Chetan left, Flush was able to check the video recording
of the front gate and learned, to his relief, that although Savita
was indeed going back to her 'native place' to attend a wedding,
it was not her own.

Not that it mattered, he told himself, suddenly facing up to
the reality of the situation and feeling like a lead weight of
despondency had been dropped on him. What would he say to
her if he actually met her? 'Hi, I'm parked over the road in a
beaten-up Bajaj, eating pizza and living in my own filth, spying
on you and your mistress.'

He tried to put her out of his mind and got back to work.

Chewing gum always helped him concentrate, and he reached
into his trouser pocket for a pack. In doing so, he inadvertently
retrieved Savita's shopping list from yesterday.

He hadn't paid it much attention but now, as he unfolded it,
something caught his eye. A square piece of paper, evidently torn
from a block of notepaper, it bore the impression of writing made
on the previous note.

There were two words: 'arrow blistered' and beneath this the
number '330'.

'Probably an anagram for a place name and the numbers indi-
cate the time, thirty minutes past three' was Tubelight's conclusion
when Flush called him to share his discovery.

'I already ran it through AI. It came up with "below rider
arts". Does that mean anything?'

'We might need a cypher. Try the usual ones. I'll pass it on
to Boss. Maybe it'll mean something to him,' said Tubelight.

Mrs Dhillon didn't seem the type to be out and about in all
weathers, especially when there was cheap labour to hand – and
Mummy was banking on her maid's duties including walking
the dogs in the morning.

Nina suggested they keep watch for her from Wanstead Flats,
the large common or park that lay directly across the road from
the McMansion.

So as to blend in to their surroundings, she suggested they go
wearing kurta pyjama, hand-knitted woollen cardigans, baseball
caps, and running shoes.

'Trust me, we'll fit right in,' she said.

Why became clear to Mummy and Rumpi when they pulled
up in a parking area on the edge of 'The Flats' and spotted small
groups of women representing various South Asian communities,
all of whom lived in neighbouring parts of East London, engaged
in different types of exercise.

They passed a group of Bangladeshis walking in a brisk forma-
tion, their dupattas blowing at right angles behind them in the
wind. Further on, some Afghans led by a fearsome matriarch
who marked out the time in staccato Pashtu were doing star
jumps. And on one of the many football pitches, some fellow
Indian aunties were attempting various stretching exercises,
though their bodies appeared loath to oblige.

Nina led the way around an old quarry filled with murky water,
past an old uncle feeding the ducks and geese, to a tree trunk
lying on its side, where they rested. From here they had a good
view of the front of the Dhillons' home – and it was not long
before Sanjiv and Tanya stepped out of the front door and drove
away in a BMW, followed five minutes later by Mr Dhillon.

Soon, a postman arrived, pushed a few envelopes through the
letterbox and departed.

Another twenty minutes passed with no further developments.

By now it had stopped raining and most of the groups of women had laid out picnic blankets on the grass and were making up for their recent calorie loss by sharing selections of fried snacks. Nina had brought along a large thermos and some treats of her own, and so the trio were able to maintain their cover at a safe distance from the house while enjoying homemade vegan samosas.

Finally, just after nine, Mrs Dhillon, wearing dark sunglasses, a long cashmere camel coat and high heels, emerged from the house, got into her MINI and drove away.

The trio waited another fifteen minutes without any sign of the maid, and then Mummy decided to go and knock on the door.

'What if Mrs Dhillon comes back?' asked Nina, alarmed.

'Just I'll say I was passing by and wished to speak further regarding the engagement.'

Mummy reached the road just as the front door opened again and three yappy, excited dogs spilled out amidst a tangle of leads.

Struggling to keep hold of them came a young Indian woman, not a day over twenty years old. Small, thin and nervous, with a sharp parting running through her hair, she wore a red bindi and the very same clothes she must have brought with her from India, the only concession to her new home being an old ski jacket several sizes too big for her.

Somehow she closed the door behind her and the dogs led her across the road and onto the common.

Mummy intercepted them a minute or so later as she stopped to pick up some dog mess in a little plastic bag.

'These dogs look like they're a handful,' said Mummy in her rusty Haryanvi.

'Yesterday one of them bit me,' the young woman complained. 'See here.'

She showed Mummy a scar on her hand. 'The one they call "Chutney" ran away a few weeks ago and it took two hours to find him. I got the blame and was punished. But it wasn't my fault – someone else left the door open.'

'Let me help you, I have some experience with dogs, they respond well to me,' said Mummy. 'Nothing bad will happen,' she added in response to the maid's reticence. 'I'm here to help. What is your name?'

'I'm Pooja.'

'Have you been here long?'

'Nearly one year, I think.'

Mummy took one of the leads and held on tight as they walked on past the quarry.

TEN

Puri's further attempts to emotionally blackmail Jags into assisting him again had still come to nothing. At eleven, however, when a car pulled up in front of the house and he saw that it was another black Mercedes-Benz minus the tinted windows, he decided to give it one last try.

'By God, don't tell me?' he said, knotting his eyebrows with concern as he glared out through the window.

Jags peered past the net curtains as a tall, well-built Indian driver, with pitted skin and dark sunken eyes, stepped out of the car.

'Do you reckon that's the bloke who was following you yesterday?' he asked.

The driver was approaching the house. It helped that he had a scar on his left cheek.

'Could be,' said Puri. 'The car make is most definitely the same.'

There came a sharp knock on the door. Jags looked around the room as if searching for an object with which to defend himself if need be.

'Don't answer the door, I'll call the police,' he said.

Puri counselled caution, however. 'Let us not be too hasty,' he said. 'I will enquire what this gentleman wants exactly. You remain hidden and if his intention proves hostile, then only sound the alarm.'

The detective went to the door and opened it ajar.

'Mr Vish Puri?' asked the driver in a deep voice.

'And you are?'

'Mr Joshi from the High Commission sent me. My instructions are to take you to him. He is waiting.'

The driver went back to his car and Puri shut the door.

'What's that about then?' asked Jags.

'I had better go with him and find out,' said Puri, sounding resigned to his fate.

'I don't know, Uncle-gee, this is well sus,' he said. 'How d'you know he is who he says he is?'

'That is a risk I am willing to take,' said Puri. 'If you don't hear from me in one hour, then be sure to inform Inspector Bromley. And Rumpi, also.'

Puri began to open the door again, but Jags stopped him. 'Hold up, Uncle-gee,' he said with a sigh. 'I can't let you go off on your own like this. Give us a minute and I'll grab my things.'

'But your mate,' said Puri. 'You gave him your word, no?'

'Shiv and me is tight, he'll understand; he's got family, too.'

A few minutes later, they were both seated comfortably on the back seat of the Mercedes, heading into central London.

Fortunately, the driver proved to be a man of few words, and Puri did nothing to encourage a conversation, lest Jags come to know that Mr Amul Joshi of the High Commission of India had messaged him soon after nine asking for a meeting and offering to send a car to collect him.

Their ride pulled up on The Strand behind the High Commission of India. The driver pointed out a dingy, easy-to-miss door squeezed between a couple of tatty shops – the entrance to 'India Club'. This was not, as the name suggested, a members-only institution, though the rooms at the top of the narrow stairs were evocative of India clubland. Black-and-white prints of Jawaharlal Nehru, Mohandas Gandhi and Bhimrao Ramji Ambedkar graced walls painted in faded banana yellow. Threadbare armchairs in the bar were occupied by men in outdated suits, taking their elevenses as they perused periodicals and slowly gathered dust. Doddering waiters in collarless white jackets with thin over-combs stood around with silver trays doing not much of anything.

Puri asked Jags to wait in the lounge and was directed to the dining room.

Amul Joshi, a young Maharashtran in a smart suit, sat by a Victorian bay window with three mobile phones arranged on the table in front of him. His card reported the nebulous designation, 'Representative'.

'I believe congratulations are in order,' he said as the two sat. 'It's my understanding you're the very first of our countrymen to receive the top award in your field – from the prestigious and esteemed International Federation of Private Detectives no less.'

Puri felt instinctively distrustful of this man, though he liked the way he framed his achievement. 'The case for which I am being acknowledged was a first in the annals of crime,' he said. 'And it is high time we non-European or Amrikan detectives receive the recognition we deserve. Frankly speaking, some cultural bias has been there in the past.'

Joshi clicked his fingers to get the attention of a waiter. 'Two teas and bring biscuits,' he said, before confiding in Puri that while the India Club food was 'not up to much', the chai was 'drinkable' compared to 'the stuff' served at the High Commission.

'Now, Mr Puri,' he said, composing himself. 'Forgive me if I come straight to the reason I've asked you here, but I'm sure you understand, I've various pressing matters to attend to.'

One of his phones buzzed with a new message, and Joshi glanced down at the screen and ignored it. Over the next few minutes, this was to happen a number of times.

'It has come to my attention that you're engaging in some private enterprise while here in the UK,' he said. 'Normally I would not presume to pry into your business, but where matters of national interest are concerned, I'm bound to do so.'

Puri had been hoping the meeting might provide him with some useful intel on Dr Bhatt, but could see now that it was going to be a shakedown – and that more than likely, Joshi's intentions were anything but sincere. He was either a spook or what Puri called a 'lizer', his role being to look after the interests of the powers that be. He was certainly no diplomat.

'Sir, I'm not sure where you're getting your information and all,' said Puri, deciding to play dumb. 'I'm a private citizen, travelling with my wife for purposes of tourism and to collect the aforementioned award. Provided some time is there, I plan on visiting Bates hat-makers of Piccadilly, also, being especially fond of their Sandown caps.'

'Come, Mr, Puri, let's not play games,' said Joshi. 'I'm aware you're involved in trying to locate the fugitive, Dr Harilal Bhatt. Yesterday you visited Scotland Yard for a lengthy discussion with

Inspector Simon Bromley; from there you went to an apartment building off Regent's Park where the fugitive was in hiding for some months.'

Potentially this answered the question of who had been tailing him yesterday.

'What all I do with my time and whom I meet exactly is my own private business,' stated Puri.

'I was told that you are a patriot and a team player,' said Joshi, dropping his pretence to congeniality.

'A patriot, certainly. As for the team, it depends upon who my fellow members are exactly.'

'I'm sure I don't have to remind you that Dr Bhatt is a criminal, wanted on numerous charges,' continued the 'representative'. 'Now,' he said, pausing for a beat, 'I should like to know the details of your conversation with Inspector Bromley. You must be aware by now that Scotland Yard has located Dr Bhatt but is refusing to share his location with us.'

'Sir, with respect and apologies and all, I would prefer not to divulge the details,' replied Puri. 'We two spoke in confidence, actually.'

'In so doing you put the interests of the British above those of your country, Mr Puri.'

'It is not that, sir. The nature of the conversation was sensitive, shall we say.'

'In what way?'

'Inspector Brom-ley confided in me regarding the details of his wife's affair with a hot yoga instructor from Tamil Nadu,' said the detective. 'These days, the poor fellow is having to iron his own shirts and prepare his own tea.'

Joshi stared at him impassively. 'You disappoint me, Mr Puri,' he said.

'I agree it is embarrassing to learn of such behaviour on the part of a fellow countryman, but what to do?' Puri stood to leave. 'Forgive me, sir, I'll pass on the chai,' he said. 'My wife is keen to see the Buckingham Palace and Westminster. The woman will not rest till she's seen all the sights in London. And no doubt she'll insist on so many selfies.'

* * *

'Chubby? Where are you?'

'We've reached the tailor.'

'It sounds like you're in traffic.'

'Not at all, my dear, I'm standing by an open window only.'

'We're going to take the metro and get off at Green Park station. Yes, Green Park, same as in Delhi. Nina says it's a short walk from there to Buckingham Palace. We will meet you in one hour.'

'Two customers are ahead of us. It will take some more time.'

'Don't be late or we won't be able to see everything today.'

'Lunch will be required, also, no?'

'Nina says there are plenty of places where we can pick up a sandwich.'

'The British sand-wich is exactly as described, the flavour of sand.'

'Chubby, for once can you please *not* put your stomach first? I'm sure we'll manage.'

'Jags was mentioning one Turkish establishment with tasty kebabs and all.'

'That's not suitable for Nina.'

'Why the rest of us should suffer? Hello? Hello?'

Rumpi, Nina and Mummy were on a slow District Line train, discussing the Dhillons' maid, Pooja.

During their walk on Wanstead Flats, the young servant had complained to Mummy about being made to work seven days a week, for up to twelve, sometimes thirteen hours a day. Often she was locked in her room and Mrs Dhillon had abused her verbally on a number of occasions.

Pooja had agreed to meet at the same time again tomorrow to discuss what might be done to extricate her from the job.

'She's a sweet girl but no clue,' said Mummy. 'Without assistance, her situation will remain same.'

'I think we have to consider Amber in all this as well,' said Rumpi.

'I agree,' said Nina. 'She deserves to know about how the Dhillons treat poor Pooja. Then Amber can make her mind up if she wants to go ahead with the marriage.'

It was not ten minutes, however, before Buggi called from

Delhi and broke the news that Sanjiv had ended the engagement.

She was sobbing hard – and it was only once Amber came on the line that Mummy was able to glean the details.

'Sanjiv said that he couldn't see it working between us, that it would be unfair to take me away from my family and friends in India,' she explained. 'He sounded so different. So cold. I can't understand it. Was it something I did?'

Mummy did her best to comfort her before the train entered a tunnel and they were cut off.

'Why would he break the engagement like that?' Rumpi asked Mummy. 'Do you think it had anything to do with us?'

'Responsibility lies with me,' said Mummy. 'Mrs Dhillon came to see me as a threat – after hearing the story regarding my part in recovering the jewellery from that Loot and Scoot Bride, that is.'

'Why a threat? You think she's worried you'd find out about Pooja? That sounds a bit far-fetched, Mummy-ji,' said Rumpi.

'Juts the issue with Pooja is one thing,' said Mummy. 'Sanjiv was in such a rush to go the marriage way. Why all of a sudden? It is suspicious, na. Some other agenda is there.'

'If you're right, then Amber is better off without him,' said Nina.

'I agree,' said Rumpi. 'At least she can take some comfort from that.'

Puri and Jags were in a taxi heading to Regent's Park to try to meet the security guard.

Knowing the building was being kept under surveillance by at least one party, they stopped two streets over from the address and split up. Puri proceeded to the alley that ran behind the building, while Jags went to the front entrance to ask for Rakesh Sharma.

Theirs was a wasted journey, however.

'He's been "redeployed", innit,' Jags reported when he went and found Puri at the back of the building. 'The new guy on duty gave me an address in Shepherd's Bush. Some big office block, their company does the security there and all.'

'So sudden?' asked Puri, frowning suspiciously. 'As of yesterday, only, he was scheduled to work at this address today. Were I a betting man, I would say someone or other does not want us speaking with Sharma, which makes it all the more imperative that we do so. Keep hold that address.'

On their way to Green Park, Puri made sure they weren't being followed and then checked his messages. These made for frustrating reading. Tubelight and Flush seemed to be in a rut. The promise of hacking Shweta Bhatt's WhatsApp and cracking the case wide open, something he had been banking on from the start, had still come to nothing. The anagram Flush had discovered on the maid's shopping list was eluding them as well. Meanwhile, his counterpart in Mauritius said he would need at least another day and around 500 dollars US for a bribe to see the file on Gladstone Global Holdings Inc.

A voice broke into his thoughts. It was the taxi driver asking where they wanted to be dropped off.

'Was that Green Park station, mate?'

'That will surely do,' answered Puri, though Rumpi hadn't provided him with the exact location of where they were to meet.

'I'll ping Mum a three-word location so she can find us,' said Jags.

'Three-word location: what is that exactly?' asked Puri.

'What3words – 'ave you never 'eard of it? At Deliveroo, we use it all the time. Let's say a customer's in the park and orders a pizza. They give us their three-word location and we can like zero in on where they're at.'

'Every three metres square on the planet has a reference – a unique combination of three words,' clarified the driver.

'That must be it?' said Puri, eyes wide as if he'd had an epiphany.

'That is what?' asked Jags, as the detective started to search hurriedly through Tubelight's recent messages.

'These words mean anything? "Arts", "Rider", "Below"?' he asked.

Jags typed them into his phone. 'That's near Chicago, Illinois,' he said, reading the result from What3words. 'Hang about.'

Next he tried 'below.rider.arts' and said: 'That's the Savoy Hotel, London.'

'By God! The Savoy, it is far?'

'Just a few minutes' walk from where you met that dodgy geezer this morning,' said Jags.

'We must reach by three,' said Puri. 'Could be Dr Bhatt will be reaching the place at 330, only.'

'But what about Rumpi and Buckingham Palace?'

'Somehow we'll have to make it a whistle-stop tour.'

'If you're going to the Savoy, they do a blinding afternoon tea,' said the driver. 'The full works – scones and cream, cucumber sandwiches, iced fairy cakes. Lovely.'

ELEVEN

Buckingham Palace turned out exactly as Puri had anticipated: a very large, grey, unremarkable building, showing
no sign of life, with a huge tarmacked area in front that
looked to him like a lot of wasted parking capacity.

Admittedly the world-famous guards in their tall bearskin hats
– the original human statues – provided some entertainment value.
But the place was not a patch on, say Jodhpur, with its magnif-
icent elephant gate and soaring sandstone ramparts glowing in
the soft, Rajasthani evening light.

This did not prevent droves of tourists from every corner of
the globe from milling about in front of the long railings, posing
for countless photographs – not least Rumpi, who thrilled to the
sight of the famous balcony where, on special occasions, those
British royals who had not fallen out with one another, waved
down at their subjects.

Puri lost count of the number of selfies and group shots his
wife took in front of the palace gates. And when a couple of
amiable London bobbies appeared, she insisted Puri pose along
with them, an image that there and then she committed to their
next Diwali card.

The following forty-five minutes brought yet more photo
opportunities: the Victoria fountain; The Mall, where a troupe of
horse-mounted guards obliged Rumpi by trotting past; and
Trafalgar Square, where she exercised her photo fetish to the full
and Puri found himself longing for the restrained and more civi-
lized days of film canisters with a maximum of thirty-six shots.

It was not until two thirty, and he was being made to pose
beneath Nelson's Column, that he sprung his surprise – 'I've a
special treat in store.'

'What sort of treat?' asked Rumpi, who could not help but
sound sceptical. After all, it had been a number of years since
he'd done anything to surprise her.

'I've booked a table at the Savoy where we will have a

proper British afternoon tea,' he revealed with a flourish of his hands.

Rumpi was completely taken aback. 'Afternoon tea? At the Savoy? You mean the hotel?'

'One and the same.'

'But we were planning to go on to Downing Street and see Big Ben.'

'It can wait till after, no?'

'Are you sure we can afford it?'

'My dear, what is money when we are on holiday? It is a once-in-a-lifetime-type thing. Such extravagance is permitted under the circumstance.'

'If you're sure, Chubby . . .'

'Certain in fact. But not much time is there. I was fortunate enough to secure a table. It is booked for three o'clock, only.'

Mummy had fallen into conversation with a family visiting from Ludhiana who had the inside edge on every discount available for all the major tourist attractions in London, not to mention Stonehenge, which they said could be viewed for free from an adjacent field, thus avoiding paying the entrance fee. It took some effort on Puri's part to prise her away and, not wanting to walk, bustled everyone into a black cab.

The ride was ludicrously short, no more than four minutes in total, most of it taken up just turning into the Savoy's private driveway.

Here the most unlikely scene greeted them, with dozens of desis waiting along the pavements behind crowd-control barriers, all of them wearing T-shirts with images of Shah Rukh Khan or placards emblazoned with 'I LOVE SRK!' – and with cameras and autograph books at the ready.

The doorman soon confirmed the obvious: the Bollywood star was a guest of the hotel and, as a result, there was extra security. This involved Puri having to show his booking for tea, the ladies' handbags being searched, and Jags confirming that he was not a SRK fan.

'Tarantino's more my thing,' he told the security guard.

Beyond the grand revolving doors, the Puris found themselves transported into a world that sparkled like the fanciful imaginings of *The Nutcracker*. Guests exuding wealth as potently as the scents of the extravagant flower arrangements placed around the lobby passed back and forth in what might have been a staged, choreographed performance. Heels sounded staccato across the glassy chequered marble floor. Designer watches and precious stones caught the light cast by brass Art Deco pendants hanging overhead. Great oil paintings arranged on the oak-panelled walls depicted scenes of antiquity co-opted to enhance the contrivance of contemporary luxury.

The Puris fell uncharacteristically quiet, suddenly feeling out of place in the midst of such unprecedented opulence, and made their way slowly and uncertainly past grand columns and Greek friezes to the hotel's central atrium.

'Chubby, are you sure we're dressed smartly enough?' whispered Rumpi, as they waited on the edge of the area where afternoon tea was served at tables arranged around a large gazebo, with trellising interwoven with fresh flowers. A pianist sat at a Steinway grand playing Debussy.

'Jags, you should definitely wait outside – look at the state of you,' said Nina, noting her son's ripped jeans and hoodie, and the loose soles on his Air Jordans.

The hostess who showed them to their table could not have been more convivial, however, and having sat them at a sumptuously laid table, sent over a young man, who possessed more the bearing of a courtier than a waiter, to take their order.

Puri, not wanting to lose face by admitting that he didn't understand the difference between Afternoon Tea or High Tea, answered, 'The High one, naturally,' when asked to choose between the two. And when it came to ordering one of the seventy types of tea available on the menu, he went along with the waiter's suggestion of Earl Grey, even though he hated the stuff.

Had not Rumpi pointed out that champagne was not included in the set price, they would have also ended up with a bottle of Laurent-Perrier La Cuvée at £120. As it was, Puri calculated that this was going to be the most expensive stakeout of all time.

Still, he could not have hoped for better cover. By sheer good luck, the table afforded a view of the main lobby. And with the ladies distracted by all the antique English silverware and fine china, not to mention the prospect of spotting SRK in the flesh, he was able to keep an eye out for Dr Bhatt without giving

Rumpi – and, he hoped, Mummy – any indication as to his real purpose in being there.

Puri always maintained that food, and plenty of it, was essential for a stakeout, and the Savoy did not disappoint. A tower of tiered plates groaning with tartlets, cakes and scones was soon set before them. Finger sandwiches followed, and then a selection of savoury pastries, which proved 'quite tasty', even if they could have done with some Maggi hot sauce.

High Tea also included a course of seared fish and salad. And though by now even Puri was stuffed, pride dictated that he ate everything put in front of him.

By three thirty, when he excused himself from the table, leaving Jags to keep tabs on the others, he stood from his chair with difficulty and proceeded into the lobby feeling bloated and gassy.

Fortunately, Puri found one of the booths for the house phones unoccupied and, having squeezed inside, kept up the pretence of holding a conversation on the handset when in fact he was burping quietly into the receiver while keeping close watch on those coming and going through the lobby.

There was no shortage of South Asians amongst the guests and visitors to the hotel. A few had a filmi whiff about them – possibly members of SRK's entourage. There were corporate types in sharp suits and well-polished shoes, shaking hands, checking their phones, settling bills at the main desk with gold cards. Puri spotted some Indian tourists, too, including one family who he summed up as 'second-tier metro, new money', meaning they were small-town India nouveau riche.

His phone buzzed with a message from Jags, which read, simply, ''sup?'

He was about to respond with 'zero' when a bellboy, pushing a brass trolley groaning with Gucci luggage, paused in front of the booth.

For just a few moments, Puri's view of the front doors was blocked, and in that time several people entered the hotel and fanned out across the lobby.

One of them, a man making his way purposefully towards the lifts, matched Dr Bhatt's height and build.

He wore a linen shirt, loose cotton trousers and a baseball cap. From behind at least, it was impossible to judge his nationality.

He might have been Lebanese or even Spanish. Puri hesitated to leave the booth and follow him.

But then, as he would frame it later, 'fate' intervened: the man passed beneath a great chandelier and the light revealed the distinct outline of a Janeu beneath his shirt, draped over his shoulder and across his chest.

On his wrist, too, Puri now spotted a red and gold thread mouli.

Knowing him immediately to be a high-caste Indian, and very likely a Brahmin, Puri left the booth and set off as quickly as he could manage across the lobby. Had his eyes shot lasers, they would have burned into this man's back. Before the detective could get a look at his face, however, he stepped into one of the lifts ahead of a large family of gregarious Italians.

Puri watched the floor numbers light up in sequence on the brass panel above the doors as the lift stopped on the third floor and finally the sixth. Then he retreated to the other side of the lobby so as to avoid being spotted by Rumpi and the others from their table.

'I ing fotos bt starting 2? whr u @' came a message from Jags.

This seemed to suggest that Rumpi was beginning to wonder where he was. But there was no way Puri was leaving now, not when he was potentially so close. If the Indian did indeed prove to be Dr Bhatt, he intended to detain him and call Inspector Bromley to come and make the arrest. The cost of Rumpi finding out about the case would be, on balance, worth it.

A long five minutes passed.

One of the lifts went up to the sixth floor, remained there for twenty seconds, and then began its descent.

It reached the lobby and there came a ping.

The doors slid open and the same man stepped out, now carrying a white sports bag. His baseball cap was drawn down tight over his forehead and he was wearing a pencil-thin moustache. But there was no doubt this was Dr Harilal Bhatt.

Though Puri had expected as much and spent the past few minutes thinking through what he would do next, he faltered for a few seconds, trying to process the enormity of his find. This was India's most wanted man. The entire country had been talking about him for months. His image had appeared on countless front pages and covers and nonstop on news bulletins.

Never a man for action, and with one leg shorter than the other, Puri now suffered from the added disadvantage of a full Savoy High Tea weighing him down and this lost him more valuable time. A group of Japanese tourists, studying a map in the middle of the lobby, and a large, multi-generational Gulf state family returning from the Harry Potter Warner Brothers Studio tour with a considerable collection of souvenirs did not help, either.

Puri went around all of them and then had to break into a trot, his big stomach bouncing up and down and gurgling like a drain.

He closed the gap to roughly ten feet as Dr Bhatt approached the front doors and one of the hotel staff prepared to open one of them for him. Puri nearly had him.

And then suddenly he heard his family pet name being shouted across the lobby in a distinct, Indian accent: 'Chubby! Stop! It is *him*, na!'

Puri threw a glance over his right shoulder to find Mummy hurrying across the lobby, flourishing Rumpi's phone. Jags was trying to keep up with her.

'He's here. Close by!' she called out in Hindi.

Her words caused Dr Bhatt to look back in alarm and then bolt.

Puri shouted: 'Stop that man! He is wanted by the police!'

But none of the guests or staff responded, and the fugitive escaped unchallenged, breaking into a run.

Knowing he stood no chance of catching him, Puri instructed Jags to go in pursuit: 'The man in the linen shirt and baseball cap carrying the sports bag, don't lose him!'

'Yeah, got it,' he said, and took off after Dr Bhatt.

Puri watched until he reached the Strand before turning angrily to his mother. 'What is it, Mummy-ji? What could not wait?' he demanded.

'The one on the plane, the Hairy One, he is close by,' she said, taken aback by his reaction.

'I've seen no one matching that description,' snapped Puri.

'See here, on Rumpi's portable,' she said, showing him her photo library. 'That is him. There at the Buckingham Palace he was. Standing some way off. Just I told you, Chubby, he's been following you.'

One look at the man's image told Puri that his mother was right: this was a prize goonda if ever he'd seen one. But he had not been in the lobby – he was sure of that. Was he waiting outside the hotel, perhaps? If so, he might have recognized Dr Bhatt. In which case . . .

Suddenly concerned for Jags's safety, Puri tried calling him, but the call went straight to voicemail.

'By God, if anything happens to him . . .' he said, contemplating what to do next. There was surely nothing for it but to let Bromley know that he had located Dr Bhatt and that he had last been seen heading west on the Strand.

Once Puri had made the call, he returned to the table to face Rumpi, convinced that he was going to have to confess all.

Fortunately, during all the commotion, she had been in the ladies, though she still wanted to know why he had been gone from the table for so long.

'Apologies, my dear, some indigestion was there,' he said, relieved not to have been found out.

'Mummy-ji, you suddenly took off and I heard raised voices,' said Nina, who sounded concerned.

'Just I thought I spotted Shah Rukh, but it was a false alarm,' answered Mummy.

'Where's Jags now?'

'He headed off, actually – said he was meeting one *mate*,' said Puri, making it sound as if he was unreliable.

'Then who's going to eat these salmon tartlets?' asked Rumpi.

'I will ask to get them packed,' said Puri, though for once he felt like he could never eat another thing.

TWELVE

The sight of Savita in a lime-green kurta with white churidar leggings tight around her shapely legs caused Flush's heart to skip a beat. She paused outside the front gate to tug out the periscope handle on her wheelie bag. Dappled sunshine danced across her face, causing her to squint and crinkle her delicate nose and adjust her glasses. Watching her, Flush knew this rare creature, who had come to dominate his thoughts and dreams, could not have anything to do with any conspiracy to assist Dr Bhatt in avoiding justice. She was a servant not long in service with Shweta Bhatt, and surely incapable of deviousness or malice.

Tubelight, though, was not so trusting. He wanted confirmation that she was on her way to her village in Uttar Pradesh for a family wedding, and had assigned Chetan the task of following her to the bus or train station.

Unluckily for Chetan, who also seemed sweet on Savita, he was on a toilet break, and Flush did not hesitate in taking on his task, even if he was sure it was a waste of time.

Locking the van, he set off after her as she started down the street, keeping to the shade cast by the high walls of the neighbouring villas.

Savita made slow, ungainly progress – one of the wheels on her bag was off-kilter and she also had to contend with a handbag and a tiffin packed with food for the journey.

When she came to the Inner Ring Road, a blur of steel and chrome, with pollution hanging so thick in the air it looked like it could be cut with a knife, she had to dodge and weave through the pitiless traffic until she reached the bus stop on the other side.

Flush, well accustomed to putting his life on the line just to cross one of Delhi's main arteries, managed to reach the other side as well, and went and stood behind the forty or so other would-be passengers waiting in the beating sun.

The first DTC bus that came roaring up looked like a vehicle for transporting prisoners that had been commandeered during a jail break and used to ram a roadblock of police cars: the front grille was torn back, the windscreen fractured as if it had been hit by a hail of bullets. The state of the next bus was not much better; it was missing most of its side panels and windows.

Fortunately, the bus to Old Delhi railway station was one of the new models, a so-called 'cluster' bus, which came with the benefit of suspension and air con and drivers who showed some modicum of regard for the safety of their passengers by keeping the bus stationary until they had been given the opportunity to board.

Still, it was no less over-subscribed than the others, and at least fifty passengers stood squeezed into the aisle, including Flush and Savita.

Standing next to her was a young man, who, with every lurch and jolt of the bus, pressed up against her. Judging by his expression, he was taking considerable pleasure in doing so.

Flush was helpless to intervene – even if he'd decided to risk drawing attention to himself, there were just too many other passengers blocking the way – and no one else appeared prepared to come to her aid. Savita's appeals for him to stop only promoted him to laugh luridly in her face and to grind his crotch against her thigh.

She endured his abuse in silence for just a few seconds more. And then suddenly Savita pushed him roughly away and, with a curse, took aim with a small bottle of pepper spray and fired a burst in his face.

A terrible scream carried through the bus as her assailant, clutching at his face with both hands, eyes burning a blistering red, fell to his knees, demanding that someone give him water.

The driver stopped the bus abruptly and opened the doors, and for a moment Flush assumed he would call the police. Instead, he ordered the young man to get off – and when he refused, two of the other male passengers, finally stirred to take action, dragged him to the door and shoved him outside.

As the bus pulled away, Flush caught sight of him frantically dowsing his face with the contents of a matka pot on the pavement – and a collective cheer went up amongst the women passengers, many of whom congratulated Savita for standing up for herself and began to share their own stories about the constant 'eve-teasing' they endured every day on public transports.

The maid, who by now had found a seat, said little, however. And over the next half-hour, as the bus passed beyond British New Delhi and through the diminished remnants of Shah Jahan's Mughal City and the Red Fort, she passed the time looking out of the window, apparently unflustered or untroubled by what had happened, a slight smile playing upon her lips.

If anything, Flush felt more attracted to her than ever, knowing that she could take care of herself, that she was beautiful, capable – even brave. But as he followed Savita through the ever-busy station, with its maelstrom of passengers, pilgrims, porters and pickpockets, and watched her board the Mahabodhi Express for Kanpur, he felt conflicted again. One voice in his head was telling him he was indulging in adolescent fantasies and that she would want nothing to do with him; while another reminded him that love was boundless and he should follow his heart.

Bromley was not at all happy about Puri having 'gone it alone'.

'We had a deal, remember?' he said over the phone.

By now Puri was back in East Ham, having accompanied Rumpi to Westminster where, in front of the Houses of Parliament, Westminster Abbey and Mahatma Gandhi's statue, he had posed for enough photographs to fill two family albums.

'Believe me, Inspector-sahib, I was acting on the thinnest of leads,' he explained as he stood once again out on the pavement in front of the house. 'The impression of a few words on a shopping list, only.'

'You still should have called me. Now let's go over this again in case I've missed something, shall we? You reckon Bombay Duck went up to the sixth floor of the hotel and, presumably, met with someone there?'

'It would seem so. That is unless he is keeping a room at the Savoy himself,' suggested Puri.

'Unlikely.' Bromley was dismissive. 'And you said he left the hotel with a sports bag?'

'Correct, white and lacking in any markings.'

'Have you heard from Jags?'

'Each and every time, his phone is going to voicemail.'

After Bromley had received Puri's call from the Savoy, he had immediately put out an alert on Dr Bhatt, but none of the mobile units in the vicinity or the Metropolitan Police CCTV control room had been able to trace him.

'We're checking what we've got from inside Charing Cross station, Piccadilly Circus, Holborn. I'll look over the Savoy's security tapes as well. Meet me there first thing in the morning.'

To Puri's considerable relief, Jags returned half an hour later – by now it was approaching seven o'clock – and went straight up to his room.

'Where've you been?' he asked, soon joining him. 'I've been calling you so many of times!'

'I lost my phone, didn't I? Must 'ave dropped it somehow when I legged it from the hotel.'

'But you followed Dr Bhatt, you know his location?' asked Puri, anxious for news.

'Should do, Uncle-gee. Give us a minute, yeah.' Jags was starting his computer.

'It is either yes or no, surely.'

'Just chill, Uncle-gee, let me explain what happened, yeah? See, I followed Bhatt into Charing Cross, and he walked into the station and went into the toilets. When he came out, like five minutes later, he'd changed hats and put on a long coat. Then he walked out the back of the station, crossing one of the two bridges over the river. All the time, yeah, he's like really cautious. Keeps stopping, checking no one's following 'im. I thought he was gonna spot me for sure, innit.'

'Then what happened?' asked Puri, impatiently.

'Bhatt reached the South Bank, and then starts lookin' round all them second-'and book stalls. Buys a paperback. Then goes sits in a cafe for like thirty, forty minutes maybe. After that he goes over Westminster Bridge and goes down the Tube, then comes up again and walks through Green Park. He kills another twenty minutes sitting on a bench. Makes a phone call. Then finally walks into the station. I reckoned by this time maybe he'd spotted me. That's when I had, like, this brain wave.'

'Brain wave?' repeated Puri, braced for the worst.

'As Bhatt went through the ticket barrier, I got up like right behind him, yeah, and slipped my AirTag – the one off my keychain – into the outside pocket of 'is bag.'

'With this AirTag you're able to trace him, that is what you're telling me?'

'Yeah, on my phone or 'puter.'

Jags launched the Find My app, and a map of the UK appeared together with a list of several devices, all owned by a certain 'J Dog'. The first was an iMac, its current location 'East Ham'. The second, an iPhone, appeared to be on Agar Street near Charing Cross in a police station, meaning someone had handed it in. And the AirTag's status read: 'No location found'.

Jags refreshed the app, but with the same result.

'Bollocks!' he declared, and pushed back from his desk. 'Bhatt either found it or it's out of range.'

'Meaning what exactly?' asked Puri.

'AirTags can only be located by Apple devices. Like iPhones, iPads, Macs, innit. It's possible he's gone into like a dead zone with nothing else in range.'

Did the app provide a record of the device's journey since Westminster? Puri wanted to know.

'Nah, it don't work like that, Uncle-gee. It's only designed to show its current location.'

'So it is totally useless, in other words,' said Puri, uncharitably. 'I ask you to do a simple thing and zero.'

Jags's face showed startled dismay. 'Yeah, well, sorry my 007 skills aren't quite up to scratch, Uncle-gee! I didn't see you firing any tracking darts or chasing after Bhatt in your invisible car.'

Puri sat down on Jags's bed. He was tired and crotchety, he realized, and had the good sense to apologize.

'You did well, beta, actually. Using the device was quick thinking on your part,' he added.

'Yeah, well, like I said, all's not lost, necessarily like,' said Jags, taken aback by Puri's expression of regret. 'I'll keep monitoring the app, yeah. Maybe we'll catch a break.'

'Let us hope by then it is not too late.'

'Why d'you say that?'

Puri showed him an enlarged image of Hairy One from Rumpi's selfie and asked if he recognized him. The answer was an indefatigable, 'Yeah! I nearly knocked that geezer down right outside the hotel, innit. What's his story?'

'Most probably he's a killer contracted to put an end to Dr
Bhatt,' said Puri, despondently. 'In which case, I've served up
Brom-ley's Bombay Duck on a platter.'

THIRTEEN

t was past nine and the family were all sitting down for dinner when the doorbell rang. Jags answered the front door – and an all-too-familiar voice, loud and cocky, boomed through the house as if broadcast from a loudspeaker with ragged bass.

'By God,' Puri sighed with a sinking feeling. 'Don't tell me.'

The voice was equally familiar to Mummy, though her reaction was in sharp contrast to her son's.

'Such a nice surprise, na!' she enthused, as she went to greet the visitor herself and invited him to join them.

But then Mummy always did have a soft spot for Rinku, Puri reflected. She still saw in him the cheeky neighbourhood kid who roamed the streets of Punjabi Bagh as head of the Yo-Yo Gang, playing Gilli Danda and buying kulfi from old Paaji's stand behind the Masjid.

It helped that the twenty-four-carat criminal was always deeply respectful of her and minded his language – and that he always came bearing armfuls of presents.

'Mummy-ji, sat shri akal,' he said, bending to touch her feet. 'No issues dropping in, ha? I came to know you were in London, taking the place by storm. I was thinking: who better to party with, yaar? Along the way, I picked up these, they're all your favourite colours.'

He handed her a huge bouquet of cut roses wrapped in plastic sparkling with glitter. At the centre nestled a small teddy bear wearing a T-shirt that declared 'Hug!' There was a matching bouquet for Rumpi (though her teddy bear T-shirt read, 'Bestie!'); and for Joni and Nina a box of mixed Barfi from the local Anand sweetshop.

To Puri he handed a bottle of Johnnie Walker Green Label, intoning his favourite line, 'Good for bad purposes!' and then embraced him with an unmistakably passive-aggressive hug.

'You've been avoiding me, you bugger. I've been waiting for your call these past days,' he said.

'We've not stopped since landing, going round all the sights and all,' said Puri, immediately on the defensive. 'Today we saw the Buckingham Palace, Houses of Parliament and some church place where they filmed Hari Pottar.'

'Not forgetting the fancy afternoon tea, Chubby,' said Rumpi, who recognized all too well the tension between the childhood friends and was trying to do her bit to be supportive. 'Chubby took us to the Savoy,' she told Rinku. 'It was a grand affair with all the trimmings.'

'Is it?' laughed Rinku. He eyed Puri with a wry expression that denoted suspicion. 'Not like you to splash out on five-star-living, Chubby. You had vouchers or what?'

'Believe me it was paid with honest, hard-earned cash,' Puri shot back.

Punjabi Bagh's most notorious son, who ate with a fork clutched in one hand as if expecting to spear a live fish, dominated the evening, regaling the company with tales of encounters with a cast of outlandish characters, close scrapes and cheeky escapades, including the time he had travelled on Air India and pretended to be blind, claiming his pet Alsatian was a seeing-eye dog.

Puri sat patiently, enduring the all-too familiar repertoire, grateful that at least Rinku left out the most sordid details given the age and sensibilities of his audience. When recalling his hair-raising tale of survival during the 2008 terror attacks at the Taj Hotel in Mumbai, for example, he omitted all mention of the two Turkish belly dancers he had been entertaining when the gunfire began to ring out. It would have been different had there been alcohol at the table, but with Mummy present, Rinku had not suggested they break open the bottle of Johnnie Walker, and Nina had served him a glass of fresh watermelon juice.

Though a carnivore with a capital C (on one occasion he had famously eaten half a goat roast in one sitting at Karim's), Rinku was also scrupulously polite about the vegan food, complimenting the chef on her tofu tikka masala.

Only later, while smoking a cigarette out on the pavement, did he let his true opinion be known.

'What the hell, Chubby, yaar?' he bawled, a little too loudly for Puri's liking. 'That woman can't cook for shit. How you're surviving? Listen, I'll take you to this place, I know. We'll get a good steak. Grass-fed, Argentinian beef, specially flown in from Patagonia. We'll order a bottle and make it a night.'

Puri rarely ate beef, though right now a steak and a peg or two sounded extremely tempting. The last time he'd gone out with Rinku, however, he'd stumbled into bed at four and been called a 'lightweight' for his trouble.

'Let us make it another time,' said Puri, turning down the invitation. 'We've an early start, Rumpi is set on taking some boat on the river and it does not do to argue with the wife.' He found himself borrowing a phrase from Jags: 'You know how it is.'

Rinku forced a plume of cigarette smoke up into the night sky. 'Know how what is? Blissful married life?'

Rinku's wife had left him and he blamed her for the disintegration of the marriage, never mind all his boozing and philandering.

'Nitu barely lets me see the kids nowadays, you know that? Says I'm a "disruptive" influence. Took out a court order against me.'

'Perhaps she'll have a change of heart,' was all Puri could think to say.

'Whatever, yaar,' scoffed Rinku, and took a hard draw on his cigarette. 'Listen, I don't need your bleeding heart, holier-than-thou sympathy, Chubby. I came here to warn you. There's a supari been sent to London, and I got to know he's on your tail. Trust me, you don't want to be taking chances with this guy. Comes with a Rolls-Royce rating, à la carte. He's the one who took out Lamboo "the Fruit" Bepari two years back. Remember? Sniper shot from 850 yards with a medium calibre. The bullet put a permanent bindi on his forehead.'

'You've a name for me?'

'Chhota Balu – the guy's short, hairy. Word is he killed his own driver after he spat paan out the window and it came in through the back window and got him in the face.'

Did Rinku know the identity of Chhota Balu's London target?

'Some big shot. I heard the hit's worth two crore.'

'Meaning someone with muscle hired him to do the needful.'

'That I can't tell you.'

'Can't or won't?'

Rinku broke into song, warbling the chorus of 'I Heard It Through the Grapevine' in an exaggerated, mocking tone.

'Tell me how my name came up at least,' said Puri, irritated by Rinku's evasiveness, to say nothing of all the loucheness.

Rinku dropped the butt of his cigarette onto the pavement and, grinding it beneath the heel of his cowboy boots, said with a patronizing sigh as if speaking to an adolescent who needed to stop questioning parental rules: 'Just keep your head down, Chubby, and stick to the tourism. You should take Rumpi to the theatre.'

Puri was sure this wasn't Rinku speaking; this last suggestion clearly originated elsewhere – and, in a flash, he could see Mummy's hand in Rinku being there. This afternoon, she had sent him the photo from Rumpi's selfie. He had asked around and confirmed from his Nexus contacts that Chhota Balu was indeed in London and had taken on a big contract. Mummy had then asked him to come to dinner and issue his warning. Or perhaps he had volunteered to do so. His concern did indeed seem genuine. And for that, at least, Puri could be grateful.

'I appreciate the information, you bugger – "Pals for Pals", right?' he said, invoking the old Yo-Yo Gang motto.

'Always, Chubby,' said Rinku. 'Now tell me, can that woman at least make a cup of decent chai?'

'She doesn't keep milk in the house. Can you believe? Uses soy substitute,' said Puri. 'Last night my bed tea tasted like turnip.'

'Shit, Chubby, you're a sucker for punishment.'

Puri slept badly again and woke later than intended. He found a note on the kitchen table from Rumpi explaining that she, Mummy and Nina had gone 'brisk walking' and would return by ten thirty.

Jags was still asleep in his clothes, having collapsed face down on his bed.

Puri gave him a shake. 'Oi! Sleepy head! Jaldi, time to rise and shine!'

The young man responded with a groan and then rolled onto his back: 'What?'

'You've checked your computer recently?'

Jags staggered bleary-eyed to his desk and refreshed the screen. 'Still nothing,' he said with a yawn.

'In which case you can make my breakfast.'

Jags went and fetched more illicit eggs and prepared his chilli omelettes.

'Your mate's a bit of a character,' he said, referring to Rinku, as he joined Puri at the table.

'That is one way of putting it.'

'Auntie says you was in a gang?' Jags sounded surprised. 'I can't picture that myself.'

'Ours was not like a street gang exactly,' said Puri with a smile. 'One year my Chacha gifted us two yo-yos and we started practising. Before long, we could do plenty of tricks – "walk the dog", "elevator" and so forth. In this way we used to keep everyone in the colony entertained and came to be known as the Yo-Yo Gang.'

Jags suddenly hopped out of his chair and left the kitchen, pounding up the stairs to his room. He returned holding a smart blue plastic yo-yo with a stainless-steel trim.

'I've got pretty good myself, Uncle-gee,' he said, bouncing the spool up and down.

Puri could not have looked more delighted. 'Very good,' he said, with a broad smile, his moustache pushed up hard against his nose. 'That is a handsome one, I must say. In my day, ours were made of wood, only.'

Jags handed it to him. 'It's called an Arcade, basically designed for tricks. I got it at the National Yo-Yo Championship.'

'There is such a thing?' asked Puri, eyes bright with enthusiasm.

'There's a world championship and all, innit.'

Puri let the Arcade drop and it came spinning back hard into his hand. 'So smooth,' he said admiringly.

He released it again and captured the yo-yo on the rebound. His attempt to make it spin at the end of the string before returning to his hand failed, however.

'Somewhat rusty,' he commented, and handed back the yo-yo to Jags.

'Keep it, Uncle-gee, it's yours,' he said.

'Most kind of you, beta, but my yo-yo days are behind me,' Puri insisted. 'Now I had better get a move on, actually.'

'I reckon I'll tag along, Uncle-gee,' said Jags. 'I'm off shift today. And let's face it, you can't manage without me. Plus if my AirTag's location updates, you're gonna wanna know, sharpish, innit.'

*   *   *

Pooja emerged from the Dhillon McMansion promptly at nine-thirty. Mummy, Rumpi and Nina met her in the copse of trees by the quarry. With the dogs kept busy with a couple of chunky bones bought at a butcher's by Nina en route, the group sat on a felled tree trunk in the drizzle, discussing the maid's predicament and how to rescue her from her employers.

She had brought with her paperwork pertaining to her employment. This included two contracts. The first was in Hindi, typed on Delhi court paper with a ten-rupee note fixed to the top of each page. It stipulated pay and working hours more generous than the vast majority of India's legions of domestic servants could ever expect to receive – a highly attractive prospect for a young woman from a village with, at best, an upper primary education. It also guaranteed one day off a week, a return ticket home once a year, accommodation, food and health care.

The second contract was in English. Pooja had been told by Mr Dhillon that it was simply a translation of the Hindi version and a requirement for a UK work visa. But the terms were barely comparable. The pay stipulated was the UK minimum wage, which was roughly six times outlined in the Hindi contract; sick pay and a month's paid holiday were also guaranteed.

Pooja received the news that she had been duped with a helpless expression suggestive of someone long resigned to exploitation at the hands of others. Even after Nina spelled out that, under the terms of the contract, she was due thousands of pounds in back pay, she sounded unconvinced that anything she could do would make a difference and admitted to being scared of the Indian agent who had found her the job.

'If I make problems, he will fix my parents in the village,' she said.

Mummy tried to assure her that she had connections of her own and the parents would come to no harm. Nina further assured her that British law guaranteed her certain rights and protection and she knew an experienced immigration lawyer who did pro bono work. The Dhillons would be held to account.

'They will face prosecution for sure, possibly time behind bars,' Nina promised.

'I'll have to think about it,' said Pooja, who still sounded unconvinced. 'I also have my duties. Tomorrow there is the engagement party and I have to clean.'

Her words caused Mummy, Rumpi and Nina to share startled looks.

'The son is getting engaged?' asked Mummy.

'To a girl from Delhi,' said Pooja. 'The two met when he was visiting India.'

'He was also engaged to our friend's daughter, Amber,' stated Rumpi. 'He broke it off yesterday.'

'I don't know anything about that,' she said. 'I only know what I overheard madam and sir saying last night. They want Sanjiv sir to marry as soon as possible.'

'You got the impression there's some urgency to him going the marriage way?' asked Mummy.

'They were saying it has to be within a month.'

'Did they mention why?' asked Rumpi. 'Did their astrologer set the date, perhaps?'

Pooja didn't think so. 'But I heard them talk about the wedding plans,' she said. 'They've booked the golf club, and there's going to be a live band and a cake covered in white icing.'

Despite all she had learned in the last twenty minutes about how she was being ruthlessly exploited, Pooja was still tickled by the prospect of a big wedding with all the frills.

Nina felt compelled to gently point out that in all probability she would be confined to her room during the festivities. 'They don't want anyone seeing you and risk being reported to the police. You have to let us help you and bring them to account,' she insisted.

FOURTEEN

Bromley was waiting for Puri and Jags in the foyer of the Savoy.

'Managed to slip the leash, did you?' he said without so much as a hello or good morning.

A few days in London had not improved Puri's grasp of English irony. Thrown by Bromley's question – assuming it was indeed one – he answered literally, 'Rumpi has gone to do some exercise, but not much time is there. Today's agenda includes going by boat to visit the Green-witch.'

'It's pronounced "Gren-itch",' said the inspector. 'Sorry to correct you, Vish, but we can't have you butchering London place names any more than you let me get away with mangling Indian ones.'

'Not that it made the slightest difference, Inspector-sahib,' Puri felt compelled to point out. 'You kept on calling Mr Bose, Bose as in Rose; and our mountains the 'Him-uh-LAY-uhs.'

'Him-uh-LAY-uhs,' repeated Bromley. 'That's right, isn't it?'

Jags waited in the lobby while Bromley took Puri to a room in the hotel where all the security cameras were monitored by a two-man team. At Bromley's request, one of them played the footage from the sixth floor at three thirty-five the previous afternoon.

It showed Dr Bhatt in his blue baseball cap heading down the corridor, checking the numbers on the doors. He reached 612 – 'a suite' – and knocked. The door opened. A hand appeared – on the wrist, a Rolex and a flash of gold cufflinks.

'No one else entered the room,' said Bromley, before asking for the recording to be forwarded by five minutes when Dr Bhatt emerged with the sports bag.

'He came straight down to the lobby where you clocked him,' Bromley clarified.

'And the individual with the Rolex?'

'Hold your horses,' said Bromley, before asking the security guard to forward the recording by another thirty minutes when a figure emerged from 612. He was dressed like a stereotypical

Cold War spy in a trench coat, scarf and flat cap, the brim of which kept his face hidden from view.

'You've a name from the hotel register?' asked Puri.

'Booked to none other than Gladstone Global Holdings Inc.,' confided Bromley.

'Very good, Inspector, sahib, now we are getting somewhere,' said Puri, a grin suffusing his features. 'Who all signed for the room?'

'The key was collected from the desk by a hospitality concierge, so-called, working for the Lux Club, a company that facilitates travel and accommodation for multimillionaires.'

'No doubt this Lux Club is not about to reveal the identity of their client?' guessed Puri.

'If they even know. But it's not a total bust, Vish. Take a look at the video from earlier.'

The security man lined up footage from the cameras at the front entrance to the Savoy, recorded thirty minutes before Dr Bhatt's arrival. This showed the mystery man in the trench coat and flat cap arriving in a taxi, and caught him side on.

'I'd say mid-forties, probably South Asian origin,' said Bromley as they studied a blurry freeze frame.

'I've seen this man somewhere or other, I'm certain of it,' said Puri. 'But owing to the quality of the image and the wig, also, I'm facing trouble placing him.'

'You sure that's a wig?' asked Bromley.

'Being myself a master of disguise, I know a wig when I see one, Inspector-sahib, let me assure you.'

Bromley leant closer to the screen, scrutinizing the image. 'You're right and all. I can see it now.'

'Could be the individual in question is bald. Certain individuals go to some length to hide their deficiency in the hair department, so to speak.'

Bromley eyed Puri's Sandown cap, which never left his head, and didn't seem to be covering much beneath. 'Must be a vanity thing, I shouldn't wonder?' he asked, stifling a smile.

'For some it is a practical necessity – a case of protecting the head from the elements. In India, the sun being so strong, a bald head is something of a liability. Now Inspector-sahib, I would need a word in private.'

They went and found a quiet corner of the lobby where Puri broke the news that a professional Indian hitman had been shadowing him and, it seemed, had been contracted 'by nefarious actors' to kill Dr Bhatt.

'What!?' Bromley's voice crashed through the lobby. 'Oh, that's just perfect. Anything else you want to tell me, Vish?' This was said with unmistakable sarcasm.

'Well, yes, Inspector-sahib, something more is there, actually,' ventured Puri. 'There is every chance he picked up Dr Bhatt's trail outside the hotel.'

Bromley ran a hand slowly through his hair. 'You mean he followed you here yesterday?' he asked, surprise giving way to concern.

'From the Buckingham Palace.'

'And you didn't think to mention this before?' Bromley tugged out his notebook form his jacket pocket and gave a sigh. 'Go on then, give us the details,' he said.

Puri explained that the hitman's real name was Sahil Yadav but went by his underworld name, Chhota Balu, meaning 'little bear'.

'You're not aware of who hired this Chow-ta Bal-oo, I take it?' asked Bromley.

'Not as of yet, but rest assured my operatives in Delhi have started making all enquiries,' said Puri.

'And you came to know he's in London gunning for Bombay Duck how?'

Puri wasn't about to admit that his mother had identified him on the plane as a potential threat, yet felt compelled to acknowledge that it had been she who picked him out from Rumpi's selfie.

'Your mother?' said Bromley, showing surprise. 'How did she recognize a professional assassin?'

'Mummy-ji is quite an observant person we can say – always watching true-life crime TV,' Puri explained. 'No doubt she saw Chhota Balu on some such trash show.'

'My mother wouldn't be able to pick out her postman in a line-up,' observed Bromley. 'Tell her "good job" from me. Oh, and I nearly forgot: the Mercedes-Benz that tailed you from Baker Street, the plate's registered as what we call a "flag number".'

'That is what, exactly?'

'It means it's a diplomatic car, but doesn't have to advertise itself as such. All embassies are allowed up to three such plates. They're usually used by the ambassador and family. What do you make of that?'

Puri told him about Amul Joshi and their strange meeting at India House.

'You think he's working for your intelligence agencies?' asked Bromley.

'Not at all, he's what is referred to in Delhi circles as "lizer", a kind of fixer if you like,' said Puri. 'Never mind who is in power, he will see to it their interests are furthered. Amul Joshi belongs to The Nexus, in other words.'

'And this Joshi is keeping watch on the apartment block?'

'More likely he has been keeping watch on yours truly, Inspector-sahib. God knows half of Delhi came to know of my visit to London. No doubt Joshi got to know of my interest in Dr Bhatt, also.'

'How?'

'That I don't know – a leak from the Ministry of Finance could be.'

'Well, he didn't get it from us, if that's what you're thinking,' said Bromley, defensively.

But Puri thought it a distinct possibility.

The morning in Shanti Niketan was passing with a certain predictability. The dhobi wallah, whose place of business was beneath a blue tarpaulin beneath a tree at the end of the road, arrived at eight, bearing a neat pile of immaculately folded kurtas for which he received thirty rupees in grubby notes from Shweta Bhatt's cook. Soon after, a plant seller appeared, pushing an old wooden cart loaded with pots of bright zinnias and begonias, a few of which he arranged along the boundary of the property. At around eleven, the local nimboo mirchi lady arrived to hang a fresh evil-eye averter from the grille of the gate.

A subzi wallah offering piles of fresh cauliflowers came and went, then a knife sharpener on a bicycle. The kabari wallah's calls brought servants from all the neighbouring houses bearing recycling; and the work of the municipality's street cleaner, who stirred up a pall of fine dust with his broom as he worked his way down the street, preceded the sight of numerous drivers diligently wiping down their owners' luxury cars with damp cloths.

It was proving a routine morning for Flush as well. He had filed his report to Tubelight, bringing him up to date with movements at the house in the past twelve hours. Shweta Bhatt had taken an evening walk and later stood on the balcony smoking her usual cigarette; at breakfast an order of fresh croissants and brioche had been delivered from L'Opéra; at ten thirty the beautician had arrived, carrying a small bag. According to the security guards' conversation, picked up on Flush's microphones, Madam was getting her weekly 'threading and waxing'.

As per the standard Most Private Investigators Ltd. 'Trash Analysis' procedure, Puri's operative was now going through the household's weekly collection of paper and cardboard, which he'd managed to procure from the kabari wallah for fifty rupees (the unfortunate Dalit having paid the cook twenty rupees for the same).

This comprised mostly old daily newspapers and news magazines. Flush found that some articles about Shweta Bhatt's fugitive husband had been removed; sections of a cover story in *India Today* titled 'DR. DEATH' had been fiercely crossed out and defaced.

Some of the society pages had been torn out as well, suggesting that the former model, despite her isolation, maintained a keen interest in who ranked amongst the Page Three people.

A collection of greetings cards sent on her birthday also suggested she retained the support of family and a few friends, with messages urging her to stay strong and resilient. 'I believe in you, Chiku, and love you always,' her mother had written.

There were a few bills and invoices as well – the latest from the electricity company, another for the servicing of the house's split air conditioning units. There was also one from Speedy Travels.

So bored had Flush grown of sifting through the recycling that at first he didn't register the significance of what he had found, but then did a double take.

'Congratulations, Mrs Shweta Bhatt, your travel is confirmed, you're travelling first class all the way! Delhi–London; London–Grand Cayman,' he read out loud, and then called Tubelight.

'She's leaving in three days! And it looks like she's booked herself one way!'

As Flush scanned the itinerary on an app on his phone to forward on to the boss, he heard the familiar pattern of sounds from the street indicating movement at the house – the clunk of steel bolts being drawn back, the squeak of the gate opening – and looked up to see the beautician leaving the property.

For once the gates were wide open – and beyond, in the forecourt, the driver was standing next to a spotless sedan, holding the back door open.

Shweta Bhatt appeared momentarily as she left the house by a side door – she wore jeans and sneakers and a pair of black sunglasses – and climbed straight into the back seat of the vehicle.

Flush scrambled into the front of his three-wheeler and brought the eight-horsepower engine spluttering to life.

The sedan turned right and he waited a minute before following on behind.

His tempo's maximum speed was thirty-five miles per hour, so it was a good job he had told Chetan to fix a tracer to the bottom of the vehicle the last time it had left the house, Flush reflected.

Puri sat on the deck of the tourist boat to Greenwich, watching the renovated wharves of the old London docks slip past. He was only half listening to the cheeky Estuary patter of the guide as he provided a potted history of 'old Father Thames' and a well-honed stock of outlandish facts.

Rumpi could tell that he was distracted, and asked him if there was something on his mind. He pleaded tiredness from 'lack of sleep'. But the truth was Puri was suffering from what he termed a 'brain itch'.

A brain itch occurred when a detail relating to a case was niggling at him. Usually it was something that constituted a crucial clue, possibly *the* crucial clue in a case. In his last significant investigation, for example, he'd suffered from an especially intense brain itch while trying to figure out the significance of the last words spoken by a dying Dalit, who, it turned out, had been killed by upper caste villagers for having had the audacity to grow a moustache. Now it was the poisoned mango he'd discovered in the fridge in the Regent's Park apartment. He was no closer to getting to grips with who had injected it with the two millilitres of deadly aconite, and badly needed to track down the security guard, Rakesh Sharma. Instead, here he was floating down this sad excuse for a river while Chhota Balu was at large and might even now be punching Dr Bhatt's ticket permanently.

The vessel passed an old pub, the guide making a good deal of fuss about the fact that it dated back to the mere sixteenth century (recent history by Indus Civilization standards), and Puri considered how best to get away for a couple of hours after they'd visited Greenwich.

Perhaps it was time to come clean with Rumpi. He could explain to her that he was acting as a loyal citizen of India at the request of the government of India, and it was his sworn duty to see justice served. Or perhaps it would be better to appeal to her sympathetic nature. He was the victim of 'unforeseen and unfortunate circumstance'. He had not been given a choice in taking on the case. If he didn't act quickly, Dr Bhatt would be murdered. A man's life hung in the balance, and he had a moral duty, not to mention a professional one, to try to save him.

No matter how he thought of framing it, however, he could hear his wife reminding him that he had given his solemn word, come what may, that he would take time away from work while in London and try to relax. She would repeat her usual complaint about the two of them never enjoying a proper holiday; that every time they went anywhere, he became embroiled in some 'horrid incident'. In Kerala, where they had travelled to celebrate their twenty-fifth wedding anniversary in a luxury hotel, a bride turned up dead in the honeymoon suite, killed by a cobra.[7] In Uttarakhand during a 'supposed break' from the punishing June heat, it had been 'even worse': Puri had become embroiled in a plot involving Iranian agents searching for seven plutonium cases lost by the CIA and Indian Intelligence Bureau in the Himalayas in the 1960s.

'Leave Dr Bhatt to the official force,' he could hear Rumpi saying. 'You have to draw the line somewhere.'

This left Puri with just one option. The nuclear one. But it was just too painful to contemplate.

---

[7] The groom was bitten, too, but survived. Subsequently, Puri discovered that he hailed from Shetphal in the state of Maharashtra, a village infested with cobras where the inhabitants have built up a strong immunity to their bites.

The guide's words broke into his thoughts: 'After the battle of Trafalgar in 1805, Admiral Nelson wasn't buried at sea but put in a barrel of brandy and brought back to Greenwich,' he said. 'From here he was taken to St Paul's Cathedral, where he was given a state funeral.'

Puri managed to nod approvingly at this tidbit and gave Rumpi a convincing smile to convey that he was enjoying himself.

'So much wonderful history,' he said with enthusiasm, giving her a pat on the hand, his brain itch growing more intense by the minute.

FIFTEEN

Protesting Punjabi farmers had blocked the major roads leading to Parliament with tractors festooned in Indian tricolours. Tear gas drifted over scenes of battle as Sikhs squared up to Delhi riot police. A journey that would normally have taken at most half an hour lasted the best part of two. It was already noon by the time Shweta Bhatt's sedan pulled into Rajiv Chowk, or Connaught Place, the colonnaded, mock-Georgian circle built by the British in the heart of New Delhi.

For anyone with a sense of history, these distinct, whitewashed buildings conjured echoes of moustachioed officers in pith helmets, and pale memsahibs carrying parasols, of punka wallahs tugging relentlessly on chics to temper the relentless heat. Yet, despite the stamp of colonialism, CP's calm elegance and long, shaded promenades made it a cherished feature of today's vast, sprawling megatropolis, so that finding a parking space here was always a challenge.

However, it was Shweta Bhatt's driver's lucky day. As he pulled into the parking area in front of C Block, a space became suddenly available. And, having let out his mistress, he docked the sedan between the other tightly packed cars with mere centimetres to spare on either side.

Flush had to park his vehicular untouchable by the kerb, along with the other undesirables, including autos, scooters and a handcart loaded with battered LPG cannisters. And with Tubelight stuck on the other side of the ongoing farmer protest – by now tyres were burning in the streets and the police were letting rip with water cannon – he was left with no choice but to leave his vehicle unattended, albeit it in the knowledge that the 'Warning Toxic Material' and corresponding danger sticked on the back door would make any thief think twice about breaking in.

By now, Shweta Bhatt was making her way along the promenade of shops, her profile appearing then vanishing then reappearing again as she passed behind the Greco-Roman columns like a figure in a crude animation created by a Zoetrope.

Ignoring the allure of new international boutiques that had, over the past two decades, replaced many of the old businesses that dated back to colonial times, she walked straight into a store selling luxury luggage.

Flush watched from a safe distance as a young shop assistant showed her several choices of brands in various shapes and sizes.

Within a matter of minutes, Shweta Bhatt had settled on the entire range of Louis Vuitton – carry-ons, suit bags, hat cases, the lot – and these were duly carried out to her car.

Her next stop was a perfume shop where she purchased a bottle of Chanel, the cost of which was enough to feed the average Indian family for months, carrying it away in a little white bag.

Her driver then took her on a roundabout route, circumventing the farmers' protests, to Sundar Nagar, the exclusive colony abutting Delhi's vast Zoological Park.

Here she was dropped in front of an exclusive Italian restaurant, where she was greeted fondly at the door by the manager.

Flush didn't even consider following her inside, dressed as he was in a T-shirt that bore tikka sauce stains from his last Peppy Paneer pizza, and cargo pants that looked like the victim of giant moths. His attempt to catch a glimpse of Shweta Bhatt and whoever she was dining with through the restaurant window failed thanks to the security guard on duty who explained in no uncertain terms that a 'kuttiya ki aulad' like him had no place hanging around the place.

Brooding over this insult, he took refuge at the dhaba on the far side of the market popular with auto and taxi drivers.

Tubelight soon joined him and commiserated – and they both ordered plates of tandoori chicken and roomali roti. They had time for a couple of glasses of extra sweet cutting chai as well before Shweta Bhatt emerged from the restaurant accompanied by her sister, Nidhi, now the owner of the bottle of Chanel.

They embraced a number of times, evidently finding it hard to say goodbye. And when finally Shweta Bhatt got into her sedan, her sister stood by her window, holding her hand to the glass and blowing fond kisses.

Everyone was standing on the Prime Meridian posing for a selfie when Jags's phone gave a loud ping. He checked for a message – and, to Puri at least, his wide-eyed reaction spoke unmistakably to his AirTag having suddenly come back online.

Puri had to endure another five excruciating minutes before he and his nephew were able to distance themselves from the group and study its location.

'It's in an area called St John's Wood,' said Jags. 'The street's Abbey Road, where The Beatles recorded their albums.'

'How long to reach the spot?' asked Puri.

'One hour, give or take.'

By now, they had visited all of Greenwich's main attractions, including the Cutty Sark, the village market and the Royal Observatory. There was now talk of heading over to – of all places – the Fan Museum. And there was still the boat trip back to Westminster to contend with. All told, this meant at least two more hours of Puri's time.

There was now nothing for it: the nuclear option was all that was left. Puri would have to swallow his pride, explain his predicament to Mummy, and ask for her help in relieving him of tourism duty.

Before he could get his mother on her own, however, Jags had to be enlisted to distract Nina and Rumpi. This he achieved by suddenly coming down with a stomach ache in Greenwich Park. And Puri was able to get Mummy out of earshot of the two of them.

'Mummy-ji, before departing from Delhi I was engaged to hunt for a certain high-profile individual while in London,' he began. 'The identity of this individual is no less than—'

'—Dr Harilal Bhatt. Yes, Chubby, that much I know,' said his mother, nonchalant.

Puri looked aghast. 'How do you know?'

'Obvious, na. From the first, I came to you were working on a case. Like your father you can't do meter down. Then yesterday in the hotel, when I came to warn you regarding Hairy One, I recognized Bhatt straight off – never mind the moustache and baseball cap.'

'Had you not made such a racket, I would have captured him,' said Puri, bitterly.

'You meant to restrain him then and there, yourself?' she asked, extremely sceptical. 'After so much khanna?'

Puri could feel his ire rising and almost launched into a (familiar) diatribe about how her interference was not appreciated or helpful, that he was the detective in the family not her, and that he did not need her protection. But he managed to restrain himself from doing so, purely in the cause of his own best interests.

'Rumpi knows?' he asked.

'She is distracted, na. Having such a nice time in London. A dream come true.'

'Thank the God, my guts would be made for garters were she to discover the truth and all,' he said before taking his mother into his confidence about the AirTag and how it might well lead them straight to Dr Bhatt.

'That is if Chhota Balu doesn't beat us to it, naturally,' he added.

Mummy listened carefully, considered for a moment and then said, 'Just I'll require one, two minutes, you stay here,' before going to speak with the others, who by now were taking a break on a bench.

Whatever she said did the trick, and Rumpi and Nina headed off on their own.

'It is all arranged, na,' said Mummy as Puri joined her and Jags. 'They are going to see this Fan Museum.'

'You don't intend to join them, Mummy-ji?' asked Puri, alarmed.

But she had no intention of doing so. 'I'll be accompanying you, na,' she said, as if this had been plainly understood.

'Out of the question, no way, final,' he protested. 'Some danger is there.'

'Exactly. Now chalo, don't do dilly-dally. You told me yourself, Chubby, time is not on our side.'

With grave reluctance, Puri started back towards the park gates.

'Just tell me what all you told Rumpi,' he said with a sigh.

'Just I told her you were hungry. That she did not question,' said Mummy.

* * *

En route to Abbey Road, a journey Puri was forced to make by Underground, this being the quickest option, he debated whether or not to now inform Bromley about Jags's AirTag. He had again broken the spirit of their agreement. With Chhota Balu at large, the stakes were high. But Puri could not be sure Dr Bhatt would be staying at the address provided by Jags. And if there was one thing Puri hated, it was being wrong. Until he could be sure that he wasn't being duped and wouldn't lose face, he would wait.

He soon got another matter straightened out as well.

'You two are to do exactly what I say, I'm in command, no argument,' were his instructions to Jags and Mummy on the Tube. 'Break ranks and I will call off the whole thing and wash my hands of the case.'

'If Chhota Balu followed Dr Bhatt, could be he's very much at large, waiting to strike,' his mother felt the need to point out, not reading the room − or rather, carriage.

'Yes, Mummy-ji, of that I'm very much aware,' Puri said, wearily.

'Either that or Dr Bhatt managed to shake him off and the hitman's following us − in which case we're going to lead him straight to him again,' suggested Jags.

'Not to worry, we're in the clear, na, I've been keeping watch,' said Mummy.

'I, too, have been keeping an eye out all day and we've not been followed, of that I'm certain,' affirmed Puri. 'In the event you spot Chhota Balu, you're to inform me immediately. I in turn will call for Inspector Brom-ley.'

'I was thinking we should try to blend in, not appear, like, too conspicuous,' said Jags. He looked Puri up and down. 'I mean, let's face it, Uncle-gee, no one could miss you in that 1970s get-up.'

'The Safari suit is ageless,' Puri stated, indignant.

He had to admit to Jags's point, however: he was instantly recognizable, to Chhota Balu and Dr Bhatt.

'You've something or other in mind, is it?' he asked.

The Circle Line train was approaching Baker Street where they needed to change for the Jubilee Line.

'Yeah,' said Jags. 'I just thought of something.'

SIXTEEN

Puri had never felt so ridiculous or self-conscious in his life. And he was not convinced that Jags's so-called 'disguise' – a Sherlock Holmes deerstalker purchased in haste at a tourist gift shop outside Regent Street station – did not make him stand out all the more. On the last leg of the journey, he'd drawn smiles from a number of other passengers. A couple of unruly teenagers had even seen fit to point at him and laugh.

Far worse still was the reaction from the barmaid in the pub from where he had decided to stake out the Abbey Road address: 'I reckon it suits you,' she said with a smile.

'That's what I said, you're slaying it Uncle-gee!' said Jags, playfully. 'Them ear flaps will come in useful in the cold.'

Puri ignored them as he perused the menu. He was starving, having binned the Cornish pasty that Rumpi had bought him for lunch – this on the grounds that it possessed no taste whatsoever – and decided to take the opportunity to try 'the famous' fish and chips.

'Mushy peas with that?' asked the barmaid.

'That is what, exactly?' Puri asked with a frown.

'Basically mashed peas, luv.'

Did the British simply have their taste buds removed at birth?

'I'll require some chilli sauce,' he said.

'We've got HP.'

Puri paid for the food and drinks and he and Jags made their way out to a table in the small garden at the front of the pub. From there they had a bird's-eye view of the address where the AirTag was still registering. A Georgian, four-storey, terraced house, it was the only one in the row with high walls and a tall front gate made of solid wood. There were other security measures as well: cameras on the gateposts, more cameras on the outside of the building and a fingerprint ID entry system. If there was any doubt that the occupants valued their privacy, all the blinds in the windows were drawn.

'No sign of your hitman,' said Jags. 'Suppose he could be nearby, undercover sort of fing. From that Mansion Block across the way he could nail anyone in the street. That churchyard's like a good spot, too, yeah.'

'Being a professional, he will remain well hidden from view, that much is certain,' agreed Puri.

'Same goes for Dr Bhatt, also, na,' said Mummy. She was wearing a 'Mind the Gap' baseball cap courtesy of Jags. 'After yesterday, he will take extra precaution when going around.'

'Let us hope he leaves the house for some reason or other,' said Puri.

Mummy could read in his tone that he knew more than he was letting on.

'Something is there you're not telling us, Chubby,' she said. 'So secretive you are.'

'You do keep a lot of secrets, Uncle-gee,' laughed Jags. 'I've lost track of what I'm not allowed to tell to who. To be honest, it's like doing my 'ead in.'

'Allow me to remind you both, I am a *private* investigator, and private means private,' said Puri. 'I'm not in the business of sharing information with all and sundry, willy-nilly.'

'We are not all or sundry, na,' insisted Mummy.

'Papa used to say, "Rule number one, never tell anyone anything they don't need to know."'

'I'm just anyone to you, Chubby?'

Mummy's words hung cold in the air. Somehow, the Abbey Road traffic suddenly seemed louder, the burst of raucous laughter from the four pint-swilling young men crowded around the next table all the more jarring. Puri kept watch on the house, fidgeting with his beermat. Mummy took out her knitting and continued work on her scarf, the needles clicking together rhythmically.

A minute or two later Puri said, suddenly, with laboured patience, 'Nothing is confirmed, but I came to know Shweta Bhatt is planning to travel this side.'

'This side? You mean here? London?' asked Jags.

'Seems she has her booking for day after tomorrow. From UK she is planning to go to the Grand Cayman island itself.'

'That's an island for like tax dodgers, yeah?' asked Jags.

'Its location is the Caribbean,' said Puri.

'So – what? – you reckon Bhatt's plan is to fly off with his missus?'

'My operatives in Delhi overheard the couple speaking about being reunited soon,' said Puri.

'That's insane – if Bhatt goes to the airport, he'll be arrested, innit,' pointed out Jags.

'Could be he got hold of a fake passport, na,' said Mummy.

'Yeah, right, makes sense. So what are we gonna do, sit here for two days?' asked Jags.

Puri knew there remained a small window of opportunity before he would have to call it a day. Leaving Jags or Mummy to keep watch was out of the question.

'We three will give it until eight o'clock; thereafter the responsibility will lie with Inspector Brom-ley,' said Puri.

'You never know, we might get lucky,' said Jags.

'At this stage, we must trust to the God.'

The same sentiment crossed Puri's mind when he sampled the bland fish and chips and mushy peas – and he made a mental note to pick up a bottle of hot sauce and carry it with him for other such British culinary emergencies.

Soon after seven it started to rain, and they relocated to a bus shelter on Abbey Road, perching themselves on the slanted, narrow, plastic seats that seemed designed to discourage anyone from making use of them.

Red double-decker buses stopped regularly in front of them, their windows steamed up like saunas, the eyes of passengers peering out through streaks and smears on the glass.

Eight o'clock came and went. And though Nina had called to say dinner was scheduled for nine, they decided to give it another ten minutes.

Finally, reluctantly, Puri called it a night and suggested they return to the pub where, out of the rain, he could make the call to Inspector Bromley.

As they were leaving the cover of the bus shelter, however, a minicab pulled up in front of the Georgian house. The gate opened, and a figure hurried across the pavement and got into the back of the vehicle.

The minicab pulled away, accelerating fast past the bus shelter.

Through the rain and the flare of headlights, it was impossible to make out the identity of the passenger.

It crossed Puri's mind that this could be a decoy, that another car might arrive in a few minutes for Dr Bhatt.

At that precise moment, however, a black cab stopped in front of them and deposited its customer on the kerb. This the detective took as serendipity, and the trio clambered inside.

His decision soon proved fortuitous. The AirTag was on the move up ahead, Jags reported after refreshing the app.

By now seven vehicles separated them from the minicab. This included a motorbike that had pulled out of one of the side streets off Abbey Road and, though it had ample opportunity to move ahead, kept behind the minicab as well.

Though the driver was wearing a helmet with a tinted visor, Mummy was convinced this was Chhota Balu. She therefore urged the taxi driver to drive faster. And when he slowed down for an amber light as he approached a crossroads near Kilburn and stopped completely as it turned red, she let him know in no uncertain terms of her frustration.

'Why you're doing such slowcoach driving?' she demanded. 'We are in a hurry, na!'

Whereas in Delhi her zero tolerance to poor driving and navigation skills generally got results, it didn't make a dent in this London driver, not even when Mummy called him 'a total duffer'. Indeed, thereafter, the taxi seemed to slow, with the man even going so far as to make way for mere cyclists.

His stubbornness, coupled with several more red lights and a showdown between a scaffolding truck driver and a white-van man at a crossroads in Cricklewood ('hardly the Queen's English,' remarked Mummy blushingly as they both exchanged abuse from their windows) ensured that the minicab reached what appeared to be its final destination, Neasden Temple, eight minutes ahead of them.

By the time Puri, Mummy and Jags reached the entrance themselves, the motorbike was parked up on the pavement further down the road, and the AirTag was registering inside the temple complex.

Fearing the worst, Puri called Bromley's mobile. The call went to voicemail, however, and he had to leave a quick message, explaining that he believed he had traced Dr Bhatt to Neasden Temple.

Brazenly flaunting the British laws of queueing, the trio then pushed past the worshippers at the security check – 'Oi! Excuse me, there's people waiting, you know?' – and quickly reached the courtyard beyond.

Stopping briefly to shed their footwear, they hurried in their socks past the ornamental gardens trimmed with neat hedges, to the bottom of a wide set of stone steps. This led up to the mandir with its lofty white shikhara, lit up bright and beautiful against the night sky.

Puri called a stop to confirm that the AirTag had been carried inside the place of worship – and then ordered Jags and Mummy to remain where they were.

'Keep watch in case Dr Bhatt slips through the net. Do not under any circumstance approach Chhota Balu. When Brom-ley returns my call, tell him "no delay",' Puri said before hurrying up the steep steps.

For some worshippers, visiting Neasden Temple was evidently something of an occasion. A couple of extended families, each three or four generations strong, attired as if they were attending marriage functions, had paused on the steps and were arranging themselves for group shots. They asked Puri if he would mind acting as photographer, but to their bemusement, he bluntly refused and climbed on.

Reaching the summit with burning knees and with his head spinning, the detective had to take a minute beneath the ornate pavilion at the entrance to the mandir to recover – and remove the deerstalker. There was no way he was going to enter wearing such a ridiculous hat. If nothing else, it was bound to offend the gods and bring him back luck. Only now did he realize he had lost his Sandown, however – perhaps in the pub, at the bus shelter or in the taxi – and had to quickly fashion his handkerchief into a kind of skull cap by tying the corners into knots.

Puri then hurried through the doors, finding himself in one of the most beautiful temples he had ever visited, with carvings to match the finest anywhere in India. The walls were graced with delicate friezes depicting scenes from the epics. A forest of white

stone pillars rose to the ceiling, branching into arches that undu-
lated like clouds. Beyond he was delivered into a hall crowned
by a central dome. Here, devotees and tourists alike, craned their
heads up at a ceiling boasting exquisite geometric floral motifs.

Puri kept to the periphery of the hall, edging towards the
temple's gilded sanctum, where a row of richly attired effigies
stood beneath brightly lit red and gold canopies.

The temple's pandits, some in white robes, others in saffron,
were conducting the evening arti. To the chanting of Vedic
mantras, the rhythmic clanging of tiny cymbals, and the alluring
aroma of sandalwood, they performed a ritualistic washing of
the divinities.

A group of fifty worshippers stood, four rows deep, making
offerings of fruit and nuts and garlands of saffron blossoms, their
collective prayers a monastic susurration.

Puri had no choice but to join the back of the congregation,
which stood six or seven people deep.

He picked out a figure at the front, kneeling in prayer in a baseball cap, certain this was Dr Bhatt; and began searching urgently
for Chhota Balu, straining his neck, scouring the congregation.

His view of one section of the congregation was obscured by
a man of considerable stature standing in the second row, however.

Puri tried manoeuvring into a better position, shuffling to his
left, and managed a foot or so at best before the tall man turned
to leave.

He was the High Commission driver with sunken eyes who had
come to Nina's house and taken him to India House to meet Amul
Joshi, Representative – and he was carrying a white sports bag
identical to the one Dr Bhatt had made off with from the Savoy.

Puri had to make a snap decision to let him leave unchallenged
– though he hoped Jags would recognize him – and continued
to search for the hitman.

Just to the left of where Dr Bhatt was still kneeling, he spotted
a short man wearing a yellow Hawaiian shirt and noticed that the
back of his neck and the backs of his ears were especially hairy.

Convinced this was Chhota Balu, he began to push deter-
minedly forward, insisting that those in front give way.

In so doing, Puri managed to crush an elderly auntie's toes
beneath his full weight.

He was getting short thrift in Gujarati when suddenly a piercing shriek echoed up into the dome above.

In a moment, the blend of chanting, percussion and prayer crashed into silence.

A man's voice shouted: 'He's having a fit, grab hold of him!'

'Call an ambulance!' cried out someone else.

Puri's bulk proved a sudden advantage as he shoved his way to the front.

Dr Bhatt, still wearing a fake moustache, was writhing in agony on the floor, his eyes glazed with terror.

Spit started to foam from his mouth, his arms flailing wildly, two pundits kneeling next to him powerless to keep him still.

Puri addressed the bank of horrified faces gathered around the stricken man.

'Is there a doctor in the house?' he called out. 'This man requires urgent assistance!'

And of the seventy or so worshippers, no less than three men and two women of South Asian origin stepped forward to answer his appeal.

SEVENTEEN

'Let me get this straight: you traced Bombay Duck to Abbey Road, didn't call it in, then followed him here?' asked Inspector Bromley, his face almost as red as it had appeared in the Delhi summer heat.

He and Puri were standing near the spot where Dr Bhatt's body lay covered in a sheet.

The temple had been declared a crime scene and a forensics team were busy dusting and swabbing the area. Every few seconds, a camera flashed and the light bounced off the white marble, dazzling the two men no matter in which direction they faced.

'Later only I will explain my reasoning, Inspector-sahib, but as of now more urgent matters are there.'

Puri had recognized an Indian High Commission driver standing directly behind Dr Bhatt just moments before he'd been murdered, he explained. This man had left the temple carrying a white sports bag, surely the same one that Dr Bhatt had taken away from the Savoy. Jags's AirTag was inside this bag and could be traced on his iPhone.

'How did it get in there? Never mind! Where is he now?'

They found Jags with Mummy in the temple garden, and Bromley asked him if he'd be willing to assist the police by travelling in a pursuit car to trace the suspect.

'Hell, yeah!' was his response. And Bromley promptly led him out of the temple complex.

A couple of minutes later, a car sped off down the street, splattering the terraced houses across from the temple complex in pulsating electric blue.

'Your suspect doesn't appear to have got far, not if your nephew's device is working properly,' reported Bromley upon his return. 'Now I want to know how the AirTag found its way into Bombay Duck's bag.'

But there were still more pressing matters to attend to, Puri insisted. His mother had positively identified Chhota Balu amongst the worshippers as he'd left the temple.

'You're sure it was him, madam?' asked Bromley

'Quite sure, sir,' said Mummy. 'He was there on the aeroplane from Delhi, na. Being so hairy and bad mannered, he was impossible to miss.'

Bromley threw Puri a look. 'He was on the flight with you?' he asked, wide-eyed.

'At that point I was not aware of his identity,' said Puri, wishing his mother would keep her mouth shut but powerless now to do anything about it without causing a spat.

'Then when?'

'Inspector-sahib, we can stand here wasting so much of time or you can try to catch hold of him. Seems he arrived here by motorcycle and I happened to note down the number plate.'

Puri handed him a piece of paper torn from his notebook.

'Make?' asked Bromley.

'BMW. Model is R1250,' said Mummy.

Bromley wrote this down, smiling to himself. 'You two make a good team; you should work together, make it a family business,' he said.

The suggestion provoked a burst of nervous laughter from mother and son.

'For cooperation day by day, we two are both too headstrong, sir,' she said.

'It would most definitely lead to disaster, no question about it at all,' affirmed Puri. 'There is an old saying in Hindi that tells us that we don't choose our family but the God gifts it to us, but where professional life is concerned, it is healthy for boundaries to be maintained.'

'But also we say, "Musibaat aane par, aapka parivar hi aapki madad karta hai" – when trouble comes around, just it is your family that comes to your aid, na,' said Mummy, pointedly.

'Very wise,' said Bromley. 'If you ask me, Vish, your mother's one of a kind. Now if you'll excuse me.'

He stepped away to call in the details about the bike, and to check in with the officers taking statement from the eyewitnesses.

Puri watched the scene in silence, struggling to find a way to thank his mother without giving her too much encouragement.

He did not accept, would never accept, Rumpi's opinion that he was the one who was 'prickly and territorial'.

Clearing his throat uneasily, he said, 'What all you said is correct, Mummy-ji, family should always be there for one another. Today you were there for me, in fact. Allow me to offer you my thanks. I'm grateful, actually.'

'Never mind, Chubby, that is what mothers are for, na,' said Mummy. 'Just I do what I can here and there. You are the professional. That I know and respect. Such a capable detective you've become. Your father would be proud.'

'Most kind of you, Mummy. If only he were here now with us in London itself,' he said.

They lapsed into silence again and Puri checked his watch.

'It is getting late, no?'

'And chilly also,' she said. 'Better you cover your head, Chubby, or a cold will come.'

Puri knew she was right, the handkerchief had been sufficient for its purpose in the temple, but he risked getting sick if he didn't put the deerstalker back on.

Bromley, upon his return, smiled at the sight of it. 'The game's afoot, my dear Vish Puri,' he teased, before confirming that officers were en route to the Abbey Road address armed with a search warrant.

'One bit of bad news: there are no CCTV cameras inside the temple and photography's not permitted,' he added. 'Assuming the poison – I'm assuming it's aconite again – was injected into the victim with a syringe, then perhaps one of the congregation can ID the murderer.'

'Aconite is easily absorbed through the skin and then passes into the nervous system,' pointed out Mummy. 'In some cases, death can arrive in minutes.'

'Provided the right potency is there,' said Puri. 'Inspector-sahib, your pathologists should be on the lookout for any corrosion to the skin marking the place where the aconite was introduced.'

Bromley's hand-held radio emitted a series of tones, and he answered it with his call sign. He and the officer calling spoke for a minute or so in British police jargon that Puri struggled to understand, and then they both signed off.

'Good news: thanks to your enterprising nephew, Bombay

Duck's bag has been located on a commercial refuse truck in North Acton, a couple of miles from here,' said the inspector. 'My guess is the Indian High Commission driver emptied it of its contents and then got rid of it – a bin outside some business premises, most probably. Lucky for us, the AirTag wasn't crushed.'

It crossed Puri's mind that Amul Joshi's driver might have recognized him in the temple and thought it best to rid himself of the bag as quickly as possible.

'The driver's prints will be there on the bag,' he said. 'He wasn't expecting it to be retrieved and will not have taken the precaution of wiping it clean.'

'The tall one with the sunken eyes carrying the white bag was wearing gloves,' said Mummy, who had watched him as he'd left the temple.

'She doesn't miss a trick, your mum, does she, Vish?' said Bromley, smothering a smile. 'Never mind. There's CCTV outside the temple and that'll connect this driver of yours to the bag. Now, tell me how you see this driver fitting into things? What was his relationship with Dr Bhatt?'

Puri gave a shrug. 'That I don't know, Inspector-sahib. As of now it is all conjecture, and I hesitate to dip my toes in such waters so to speak.'

'My guess is it was blackmail,' said Bromley, regardless. 'Somehow he gets to know of Bombay Duck's whereabouts, threatens to give him up. They arrange to meet here at the temple. Dr Bhatt brings along the pay-off. But then why would this driver, having got what he came for, murder him?' He paused and made a face, his forehead corrugated. 'Nah, I'm not buying it,' Bromley went on. 'It's far more likely this Chow-taa Ba-loo's our man. He's the contract killer. We can place him in the vicinity at the precise time of the murder.'

'Chhota Balu is a supari, na, a shooter,' said Mummy. 'Poison is not his style.'

'I have to agree with my mother,' said Puri, as much as it pained him to do so. 'Such types don't go in for poison and all. When they do the needful, they'll make it messy. Up close and personal.'

'Perhaps he's taken a different approach, seeing as this is London. Think about it. He stands out here, this isn't his usual hunting ground. If he goes blasting away in his usual fashion, he knows full well he's going to be picked up on CCTV. We've got thousands of them across London. *And* he knows he can't buy his way out of trouble through his political connections. He gets smart, bides his time, knows that Bombay Duck visits the temple – you said so yourself yesterday that you could tell he'd been owing to the what's-it on his wrist—'

'A mouli, Inspector-sahib,' said Puri.

'Right, exactly – that thread thing you people wear. So Chow-taa Ba-loo counts on Bombay Duck going again and, when it comes to it, gets right up behind him. A syringe in the back of the arm. Job done.'

'What you're suggesting is possible but not probable,' said Puri. 'To my mind, only, we're missing some ingredients for the full thali.'

Indeed, there were too many unanswered questions to start trying to draw conclusions, Puri reflected. For one thing, they still had no idea who had poisoned the mango in Dr Bhatt's fridge, though, surely, it had not been Chhota Balu. The driver was a far stronger suspect, given that he worked for the shadowy Amul Joshi. The identity of the South Asian male who had occupied suite 602 at the Savoy through Gladstone Global Holdings Incorporated remained an unknown as well – surely a key piece of the puzzle that could not simply be ignored.

Puri refrained from sharing his thoughts with Mummy present, however. She already knew far too much and, if possible, he wanted to keep her from any further involvement in the case.

He gave a yawn and said, 'For now, Inspector-sahib, I believe we will call it a night.'

'About the High Commission driver, I'm going to need a name,' said Bromley.

'Give me one, two hours and I'll revert,' Puri assured him.

He and Mummy left the temple complex and emerged into the street to find it blocked by police cars and vans.

They asked one of the constables manning a cordon in the form of plastic tape stretched across the road if he knew how they could find a taxi, and were directed to a nearby minicab office.

Once they were on their way back to East Ham, Mummy asked about the reference Bromley had made to aconite being used 'again' and he had to tell her about the apartment and the poisoned mango.

Inevitably, she wanted to know more. Who had delivered the mangoes, for example. But Puri pleaded exhaustion and suggested they 'take some meter down'.

Mummy agreed but there was one thing she simply had to know.

'It is puzzling me, Chubby – why Inspector Brom-ley keeps talking about Bombay Duck?' she asked. 'It is a dried fish, na?'

By the time Puri and Mummy reached East Ham, it was past ten o'clock. By then, several witnesses from the temple, having recognized Dr Bhatt, had spoken to a couple of local reporters who'd reached the scene. And although Scotland Yard was yet to corroborate the identity of the victim, the news was making headlines nationally and internationally.

Thankfully, Nina and Rumpi hadn't heard about the murder yet, and both seemed preoccupied. Indeed when Puri apologized for being late and explained that he and Mummy had, after going for a nice meal, taken a stroll and then gone to watch a movie (something they enjoyed doing together in Delhi from time to time), Rumpi just smiled and said, 'That's nice, Chubby. Tomorrow we're all planning to go to Windsor to see the castle.'

Once he had gone up to bed, however, Rumpi and Nina explained to Mummy that they were preoccupied with good reason: Pooja had called an hour ago on the phone they'd lent her.

'She was in tears, Mrs Dhillon locked her in her room this afternoon while Sanjiv's new fiancé and her family visited,' said Nina. 'She wants to speak with the lawyer tomorrow. I've set up a meeting for nine. Same place.'

But that was not all. Pooja had shared more, troubling news. In the early evening, while she'd been cleaning up the kitchen, she'd overhead Mr and Mrs Dhillon speaking in Hindi in the next room.

'She said they were drinking a lot and their voices got louder and louder,' said Rumpi. 'Pooja said they were speaking very badly about the fiancé and her family. They called the girl, Smita, "chinaal", mocked her "carrom board" chest, and referred to her father as "suwar ki aulad"!'

'Just we must warn them somehow,' said Mummy, alarmed.

'You haven't heard the half of it,' said Nina. 'Pooja says they're planning to hold the wedding in a fortnight – and after twelve months, Sanjiv plans to divorce her.'

'Is the other family rich, are they giving the Dhillons a huge dowry, is that it?' Rumpi speculated. 'It does happen sometimes, families conniving to rob the girls' parents of money and jewels.'

With Amber, there had been no promise of a dowry, Mummy pointed out, and Buggi had no money at all.

'Every time, she is borrowing a few bucks from me,' she said.

'What then?' asked Nina.

'The two girls – Amber and this second one – share something in common, na,' said Mummy. 'That is why Sanjiv chose them. It is for us three to find out why.'

There was a pause and Rumpi breathed a sigh into it. 'I agree, we can't just stand by and do nothing,' she said. 'But I do hope it doesn't take too long. We've only got a few days left and there's so much more of London that I promised to see with Chubby.'

EIGHTEEN

nspector Bromley was fast becoming a recognized public figure amongst tens of millions of Indians – from Srinagar to Trivandrum; from Mumbai to Guwahati – watching the news on their TVs, tablets and mobile phones. Twenty-four-hour news channels broadcasting in dozens of languages had got hold of the clip of Scotland Yard's man emerging from Neasden Temple and making a brief statement – and they were all repeating it over and over again.

Assaulted by a cannonade of press flashes, Bromley could be seen standing in front of a small press corps of local reporters, gathered on the street in front of the temple. In his plodding, matter-of-fact vernacular he stated: 'Soon after eight o'clock this evening, a male in his mid-fifties of South Asian extraction died while attending Hindu prayers at Neasden Temple. Emergency services attended the scene but were unable to revive the individual. A team of specialists are investigating the scene. Several witnesses are helping us with our enquiries. We are asking anyone who was present inside the temple during the incident to contact us. Meanwhile, I would ask the representatives of the press to refrain from speculating as to the identity of the victim which, at the present time, is not confirmed, pending further enquiries. I will update you on our progress at the appropriate time.'

Bromley's appeal for responsible reporting and his refusal to answer any questions had not deterred India's news editors from declaring that the victim was none other than fugitive Dr Harilal Bhatt. And they weren't shying away from suggesting he had been murdered, either – this based on testimony of a single witness who, having recognized India's most wanted man as he lay dying, had spoken to a local reporter from the website, Neasden Live.

'INDIA'S MOST WANTED: SHOCKING LONDON TEMPLE MURDER' ran the headline on Action News! accompanied by a hyper commentary that sounded like it belonged in a trailer for a superhero movie. 'DOCTORS AT SCENE FAIL TO SAVE DR HARILAL BHATT', ran the onscreen ticker tape. 'WITNESSES DESCRIBE DRAMATIC LAST MOMENTS'.

Channel-surfing in his tempo, Flush watched panels of commentators speculating about events in London and who might potentially be behind the murder. File footage of Dr Bhatt – in his lab, at his desk, playing with his kids from his first marriage, at a huge society wedding standing next to Céline Dion – kept playing over and over again. A son who lost his father to Bio Solutions' Dia-Beat lamented the former executive's death as he would not now face justice, calling him a 'fraud, crook and a murderer' who 'got off lightly'. A lady who lost her husband and had been one of the chief campaigners demanding justice and Dr Bhatt's extradition to India, vowed to continue to press the government for answers and compensation.

'Why?' asked one irate commentator, 'are the British police being so tight-lipped? What do they have to hide? My suggestion is that malignant state actors played a part here!'

It was typical how much noise the press wallahs were making based on little corroborated information, Flush reflected. And it struck him as highly ironic that, so far at least, they had failed to pick up on one juicy element of the story hiding in plain sight: the presence at the temple of India's most celebrated private detective.

'You're right!' said Tubelight after Flush told him to watch Action News! and look for the shot of Puri emerging with Mummy-ji from the temple. 'But he's not wearing his usual cap.'

'What is that thing?'

'Must be part of a new disguise.'

'It's got ear flaps. Makes him look like the donkey in *Shrek*.'

Flush also reported that he had been joined outside Shweta Bhatt's residence by no less than eleven uplink trucks – and he counted at least twenty cameramen and still more photographers waiting for a shot of the bereaved widow, or better still a statement from her.

'When her sister arrived an hour ago, her car was mobbed,' said Flush. 'The ANI cameraman got up on the bonnet, trying to get a shot through the windscreen, and when she braked hard, he was thrown onto the road. I tell you these press wallahs are crazy.'

Flush asked him what he wanted him to do, now that their part in the case was surely over.

'You know Boss, he won't call it till he's one hundred per cent done with the case,' said Tubelight.

Flush put his feet up and reached for one of Chetan's *Iron Man* comics, which he'd left behind after the night shift. It was an old one that he had read numerous times before, and he flicked through it, thinking mostly of breakfast, before tossing it to one side, bored. For a while, he watched the press outside the gate – in-earnest, on-air reporters addressing their respective cameras; producers constantly on their phones; photographers standing around bantering amongst themselves and forever fiddling with the settings on their digital SLRs.

Into this scene appeared unexpectedly Savita, pulling her wheelie bag – and Flush sat up suddenly straight and alert, his heart pounding, his eyes fixed on the screen.

What was she doing back so soon? he wondered. To reach Shanti Niketan, she must have set off from her village before dawn. Had she been sent for by her mistress? If so, she had not forewarned Savita to expect the media circus infesting the usually quiet lane, not going by her expression, which was one of bewilderment. She had not been told, nor learned for herself, about what had occurred in London, either – this was evident from the manner in which she raised a hand to her mouth as if to stifle a scream after learning the news from the security guard.

Flush watched her pass through the gates – and immediately reviewed his recording of the street from the last couple of minutes, smiling, love-struck, as he slowed this latest footage of Savita in the street.

She looked as beautiful as ever, more so now that her hands and ankles were decorated in intricate mehndi designs from the wedding she'd attended, and her lush lips bore the trace of rouge lipstick. After the bus ride to the railway station, he had tried his best to put her out of his head. But it had been impossible, and he had made up his mind to follow his heart. As soon as the opportunity arose, he would ask her out on a date – and he spent the next hour or so practising what he was going to say to her when the time came.

He also called Tubelight. 'Listen, I've been thinking,' said

Flush, 'don't bother Boss on my account, there's no rush; I'm happy to stay for as long as I'm needed.'

'She's back, isn't she, that dilrubaa of yours?'

There seemed no point in pretending any more. 'An hour back,' he said.

'What is it about her?'

'She's like the moon, I can't stop staring.'

Tubelight broke into the song 'Chaudvin Ka Chand Ho'.

But Flush wasn't laughing. 'Don't tease, I've got high fever,' he said.

Puri was woken by the blackbird at five and, having retrieved his spare Sandown cap from his luggage, went down to the kitchen to find Joni getting ready to leave the house for work. The latter had made a big batch of strong, sweet chai. It was easily the best that Puri had drunk since arriving in London.

'I've a secret ingredient,' revealed Joni, and showed him his stash of milk powder, which he kept hidden in the cupboard in a tin marked 'screws'.

'That's not all I've got in there,' he whispered with smiling eyes. 'Next time Nina is out, we'll have a drink for old times' sake.'

'Splendid,' said Puri.

At seven, Bromley called and Puri took the call on the pavement.

'It's another positive for aconite,' he reported. 'And you and your mother were right about the application: it was introduced to his system via the skin. A few millilitres is all it took. Entered his bloodstream in seconds.'

'Where exactly it was applied on the body?' asked Puri.

'Just above the ankle, presumably while Bombay Duck was kneeling. A quick squirt from a pipette would have done the job. He must have felt it when it was applied. The pathologists found traces on his hands as well, meaning he reached back and wiped it off.'

Bromley sounded strung out; he could hardly have slept. 'What else?' he asked, rhetorically, with a heavy sigh as he could be heard flicking through the pages of the report. 'The poison caused his heart and lungs to fail inside of three minutes. It's a match with the aconite injected into the mango. Which means, as you pointed out yourself, Vish, the origin's India. I reckon we can rule out the Indian High Commission's driver.'

'Thus far we know nothing of this man, Inspector-sahib,' Puri felt compelled to point out. 'Could be he is a killer himself. Let us keep an open mind until we have gathered all the facts, no?'

'Listen, no one's ruling him out entirely,' said Bromley, impatiently, 'but CCTV has the professional hitman entering the temple not thirty seconds *after* Bombay Duck. Plus we've got two eyewitnesses who can place him standing within a few feet of Bombay Duck in the minutes before he died.'

Puri was almost afraid to ask about what he had learned about the driver's movements.

'Arrived about five minutes ahead of Bombay Duck,' said Bromley. 'Incidentally, we retrieved the white sports bag and lifted two sets of prints. Surprise surprise, the first set are a match for Bombay Duck. And we've drawn a blank on the second, but I'm betting they belong to our mystery man from the Savoy.'

'Very good, Inspector-sahib,' intoned Puri. 'Piece by piece we are making progress. Now what of Chhota Balu? You were able to trace him?'

'Cool as a cucumber, your hitman,' said Bromley. 'Strolled out of the temple along with everyone else. Goes out into the street and takes a wazz against the wall, never mind there are people walking past. Then mounts his bike – your mother was on the money with the model, FYI – and drives off. Ten minutes later, ANPR cameras have him heading north through Brent. After that, we've got nothing. My guess is he ditched the bike. Now your turn. Did you get the driver's name for me?'

'One Arjun Prakash,' said Puri. 'According to my contact in the Ministry of Foreign Affairs, he is listed as a "dependent household member of a diplomatic agent".'

'Christ alive,' breathed Bromley. 'Let's just pray he didn't do it. The last thing I need is another bleeding diplomatic incident.'

'Another one?'

'Don't ask. I'll put in a request for an interview with this Arj-oon Prak-ass. My superior's in direct contact with the Indian High Commissioner. He's piling on the pressure for us to ID the body. We keep reiterating that in the case of an autopsy, the coroner requires a family member to confirm the identity of the deceased. But is he listening?'

Bromley also shared the news that Shweta Bhatt would be arriving on a flight from Delhi in the evening – and the plan was for her to proceed directly to the morgue to identify her husband's body.

'I would not be at all surprised if I get stuck with chaperoning her as well,' he grumbled.

Rumpi's words over breakfast – 'I think we should leave Windsor Castle for today, Chubby, there's heavy rain forecast' – could not have been more welcome. 'Why don't you go and visit that nice hat shop you wanted to go to this morning,' she suggested. 'We can meet up again for lunch and go and see a couple of exhibitions. Nina was recommending the National Portrait Gallery and the Victoria and Albert Museum.'

Before anyone had a chance to change their minds, Puri ordered a cab.

He was in no doubt that Mummy had helped engineer his escape and that Jags was accompanying him again at her behest. Given all the whispers in the house last night and this morning, and sudden changes in the conversation whenever he came into a room, he suspected, too, that the women were cooking up something together. It might be a surprise, he thought, to celebrate his award.

Still, in the car en route to central London, Jags swore he knew nothing about any secret plans. And he denied being coerced into spending the day with him.

'You're making out Mummy-ji to be, like, this devious auntie who's out to take over the world or something,' he said.

'I would not put it past her, actually,' said Puri. 'She can be the most manipulating person, believe me.'

'All I see is her like trying to help you out, innit,' said Jags. 'Seriously, Uncle-gee, you've got like these latent childhood mother control issues. I'm here 'cause I've chosen to be here, yeah. We're like hot on the trail of a murderer. Right now, you couldn't drag me away.'

Puri looked pleased. 'Finally you've been bitten by the bug, we can say.'

'Last night, I got to ride in a squad car, racing through north

London doing like ninety, chasing after a murder suspect. And that was down to me slipping the AirTag into Bhatt's bag.' Jags was grinning now. 'So, yeah, I don't mind admitting, I'm feeling pretty good about myself just now.' He paused for a beat. 'Seriously, Uncle-gee, hanging out with you is not at all what I expected.'

'How so?'

'To be honest, I sort of always got the impression that some of your stories – don't take this the wrong way, yeah – they just sounded like . . . well, you know, a bit exaggerated sort of fing.'

Puri showed surprise. 'Exaggerated in which way?' he asked.

'Like the time you said you stopped a plot to assassinate the Dalai Lama – and you said you was disguised as Richard Gere's bodyguard?'

'That is not totally accurate, actually.'

'Yeah, somehow I didn't think so.'

'In fact I was acting as Mr Gere's interpreter.'

'Straight up?'

Puri said in an avuncular tone, 'Beta, I don't deal in fictions. My life is like this, only.'

'Bit of a non-stop roller-coaster ride, innit?' said Jags. 'Don't you get tired of it all sometimes?'

'I cannot argue with my dharma, and, what is more, only a foolish man does not accept his fate,' said Puri. 'I came to London to collect an award but somehow this case also came to me. Why, I cannot tell you. All I know is I must find the truth, that is my duty. And to do so, no stone can go unturned, so to speak. Today come hell or the high water we must track down the security guard, Rakesh Sharma, from the Regent's Park address.'

'You can't go all the time, though, like full throttle, not at your age. You've gotta learn to put your feet up now and again; enjoy life, look after yourself, Uncle-gee,' said Jags.

'Rest can come once work is done,' said Puri, mechanically.

'Mum said you've got high blood pressure,' said Jags. 'Seriously, you wanna look after yourself. Your health's gotta come first, innit. Keep off the butter chicken, yeah.'

But to this Puri said nothing.

*   *   *

Nina's lawyer friend, Isha, had the bearing of someone who had
seen and heard it all, and could handle any situation while main-
taining the most impeccable fingernails painted in high-gloss red.
Empathy was not on offer, but no-nonsense practical solutions
were. She looked over Pooja's employment contracts, confirmed
that she had a strong case against the Dhillons, and offered to
represent her on a pro bono basis.

'Before you start thanking me, you need to understand what
you're getting yourself into,' she warned.

Unless Pooja had friends or family in London, she would likely
have to stay in a shelter while her case was heard. It would be
lonely and the Dhillons would probably throw all kinds of accusations her way. She might also come under pressure from family
back home to drop the case. There could be threats, too.

'I've known families blame their own for not putting up and
shutting up, even when they've suffered physical abuse, and not
risk losing the income,' she said.

Was Pooja strong enough to cope with the challenge?

The question was put to her in Isha's cramped, cluttered Fiat
with Nina also present.

Rumpi and Mummy were on dog duty. Through the car's
steamed-up windows, they were blurred smudges a little way off.

'I suggest you think it over and give me your answer in forty-
eight hours,' said Isha after she'd answered Pooja's questions
concerning how long the case would take, what she could expect
in terms of compensation, and what would happen to her afterwards.

Pooja didn't need any more time to consider Isha's proposal,
however. She was ready to file a complaint with the police and
a civil suit against the Dhillons. It was also agreed there and then
that she would escape from the house the next morning. Nina
would pick her up from the same spot. From there they would
go directly to the police station.

'I'm going to hang on to the employment contracts for safe
keeping and I'll see you tomorrow,' said Isha.

Nina and Pooja decamped from her Fiat and waved her off,
and then gathered with Rumpi and Nina. They went over the
arrangements for the following day and reassured Pooja that she
was making the right decision. Then they spoke about Sanjiv
Dhillon's engagement again.

Had she been able to find out anything more about his new fiancé's family? Mummy asked.

'I learned they're from Delhi and their last name is Kitchloo,' said Pooja. 'Also, I found this.' She handed Mummy a hotel room key card, saying, 'It was between the cushions in the living room, I think one of them must have left it behind.'

Mummy turned over the key and read the name on the back: 'Royal Lancaster, Hyde Park.'

'That must be where the Kitchloos are staying,' said Nina, stating the obvious. 'Very fancy.'

NINETEEN

Puri sat in an insipid office in the bowels of Scotland Yard, a plastic cup of vending-machine tea untouched on the desk before him. A junior detective was helping him view the CCTV footage from Neasden Temple. This came from three cameras – the first at the security check at the main entrance; the second trained on the court and garden; and a third at the top of the steps going up to the mandir.

The Indian High Commission driver, Arjun Prakash, standing a good head above the other worshippers, and smartly dressed in jacket and tie, arrived first. Six minutes later, Dr Bhatt made his way through security in baseball cap and fake moustache, carrying his white sports bag, blending in seamlessly amongst his fellow Indians. Finally came Chhota Balu, who had not made the slightest attempt to alter his appearance, and wore a garish, Hawaiian shirt open at the neck. On his belt, Puri noted, was a large silver buckle fashioned into a cobra head.

The junior detective forwarded to the time code that corresponded with Arjun Prakash exiting from the mandir with the bag (and wearing gloves as Mummy had spotted) and hurrying towards the exit. Chhota Balu left the building without the slightest indication of urgency on his part. Additional video from the street showed him unzipping his fly and urinating on the temple wall in plain sight of several passers-by.

Puri insisted on watching all the footage for a second time, now concentrating his attention on everyone else coming and going from the mandir. Of the hundred or so worshippers and visitors, he picked out three as being people of interest. The first was a young man who had loitered on the steps for a good ten minutes before entering the temple after Dr Bhatt; the second a large, middle-aged man who hurried from the complex around the time Dr Bhatt had been poisoned. And the third, a woman, traditionally dressed in a simple blue kurta pyjama and chunni, making her way slowly across the inner courtyard to the temple.

'That lad's a known pickpocket; has a record as long as my arm,' said Bromley when he joined Puri. 'The other bloke, lives very close to the temple and remembered he'd left something on the stove. As for the woman, I don't get what you think's so remarkable about her.'

'She arrived ahead of Dr Bhatt and departed moments after he was poisoned,' explained Puri. 'Throughout the footage, she can be seen with her head bowed down. Not once is her face visible.'

'She's elderly, got a bad back,' said Bromley, dismissively.

'She does not move like an elderly person,' Puri insisted.

'Look, Vish, I appreciate your help, but we're wasting our time here,' he said. 'Chhota Balu's our man. He had motive; we can place him there at the time of the murder – what more do you need?'

'Inspector-sahib, over my long and illustrious career, during which I have dealt with every type of crime under the sun, I have learned one thing above all else: never accept the obvious at face value,' said Puri. 'Face value is generally worthless.'

Bromley's hand shot up. 'Spare me the pet homilies, will you? I'm not one to go jumping to half-baked conclusions, either. And we'll need more than some CCTV footage to convict this bastard. But some cases are just *that* clear-cut.'

'Agreed, some cases, but most definitely not this one, Inspector-sahib,' protested Puri. 'A prior attempt was made on Dr Bhatt's life with the very same supply of poison, and definitely, Chhota Balu was *not* the responsible person.'

'You don't know that for sure, Vish,' said Bromley. 'He might have been in London at the time. His record came in from Delhi overnight and he's known to have travelled internationally under several aliases. I'm checking all of them to see if he came through London earlier in the year.'

Puri said with patience: 'I'm telling you, Inspector-sahib, you are barking up a wrong tree. Poison is not this goonda's MO.'

'He's not just a shooter either,' Bromley insisted. 'According to Delhi, he's connected with thirty-seven murders. He's suspected of strangling one victim with barbed wire. Another, a groom who he claimed insulted him at a wedding, he took to a zoo and dropped in the tiger enclosure.'

'He's a blunt tool, Inspector-sahib, that is my point,' said Puri. 'Meantime, so many unanswered questions are there. Who all did Dr Bhatt meet with at the Savoy? What was Arjun Prakash's motive for going to the Neasden Temple? What all was in the sports bag he made off with? Not forgetting: who all was responsible for poisoning that mango?'

Bromley was fast losing patience. 'You don't think I know all this?' he asked, his voice raised. 'For now, my top priority's locating Chow-ta Bal-oo before he skips the country. Now, we're done here. I've got a meeting with the chief in ten minutes. You said you wanted to look round the Abbey Road house. I can have a car take you over there. And if you do come across anything of interest, I want to know about it. Quid pro quo, Vish. Don't go AWOL on me again.'

Bromley accompanied him to the lobby to sign him out. Jags, who had been to Charing Cross police station to retrieve his phone, was waiting in the seating area.

'By the way, the ownership details on the Abbey Road house just came in,' said the inspector. 'You'll never guess who owns it?'

'Gladstone Global Holdings Incorporated by chance?' asked Puri.

'Right. Looks increasingly like whoever owns this shell company was acting as Bombay Duck's guardian angel here in London. The sooner we get a name, the better. Any luck from Mauritius on that score?'

'Luck is not a factor, Inspector-sahib, the work will get done, no tension,' said Puri.

'Sure, no tension, that's a good one,' murmured Bromley – and for once Puri was in no doubt that the Englishman was employing sarcasm.

Puri stood in Dr Bhatt's bedroom in the Abbey Road house, reading the list he'd received from Bromley of the items removed by the police as evidence during their early morning search of the property. It included a password-protected laptop; a file containing confidential legal advice, courtesy of a top British firm that specialized in extradition law; and from inside a large safe – forced open by the police with an arc grinder – Dr Bhatt's Indian passport and $75,000 cash.

In amongst some papers on a desk where Dr Bhatt had evidently been working, Bromley's men had also discovered a printout for a booking for a certain 'Sandip Patel' on a Virgin Atlantic flight to Grand Cayman from Heathrow the following day.

'That is the very same flight Shweta Bhatt got herself booked on,' Puri told Jags. 'So now there can be no doubt: definitely the two intended to reunite here in London before departing together to paradise for happily ever after.'

'Hang about, Uncle-gee, who's this Sandip Patel?' he asked.

'I believe Dr Bhatt intended to travel under that name, only.'

'You're saying he got 'imself a fake passport? Then where is it?'

'Two possibilities are there,' said Puri. 'Number one, Shweta Bhatt was to bring a new passport from Delhi having procured it in the black market. Second, Dr Bhatt found ways and means to procure a passport here in London in the name of Sandip Patel. Either from a broker. Or—'

'—from the driver, Prakash!' Jags suddenly blurted out. 'Uncle-gee, that's it, innit! He went to the temple to rendezvous with Bhatt and hand over a fake passport! Bhatt paid him with cash. That's what waz in the bag!'

'It is certainly an interesting theory,' said Puri. 'However I should point out—'

'—There was no passport found on Bhatt. Yeah, I get that,' said Jags, the enthusiasm draining out of him like air escaping a balloon.

But a moment later his face lit up again: 'Hang about, Uncle-gee,' he said. 'Maybe Prakash didn't bring the passport. He couldn't deliver it . . . didn't wanna risk it . . . Instead, he kills Bhatt and grabs the cash.

'*Or*,' Jags went on before Puri could respond, 'someone nicked the passport! Bhatt's down there on the ground of the mandir, like writhing around dying sort of fing, and someone pulls it.'

'As it happens, beta, Brom-ley confirmed there was indeed a certain young pickpocket present inside the temple at the time of the murder,' said Puri.

'That's gotta be it, Uncle-gee.'

Puri smiled with slow deliberation, touched by Jags's new-found enthusiasm. 'We'll make a detective of you yet,' he said. 'Most certainly it is worth speaking with the pickpocket. I'll gladly advise Bromley as much.'

They ventured next into the kitchen where every surface bore traces of powder used by crime-scene investigators in their search for telltale prints.

In the recycling bin, Puri found a couple of dozen discarded vegetarian ready-meal containers. He then went through the cupboards.

'Chilli flakes, salt and pepper – no other spices are there,' he observed. 'That in itself is highly suggestive, no?'

'Of what?'

'The Regent's Park kitchen was stocked with every Indian spice – black cardamon, hing, freshly ground garam masala, atta also – indicating someone was cooking proper, Indian khana. There, also, we found so many of microwave meal containers which, must be, Dr Bhatt purchased during his last week of residence in the apartment.'

Jags looked lost. 'Meaning Bhatt did some cooking at the other place, but didn't bother once he moved over 'ere?' he ventured.

'No, I believe Bhatt did *no* cooking whatsoever. Not here, not there.'

'You're saying someone else was doing the cooking at Regent's Park?'

'For some time, at least, but not during the last week or so before he fled the place.'

Jags reminded him that only fingerprints belonging to Dr Bhatt and the cleaning lady had been found by the police.

'Meaning all trace of the cook's prints were wiped away in the week before Scotland Yard came knocking,' said Puri.

'OK, I can buy that, but from what I remember, yeah, the security guards on the building never told your mate Bromley about any cook.'

'Could be he or she entered through the backside, coming up the elevator from the subterranean parking area and all.'

'I guess if the cook was like an illegal alien with no paperwork, maybe that might be a reason.'

'That is one possibility certainly,' said Puri.

After Shweta Bhatt departed for Delhi Airport with the Indian press pack in hot pursuit, Tubelight called an end to the stakeout and accompanied Flush in his tempo to the easternmost edge of Gurugram.

Their new target was a small, one-storey structure, crowned ignominiously by a black plastic Sintex water tank. It sat, isolated, next to the entrance to a vast construction site with the superstructures of three vast apartment blocks rising phantom-like in the smog. A sign on the outside of the building read, 'BLOSSOMING REALTORS CO'.

It was owned by one Veer Sindhu, aka Chaddi, a broker of both property and contract killings.

'My source says Chaddi handles big contracts, nothing less than twenty lakh a hit, and Chhota Balu's in his stable,' said Tubelight as they pulled up near the site. 'Boss wants us to find out who hired him to take out Dr Bhatt.'

They had not been there long before an Audi pulled up outside the building, and a man in his mid-forties emerged. He was stocky with a beach-ball stomach. A great mop of black hair came down over his forehead, almost connecting with a pair of questioning, thickset eyebrows.

'That's our guy,' said Tubelight as they watched him on the monitor. 'By all accounts, he's a real charmer.'

By now, Flush had a laser microphone trained on the window of the building and, as Chaadi entered, his voice came through loud and clear.

'Oi, *kuttiya!*' he bellowed. 'Get your filthy monkey backside off my chair! What am I paying you for? Go bring me a tambaku paan with extra mulethi!'

Chaddi's peon hurried outside – he was just a kid – and mounted a scooter, heading off down the dusty road, past empty plots marked by rows of lonely streetlights.

A couple of minutes passed before Chaddi made a phone call to a 'Mrs Bakshi'. His tone was ingratiating to the point of grovelling, the lady evidently a prospective buyer of a penthouse apartment in one of the new blocks 'coming up'.

'Madam-ji, kindly adjust, I'm prepared to come some way to accommodate, but my family must eat,' he said, before ending the call with the words, 'Very good madam, I'll revert, no issues my side.'

The next call was to his partner, and to this man he cursed

Mrs Bakshi as everything from a 'cheap whore' to a 'ball-crusher'.

'That one is eating my brain,' Chaddi complained. 'I can't wait to screw her over.'

So it went for the next couple of hours, call after call, providing constant corroboration that Chaddi was a bent property broker, a serial philanderer, an abusive employer and an 'all-round scumbag,' as Flush put it.

None of the conversations the duo overheard related to any contract killings, however.

'You're sure he's the guy?' asked Flush at long last.

'He'll be cautious about communicating with clients,' said Tubelight. 'I'll go over his call history, you hack his computer.'

Flush got on with the work, but just hoped he could have his day off tomorrow. After a good wash, he planned to return to the Bhatt house and wait for Savita when she went to fetch something from the market. Tubelight would surely not object, though he was not about to ask him for permission.

Puri was hungry. There was nothing new in that. But in the absence of a proper hearty meal (for breakfast he made do with a croissant on the go), he felt that his ability to focus, to make connections and see the whole picture, was becoming increasingly challenging. He was reminded of one of his favourite short stories from Mrs Pathak's high school English class, *A Piece of Steak*,[8] in which an ageing boxer, in the absence of a good solid meal, lacks the energy to win his last, big fight. What he needed was a big, juicy mutton kathi roll dripping in fiery green chutney.

There was no time to stop, let alone find an Indian restaurant or kebabery, however. He had just one hour left before he was due to meet Rumpi in Knightsbridge – and with the award ceremony tomorrow, this might well prove his last opportunity to find Rakesh Sharma, the security guard, and remedy his stubborn brain itch once and for all.

'You're all moan, moan, moan, innit, Uncle-gee,' said Jags when he presented him with something called a 'meal deal' purchased at a mini market.

---

[8] Jack London

By now, they were travelling in a black cab to the address in Shepherd's Bush where Jags had been told Sharma now worked.

'This is neither a meal nor a deal,' complained Puri, holding up the packaged sandwich as he might have done a soiled diaper. 'Tell me at least you purchased some hot sauce?'

'Chill, Uncle-gee, I got you some Tabasco, innit,' said Jags, handing him a small bottle.

Puri was not impressed. 'On a mirchi scale of one to ten, Tabasco ranks down at the bottom along with jalapeños.'

'Best I could do at short notice. Like it or lump it,' said Jags.

Puri had no choice but to lump it and spent the journey dowsing the so-called 'Chicken tikka' sandwich in half the contents of the bottle.

He had started to drip the rest on individual crisps when the taxi reached their destination.

'Here you are, gents.'

Puri and Jags stepped out of the cab and found themselves presented with their own reflections in the blue reflective glass of an ultra-modern office block.

At their approach, automatic doors swished open, and they were delivered into a huge space-age atrium with a long, sleek reception desk. Up on the wall was emblazoned, 'CENTURION LABS (INDIA) Ltd.'

Puri stopped suddenly in his tracks and murmured, 'By God', before leading Jags over to a waiting area furnished with black leather couches and a giant bronze sculpture of a naked man and woman entwined around one another.

'This cannot be a coincidence,' he said.

'So this is an Indian company, big deal,' said Jags with a shrug.

'Not *any* Indian company, beta. Nowadays, Centurion is the largest producer of pharmaceuticals in the country. A world-beater, in fact. Only Dr Bhatt's Bio Solutions was larger.'

Puri picked up a copy of the company's prospectus that was lying on the designer coffee table to one side of the couch. Page One featured a message from the company's new CEO, Nikesh Narayan, the eldest son of the founder, along with a portrait.

Narayan was in his late forties and as bald as a billiard ball – and Puri recognized him immediately as the mystery man from the Savoy who had met with Dr Bhatt.

'I knew he was familiar somehow,' said Puri. 'He has become a high-flyer, often appears on TV doing interviews and all.'

'That's, like, a massive development, innit,' said Jags.

'Just how massive I cannot yet tell,' said Puri. 'For now, let us keep to the plan. We must find Rakesh Sharma. See the security guard standing over there close to the reception? Could be that is him. I want you to go and get a look at his name tag.'

Jags did as instructed, and returned a couple of minutes later.

'Yeah, you're right, that's him, that's Sharma. Let's go talk to him, yeah?'

'In this instance, the direct approach could backfire; that is if he was not entirely honest with the police when he claimed he had not recognized Dr Bhatt,' said Puri. 'We should consider also that he could have been remunerated for keeping quiet about others coming and going from the apartment. Perhaps Nikesh Narayan himself.'

Jags could see where this was going. 'What is it you want me to do, Uncle-gee?' he asked.

'Stay here and find a way to make friendship with Sharma, get him talking somehow. It is more likely he will share with you than some old Indian uncle nosing around,' said Puri in a rare moment of self-deprecation. 'You can call Deliveroo, tell them you've other commitments is it?'

'I've got it handled, Uncle-gee,' said Jags. 'Don't sweat it, I'm vibin, yeah. You go have a good time with Auntie.'

TWENTY

Rumpi could always tell when Puri was working on a big case, never more so than when he had a brain itch. He did not possess, as she put it, 'a poker face'. So as they toured the Victoria and Albert Museum, he had to muster every last ounce of mental resolve to prevent himself from churning over the details in his mind, and pay keen attention to the exhibits.

Somehow – and this he would have found challenging at the best of times – he even managed to feign interest when his wife spent thirty whole minutes in the V&A gift shop perusing tea towels and dainty china mugs, and deliberating over which William Morris coasters to buy for her mother and sisters.

Not once did he dare to so much as reach for his phone – this despite feeling frequent vibrations against his thigh inside his pocket.

When Rumpi, having finally solved her coaster conundrum and paid for her gifts, suggested they go to Harrods, he managed to answer genially with a big smile, 'Splendid, my dear, why not?'

En route, Puri braced himself for an experience that would, he was sure, prove to be the very opposite of shopping therapy. But to his surprise he found himself quite taken by the store, especially the Food Halls, where there were free samples of excellent fudge on offer in the chocolate department, and slices of spicy Italian salami to try at the charcuterie counter.

In the perfume department, he had the good sense to purchase Rumpi a bottle of Shalimar after she had tried a few testers and hinted that she would be extremely happy to take home a bottle. And after travelling in the store's old period lifts – 'wonderful, old-world charm' – Puri was only too pleased to receive a counter-gift from Rumpi in the form of a polka-dot silk cravat to add to his collection.

By the time they called it a day and started towards the nearest Underground station, the two were holding hands; and Puri felt himself starting to relax, the case and all its nagging, unanswered questions proving less obtrusive in his mind. It occurred to him then that perhaps he should have allowed for spending more quality time in London with Rumpi. The demands of the past few days had not allowed him to even visit Bates or the Inns of Court, where Gandhi had been a starving student – and it occurred to him that he might delay their return.

Puri's reprieve from all the stresses of the case were short-lived, however, with Dr Bhatt popping up at every turn during the return journey to East Ham. His image was there on the newsstands; on video screens playing on the walls of the down escalator for the Piccadilly Line; on the front pages of the evening London newspapers being read by any number of fellow passengers in the trains.

In East Ham, too, up on the wall inside a pub frequented by Sardaar-jis drinking pints of Guinness, a huge screen displayed video of Shweta Bhatt in Jackie Onassis sunglasses surrounded by microphone-wielding press wallahs as she departed from Delhi. 'LATEST: BHATT'S WIDOW TO BRING BODY FROM LONDON'.

All of this seemed to pass Rumpi by, and gave no indication whatsoever that she knew anything about what had happened. She spoke instead about what they had seen in London so far, and discussed with him plans to go to the theatre the night following the awards dinner. It was only when they were approaching Nina's house that she said, suddenly, out of the blue, 'Terrible the news about Dr Harilal Bhatt's murder; what a sorry story the whole thing is.'

'Oh, yes, terrible indeed,' said Puri, feeling as if he might just have a heart attack.

'I don't suppose they know who did it yet.'

'Last I heard they didn't have a clue,' said Puri as they reached the front door.

'I hope they find whoever it was. Even Dr Bhatt didn't deserve an ending like that.'

'No, my dear,' he said – and just for a moment Puri considered coming clean and telling her about his involvement in the case. But it had been a perfect afternoon and she seemed so happy, and he knew she would not forgive him. Not while they were still in London. If she found out later, once they were home, then it would not matter to her quite so much, especially if he extended their stay.

Mummy was out (apparently she had gone to visit some distant relative and was due back soon), which saved Puri the trouble of having to answer questions from her about how the case was progressing.

Complaining of his 'paining' knees after all the walking they had done in the afternoon, he went upstairs to 'take rest', while Rumpi gave Nina a hand in the kitchen.

Puri was about to catch up with his messages when there came a timid knock on the door.

It was Joni who had brought with him a bottle of Johnnie Walker Red and a couple of glasses.

'Just one peg, for old times' sake,' he said with a twinkle in his eye.

Puri could hardly refuse and sat on the end of his bed while Joni pulled up a chair, poured them both a double peg each, and began to reminisce about his childhood in Delhi and some old mango tree he used to climb. Soon, he was telling the well-worn story of how he'd arrived in London with just fifty pounds in his pocket and worked as a bus driver. This led to another lament about Jags's lack of direction in life.

'He doesn't appreciate the advantages we've given him,' said Joni. 'I'm just a shopkeeper, but you, he respects, I can see that. Make him understand.' He picked up the bottle and held it out for his guest. 'Come. One more peg.'

'Joni, listen, I—' was as much of a protest as Puri could muster before his glass was filled again and Joni started on a whisky-induced lament about Nina's vegan cooking and how, though healthy, it was 'depressing as hell'.

'It has been six months, and now I can't perform. You know, down there,' said Joni.

Puri stared into his glass, pretending he hadn't understood what he was talking about.

'I agree vegan does not offer enough variety in cooking,' was all he could think to say.

'I ask you what is wrong with drinking milk? It is just milk. Or honey? There is no harm in it. Last I checked we were Punjabi, not Jain. Speak to her, Chubby. She respects you, I can see that. Make her see some sense. For old times' sake.'

A shout up the stairs from Nina for help in the kitchen brought the drinking session to a premature – but from Puri's perspective welcome – end, with both men draining their glasses hurriedly.

Joni then headed into the bathroom to gargle with mouthwash, leaving Puri to catch up with his messages.

An SMS from Jags sent an hour earlier informed him (in barely fathomable text slang) that he was still hanging around in the McDonald's across from the Centurion Pharma building in Shepherd's Bush, waiting for security guard Rakesh Sharma to finish his shift.

Tubelight and Flush had followed Chaddi, the property broker, to Faridabad where he lived with his wife and four children. The team were keeping across his calls and analysing his call record. Most promising of all, they were also searching his dark web browsing history.

Bromley had also left two voice messages. The first was a thankful acknowledgement of Puri's tipoff regarding Nikesh Narayan, the CEO of Centurion Labs, having been the one who met Dr Bhatt in the suite in the Savoy. And in a second message, left just an hour before, Bromley explained that the Indian High Commission, having received the Yard's request for an interview with the driver, Arjun Prakash, had responded with a request for assistance in locating the individual concerned who had not reported for work and was uncontactable.

There was no further trace of Chhota Balu, meantime.

'Call me when you get this, Vish. I'll be working late. Dr Bhatt's widow lands at Heathrow at nine.'

Puri turned off his phone and closed his eyes, intending to take ten minutes before heading downstairs to endure more vegan gruesomeness.

The Johnnie Walker had hit him hard, however, and before he knew it he had drifted off to sleep.

Puri was woken unceremoniously just before midnight by some-one poking him repeatedly in the arm.

'Chubby, wake up, na!' a voice hissed in his ear. 'This is no time to be doing sleeping.'

'Mummy-ji?' he asked, groggy.

'Shhhh! You wish to wake everyone?'

He took a moment to gather his thoughts. 'What time is it? What do you want?'

'Your presence is required downstairs, no delay,' she said and left the room.

Puri considered ignoring her, but knew it was a lost cause: his mother would be back for sure.

He heaved his heavy, reluctant body off the bed and checked that Rumpi was still asleep before braving the infuriatingly creaky stairs.

His mother scowled at him as he entered the kitchen. 'You failed to bring your night suit, Chubby?'

'It was not my intention to fall asleep in my clothes,' Puri heard himself explain before it occurred to him that he was a grown man and was not obliged to account for his attire to his mother.

'Also, your portable is in off mode. How anyone can reach you?'

'Mummy-ji, please, it's the middle of the night, what is so pressing?'

'An emergency-type situation concerning Rinku.'

'He's in trouble again, is it?' Puri could not have showed less surprise. 'How many times I'm expected to bail him out. He's on his own this time'

Mummy interrupted with a sharp tut. 'Listen, Chubby, na. He's present at a private club in the Mayfair and says Chhota Balu is very much there with him in attendance.'

Suddenly she had Puri's attention.

'By God, why you didn't tell me, Mummy-ji?'

'Rinku made me promise you would arrange immunity on his part. The club is an illegal-type place.'

A gambling joint or brothel, or probably both, in other words.

'Understood, Mummy-ji, no issues, leave it with me, I'll do the needful,' said Puri.

He called a sleeping Bromley, informed him of the situation and provided the club's address. He then tried Rinku's mobile to warn him that the police were on their way. But it went to voicemail and Puri realized he would have to race to the scene himself if he was going to ensure Rinku did not end up in a cell for the night.

A minicab took a few minutes to reach the house, by which time Mummy had packed him some of Nina's leftover pakoras and chutney in a Tupperware container.

She stood by the door to see him off, just as she had done when he had left for school as a boy.

Puri gave her a perfunctory, side-on hug before hurrying out into the street.

'Chubby, your shoelace requires tying, na,' she called after him, but he waited to take care of it until after the car had pulled away.

Puri was a strong advocate for observing the rules of the road – as his many letters to the honourable editor of the *Times of India* on the subject attested. But along with 1.4 billion of his fellow Indians, he saw no earthly reason why anyone should ever have to stop at a red light in the middle of the night.

There was, apparently, no such understanding amongst Britishers, however. And on the way to Queensway, Puri found himself sitting at four red lights on all-but deserted streets, while his appeals to the driver to see sense went unheeded.

Had the journey taken even another minute, he would have missed seeing Chhota Balu being dragged, bloody-faced, from the smart Regency townhouse that housed the private, members-only club.

Two burly officers held the hairy, diminutive hitman by both arms as they led him, kicking and spitting Bhojpuri obscenities, to a waiting van.

'Tough little bugger,' were Bromley's first words as Puri joined him inside the police cordon. 'Pulled a knife on one of my men; lucky he was wearing a stab vest.'

Chhota Balu's insults continued inside the van as it rocked from side to side.

'You wouldn't care to translate, would you Vish?'

'I would prefer not to, actually, Inspector-sahib,' said Puri, who was close to blushing.

'About your mate, they're bringing him out shortly. Get him out of here sharpish, will you? And tell him to stick to regular bars and pubs next time.'

Rinku emerged from the building ahead of a dozen long-legged young women, ungainly in high heels, like new-born giraffes learning to walk. Half a dozen men followed behind, all in black leather jackets and sporting similar buzz cuts.

'Chubby, where were you? You missed all the action, yaar,' said Rinku, exhilarated. He sparked up a cigarette as Puri led him from the scene. 'You should have seen the cops come busting in. They were hard asses, man! Like commando-types armed to the teeth. "Get down on the floor! Nobody move!" I swear the guy on the couch next to me getting a lap dance crapped himself.'

They turned a corner and found themselves on a quiet, cobbled mews.

'So where you taking me, you bugger?' asked Rinku. 'I could murder a burger.'

By now it was past one. Puri was desperate to get some sleep ahead of tomorrow. And he didn't want any part of Rinku's sleazy existence. The sight of the young prostitutes exiting the club had turned his stomach and dampened his spirits.

'It is late, no, everything is closed,' he said, but he was forgetting with whom he was dealing.

'Bullshit, yaar, I know a place – chalo.'

Soon, they were seated in a five-star hotel lounge nursing tumblers of fifteen-year-old Dalmore Old Highland single malt.

Puri had produced Mummy's pakoras and Rinku was devouring them ahead of his burger.

'I tell you Chubby, when that bloody saala kutta appeared, I couldn't believe my eyes,' said Rinku. 'Of all the joints, he walks straight into that place. What are the chances?'

'You interacted with him at all, is it?' asked Puri.

'I had my own party going on.'

'He came with someone or other, by chance?'

Rinku shrugged. 'Not that I noticed, but another member must have signed him in. God knows why. That guy's got no manners.'

'Manners are required in such an establishment?' Puri could not help but ask, doubtingly.

'So it's not your bloody Gymkhana with your bridge and cucumber sandwich, OK,' snarled Rinku. 'Same old Chubby, always playing judge and jury.'

'By chance Nikesh Narayan, the young Centurion Labs CEO, frequents the place?'

'Not that I know if. Why, Chubby? He's been a bad boy?'

'I believe so.'

'Corporate types, yaar, I tell you they're the worst. If I hear anything about him, I'll let you know.'

Puri lifted his glass. 'Cheers Mr Big Ears, I owe you one,' he said.

'No no, you owe me three, you bugger!'

'Two, I took care of you in Goa that time, remember?'

Rinku's lips buckled into an ugly grin. 'That was a wild weekend, yaar,' he said. 'I tell you that Uzbek exotic dancer could—'

'You've the proper attire for the gala dinner tomorrow night?' asked Puri, changing the subject.

'So now I've been a good boy, I get an invitation, is it?'

'I've one ticket, only. No girlfriends or escorts – or Uzbeks. You can act as Mummy-ji's chaperone. I want one hundred per cent best behaviour.'

Rinku sank back into his chair with a second drink: 'Sure, Chubby. I'll be sure to fish out my halo,' he said.

TWENTY-ONE

With the award ceremony slated to begin at eight o'clock, Puri didn't have to conjure an excuse to get out of the day's sightseeing agenda. Rumpi, who planned to visit Kew Gardens with Nina and Mummy, was sympathetic to his need to practise his acceptance speech, which was still in draft form. He also had to collect his dinner suit, he reminded her – though he neglected to mention that he was yet to even find one.

He did not anticipate dedicating much time to the case himself, either. Jags had ridden with the security guard, Rakesh Sharma, on his way home last night, and managed to strike up a conversation, but had nothing useful to report so far. Similarly, Tubelight and Flush were working on who had hired Chhota Balu but had yet to identify the guilty party.

There was just one matter he wanted to follow up on himself, and Puri fancied he had enough time to do so before finding a tailor.

At ten, he took a cab back into central London and had himself dropped again on The Strand.

At around the same time, Isha, the immigration lawyer, called Nina with bad news: Pooja had been arrested.

'I was waiting for her on Wanstead Flats,' she explained. 'But as she crossed the road, a police car raced up and a couple of officers detained her and searched her suitcase. They found some jewellery inside that was reported stolen by her employer. Pooja swore she hadn't taken it, but the police say charges are being brought against her.'

'I can't believe Pooja would steal anything; she seems perfectly honest to me,' said Rumpi as she, Mummy and Nina crowded around the speakerphone in the kitchen.

'It is a set-up – whole thing has been arranged, na,' said Mummy.

'You're saying Mrs Dhillon planted the jewellery in her bag?' asked Nina.

'No question,' said Mummy. 'She came to know Pooja planned to alight. Could be she spotted us all speaking yesterday.'

Nina asked Asha where Pooja had been taken. The answer was Waltham Forest Police Station – it was from there that she was calling.

'I've applied for bail, but it'll take a few hours until she's released,' she explained.

'Poor girl, she must be so frightened,' said Rumpi. 'What can we do?'

It was agreed that Nina would go to the station, while the others tried to speak with Mrs Dhillon and get her to drop the case.

'Just I've one card to play,' said Mummy.

After working all night with Tubelight to identify the individual who hired Chhota Balu, Flush went home and caught up on some sleep. He awoke at lunchtime, took a bucket shower, and then went for a trim and a shave at the barber wallah's down in the street.

By the time he had donned a pressed cotton shirt and new trousers and swapped his usual dirty sneakers for a pair of brown dress shoes, his mother barely recognized him.

'You're taking Savita on a date?' she asked, all anticipation. 'Are you going to propose? Should I tell Simi you're definitely not available?'

'Who?'

'The Rajput, slim, gori one.'

'I told you already, Ma, take down that Tinder account!'

'I will after the engagement is confirmed. At my age, I have to keep my options open.'

On the Metro, Flush debated whether to approach Savita and tell her straight out that she was the most beautiful girl in the world. Or whether it might not be better to wait for her in the market and, rather than laying some line on her (he was bound to get all tongue-tied and mumble), strike up a conversation over something incidental. If, say, she was walking the dog, he could profess some interest in canines in general. Then he might offer to help her carry home the groceries from the market, and summon up the courage to ask her out on a date.

As the train raced through the tunnel towards Sir M.

Vishweshwaraiah Moti Bagh station, he imagined her saying yes and the two of them strolling around India Gate on a cool summer evening amongst the other courting couples. After buying her a balloon and treating her to golgappa at one of the stands, he would take her to a ride on the paddle boats on the reflecting ponds along Rajpath. She would smile at him and he would reach out for her hand . . .

. . . and they would run into one another's arms across a meadow of wild flowers; she in a tight sari blouse, he in a muscle shirt. They would embrace and press their cheeks together. A herd of cute goats would appear and she would pet one of them and giggle sweetly at its silly antics . . .

The waiters in India Club were gathered around the TV behind the bar glued to Action News! Puri paused to watch the video of Shweta Bhatt arriving at Heathrow the night before, looking sombre yet chic in her designer sunglasses. Mobbed by the press pack and assaulted by rapid-fire camera flashes and invasive questions, she was escorted by the police to a waiting vehicle outside the terminal.

From there she had been taken, the anchor announced, to Northwick Park mortuary in the London area of Harrow, as if that was detail that meant anything to an Indian audience.

'London's Metropolitan Police have confirmed that she positively identified the body of her late husband. A post-mortem has already been carried out, with sources telling us they believe Dr Harilal Bhatt succumbed to a toxin introduced to his skin.'

Puri continued into the dining room, where he found Amul Joshi, the representative, seated in his usual spot next to the bay window with his three mobile phones arranged in a row on the table in front of him.

He watched the detective's approach with an expression that suggested wry interest. 'Mr Puri, I hadn't been expecting you,' he said.

'You surprise me, sir. Somehow I got the impression you're a man who keeps close tabs on everyone's movements,' he responded.

'Only when I deem it necessary. Please.' He gestured to a chair.

'A terrible business, this murder at Neasden Temple. I understand you were there at the time and witnessed Dr Bhatt's last moments. Do you know yet who was responsible? Scotland Yard seems to believe it was a professional hitman sent from India.'

'Several lines of enquiry are there,' said Puri.

'The Brits are lucky to have your expertise at their disposal.'

'Had Dr Bhatt's location been known at an earlier date, no doubt this tragic event could have been avoided.'

'The blame lies squarely with Scotland Yard. They had months to locate him.'

'It is my impression the British have been working diligently to locate Dr Bhatt, actually,' said Puri. 'Their resources are stretched thin, no doubt, but their operation met with some success. Some weeks back, they traced the fugitive to a penthouse apartment in Regent's Park where he was holed up. Inspector Brom-ley believes Dr Bhatt spotted his men in the lobby thanks to the CCTV and thus escaped. I'm inclined to believe he got a tipoff some time earlier.'

'That would mean Dr Bhatt had an informer inside Scotland Yard?'

'I believe there was an informer, yes. But my guess is he did not alert Dr Bhatt directly.'

'Who then?'

'An individual working on behalf of certain interests in India who did not wish under any circumstances to see Dr Bhatt extradited to answer questions regarding illegal loans made to Bio Solutions to the tune of tens of crores,' said Puri. 'This man operates his own network of informers within the desi community in London, and thus came to know Dr Bhatt's location, having traced him after he arrived in London. When this man received a tipoff that Scotland Yard was sending detectives to the apartment in Regent's Park, he forewarned the fugitive.'

Joshi said with measured coolness, 'It all sounds a bit far-fetched, Mr Puri. And surely impossible to prove. By the way, I understand your Inspector Bromley wishes to speak with one of the High Commission drivers who happened to be at Neasden Temple the other night. Do you have any idea what that's about?'

'Most certainly, sir,' said Puri. 'Arjun Prakash was acting on the instructions of the aforementioned lizer. His task was to deliver a new passport to the fugitive at Neasden Temple in the name of Sandip Patel, and in return collect payment, bribe money being required for corrupt officials within the Home Ministry who supplied the passport.'

'Surely, Mr Puri, no such passport could have been found on Dr Bhatt's person – Scotland Yard would have informed the High Commission had this been the case.'

'You are right, no passport was discovered on Dr Bhatt's person,' said Puri.

'In which case your theory sounds a bit flimsy. I'd suggest that, being a regular at the temple, Arjun Prakash spotted Dr Bhatt amongst the congregation and decided to blackmail him.'

'Mine is not a theory and it is certainly not flimsy, sir, let me assure you. Inspector Bromley has traced the passport, in fact. It was taken by a local pickpocket from Dr Bhatt's trouser pocket while he was praying. Furthermore, this pickpocket witnessed Prakash hand the passport to Dr Bhatt, who passed him a white sports bag in return.'

'Ah, I see,' said Joshi, just the faintest flicker of irritation in his eye at having been outflanked. 'Well, I can see why the police wish to interview Prakash. But I understand he is proving difficult to trace.'

'Yes, sir, I should hazard a guess and say that he has returned at short notice to India.'

'If that is the case, he could be hard to locate.'

'No doubt, sir,' said Puri. 'But the fake passport, created for the purposes of aiding and abetting India's most wanted man, is something of a smoking gun, we can say. Once the media comes to know of its existence and the pickpocket's eyewitness testimony, a full enquiry will be inevitable. Who knows what names will come out of the woodwork?'

'Indeed, I should say an enquiry would be justified, if as you say a passport was provided to Dr Bhatt,' said Joshi. 'Let us just hope the guilty party has not covered his tracks to ensure that he is not implicated in any such corruption. Or worse still, he should threaten in some way the safety of any person speaking out against him.'

Puri stood, untroubled by the threat, and smiled indulgently. 'Future will tell, sir, but while I have a breath left in my body,

I'll not shy from standing for justice so the rot is removed from the body of our great nation,' he said. 'Now unfortunately, I must get a move on, actually. Tonight is the award ceremony gala dinner and I need to work on my speech to be delivered before so many of distinguished guests.'

Puri paused again at the bar to catch up with the latest on Action News! The last he saw of Joshi, he was speaking quietly into one of his three phones, his eyes unblinking, his expression impassive.

Mummy and Rumpi tried the Dhillon McMansion and found no one at home, but were told by one of the neighbours that Mrs Dhillon was usually at her country club.

They reached it in a minicab, travelling down a long driveway that bisected pristine fairways.

Amongst the other luxury vehicles in the car park in front of the mock Tudor clubhouse, they spotted Mrs Dhillon's MINI Cooper with its personal registration plate, PUNJGAL.

'Oh, yes, Mrs Dhillon said she was expecting two guests,' said the receptionist inside, 'I'll take you straight in.'

Rumpi and Mummy, certain that they had been mistaken for other visitors, were escorted into a lounge overlooking the golf course.

Mrs Dhillon, who sat amongst a coterie of ladies enjoying a late morning coffee and a selection of choux buns, did not appear in the least surprised to see them, however.

'These are the ladies visiting from Delhi I told you about,' she told her group, drawing quiet 'welcomes'. 'Mrs Puri here is quite the amateur detective. The other day, she was telling us about how she foiled a robbery in Delhi at a wedding.' She motioned to Mummy and Rumpi, saying, 'I'm sure everyone would love to hear how you did it. Do join us and I'll order some more coffee.'

'Thank you, but we would prefer to speak with you in private,' said Rumpi.

'Might I ask what it's about?' asked Mrs Dhillon, all innocence.

'Regarding your maid, Pooja. You got her arrested, na,' said Mummy.

'Oh, yes, that.' Mrs Dhillon spoke to the group again: 'My live-in maid has been stealing from me,' she said. 'At first it was just a pair of earrings and I thought I'd lost them myself. Then, this morning, I discovered my favourite kundan choker was missing as well. What choice did I have but to call the police?'

'Pooja is not a thief; she is totally innocent,' Mummy protested over a murmur of sympathy. 'We have come to appeal to your better nature to drop the charges.'

'But the girl was caught red-handed with the jewellery in her case as she was sneaking out of the house,' said Mrs Dhillon. 'I would dearly love to show leniency, but she betrayed the trust and kindness we showed her. Perhaps if she was able to give me some indication that she was sorry, that she understands the gravity of what she's done, then we could forget about the whole matter? I could have my lawyer draw up something for her to sign.'

Rumpi and Mummy understood the subtext of Mrs Dhillon's proposal: she would drop the charges if Pooja agreed in writing not to pursue claims against the family for wrongful employment.

'You've been exploiting that poor girl, paying her slave wages and locking her up in her room,' said Rumpi, letting her emotions run away from her. 'You should be ashamed of yourself.'

'I beg your pardon?' replied Mrs Dhillon, feigning hurt. 'I'll have you know that we treated that girl like a daughter – gave her a job, her own room, paid for her English classes. Now I think it would be better if I show you both out. Excuse me, ladies.'

Mummy and Rumpi followed her through the reception to the front door of the clubhouse.

'I think you'll find that Pooja has a lot more to lose than we do,' she said, standing on the steps. 'If she were to pursue her claim, the most I'd receive is a fine, whereas she will face a prison sentence and then deportation.'

'You yourself have some thinking to do, na,' said Mummy. 'That is regarding the Kitchloo family staying at Royal Lancaster Hotel. Yesterday I caught up with them and came to know their daughter, Anita, got engaged to Sanjiv.'

Mrs Dhillon smiled with an expression of weary patience. 'And?' she asked, as if she could hardly be bothered to do so.

'Drop all the charges against Pooja or we'll tell them about Amber and how Sanjiv dumped her a couple of days ago,' said Rumpi.

'Too late,' purred Mrs Dhillon with a cat-got-the-cream smile. 'The Kitchloos know all about Amber. I told them she became obsessed with Sanjiv and cooked up some delusional notion that he planned to marry her – even dispatched her poor, naive family to London to meet with us. Now . . .' She paused for a beat. 'I'll get my lawyer to draw up the declaration for Pooja to sign and then you can both scurry back to Delhi and I never expect to hear from you again. Toodeloo.'

Mrs Dhillon walked back into the club, leaving Mummy and Rumpi on the steps, silent in defeat.

They returned to their waiting minicab.

'I suppose we've no choice but to advise Pooja to sign,' said Rumpi.

Mummy sat back in furious repose, clasping her handbag on her lap. 'That is the last resort,' she said.

It was past six by the time Flush reached the market in Shanti Niketan where Savita came most evenings to pick up something or other for the house. The place was as busy as usual, and he stood near the sweet shop watching the jalebi maker creating orange, sugary swirls in his pan of spitting oil. Customers crowded around the paan stand, buying lottery tickets and foil sachets of gutkha. Hawkers moved through the crowd, some with leather belts draped over their shoulders, others wearing waistcoats stuffed with knock-off sunglasses and packs of men's polyester underwear.

Flush recognized one of the security guards from the house eating at a barrow that sold matar kulcha, his tobacco-leaf plate almost overflowing with chopped red onion, tomato, green chilli and chaat masala.

Shweta Bhatt's driver soon appeared as well, making a beeline for the paan stand, where he purchased a single Gold Leaf cigarette before going over to chat with the cobbler whose place of business was a patch of pavement below the market's banyan tree.

By seven, there was still no sign of Savita, and Flush began to worry that she might not appear. Tomorrow he had to be back at work, and it could be days before he would be able to get over to this part of Delhi again.

He decided that if she didn't come in ten minutes, he would buy a bunch of roses and then go and knock on the gate and ask to speak with her.

This deadline came and went.

Flush procrastinated for another few minutes, before finally approaching the flower stand and ordering a bouquet.

The phool wallah was preparing it for him, and Flush stood ready to pay, when, out of the corner of his eye beneath the smoggy beam of a streetlight, he caught sight of Shweta Bhatt's dog, Muttu, scurrying towards him straining on his lead.

The young woman who followed behind the animal was attired in exactly the same clothes that Savita had worn that first day Flush had laid eyes upon her – a green cotton kurta with a blue dupatta and a pair of identical glasses.

Her hair matched as well: braided at the back, with jasmine flowers tied in the end. A silver anklet jangled from her left ankle. She was the same height and strikingly beautiful.

But this was not Savita – and the dog, usually so obedient, knew it, too.

Flush's first thought was that Savita had a twin sister and that she must have come to stay with her while Shweta Bhatt was away in London. But then the driver, who was making his way back from the market in the direction of the house, called out to the young woman. And there was no mistaking the name he used to address her.

'Savita! Keep the lead tight, don't let him stray into the road!'

Flush felt suddenly numb as he watched the maid and the dog continue on into the market. For a while, even after she had vanished from view, he stood in front of the stand, the bouquet forgotten in his hand, staring at nothing in particular, feeling like his world had splintered into pieces.

At around the same time as Flush reached the market, Puri stepped into a posh tailor's off Regent Street to enquire about hiring a dinner suit.

A helpful young assistant took his measurements, checked the shop's stock, and returned with the regrettable news that nothing was available in his size.

Puri tried two other tailor's without luck, and finally an establishment specializing in 'plus-size attire for gentlemen'. Here he tried on a dinner jacket that fitted him perfectly, and though the trousers were a little tight around the waist and thighs, he decided they would do for the one night.

Puri rented a shirt and clip-on bow tie as well, and then headed to an Indian restaurant off Tavistock Square recommended earlier by Rinku.

Bromley, whom he had invited to lunch, was already sitting at a table near the window.

'Nothing too spicy for me, Vish,' he said as he looked over the menu. 'I can't be dealing with a dodgy tummy, not with the kind of afternoon I've got ahead of me.'

'Surely you are on safe ground here in UK,' said Puri, opting for the buffet, the aromas coming from the kitchen driving him ravenous.

In fact, the food proved pleasingly mirchi, at least for Puri's palate, and the butter chicken, palak paneer and gobi aloo all met with his approval. The rotis, too, which he ordered fresh to the table, were prepared with good quality atta. And to top it all, the waiter responded to his request for some fiery green chillies, and the detective proceeded to dunk the exposed flesh in salt.

Each mouthful felt restorative, like water for a wilting plant – and no sooner had Puri cleared his plate then he was up at the buffet again.

Bromley, having complained that the daal was 'scorching', watched him tuck into his second helping with a look of quiet bemusement as he brought him up to date with the morning's developments.

Chhota Balu would be arraigned in court at four o'clock, and had hired himself a top criminal lawyer. The Indian High Commission was now saying that the driver, Arjun Prakash, had returned to India. Scotland Yard had started a parallel investigation into the young, bald CEO of Centurion Labs, Nikesh Narayan, and Bromley expected to interview him by the end of the day regarding his meeting with Bombay Duck. Dr Bhatt's body would be flown to India tomorrow. His wife was planning to return to Delhi in a few hours to arrange the funeral.

Puri was now able to share some dramatic news of his own. 'The hit on Dr Bhatt was arranged through a property broker called Veer Sindhu, aka "Chaddi",' he explained. 'Furthermore, my operatives have come to know that Chaddi was contacted by a certain senior Indian bureaucrat by name of Dilip Shrivastava, the very same individual who requested me to locate Dr Bhatt in the first place,' said Puri.

'You're pulling my leg?' was Bromley's reaction. 'So basically you're saying your client, this Shreev-ash-tav-or, hired you to locate Bombay Duck, then got Chow-ta Ba-looo to follow you in the hope that you would lead him to his target. What was his motive?'

'On that point I'm not precisely one hundred per cent in fact. But I've come to know his father suffered from Type One diabetes and fell victim to Dr Bhatt's so-called cure. Revenge would therefore appear to be a strong motive.'

Bromley had bit into a stray piece of red chilli in his rojan ghosh, and with a look that suggested he might be having a heart attack, reached urgently for a glass of water and glugged down half the contents. After a moment, he said in a croaky voice, 'I'd imagine he wasn't alone in wanting revenge. Bombay Duck was directly responsible for at least three hundred deaths, from what I understand.'

'That is the official figure, most probably it was higher,' said Puri.

'I take it you've got enough to tie them both to the murder – the broker and Shreev—'

'Not to worry, Inspector-sahib,' interrupted Puri, before he could mangle Shrivastava's name again. 'Phone records and messages exchanged on a dark web forum are there. I'll have them forwarded to you, no delay.'

But that was not all: in the past hour Puri had also heard back from his colleague in Mauritius.

'He learned that Gladstone Global Holdings is owned by Centurion Labs, no less,' said Puri. 'So it would seem CEO Nikesh Narayan was acting as Dr Bhatt's guardian angel in London, providing him with safe houses.'

'Good work, Vish!' exclaimed Bromley. 'So why do you think Narayan was sheltering him, then? Are they old friends?'

'Not especially is my understanding,' said Puri. 'But they were in the same business, no? Pharmaceuticals. Could it be that Dr Bhatt provided him with his Dia-Beat research? That I leave with you to investigate yourself, Inspector-sahib.'

Bromley called his number two to update him on Puri's intel and then gulped down a cup of milky British tea.

'Before I go, are you absolutely sure about not wanting your name mentioned in connection with the investigation?' he asked. 'I gather you'll be passing on a substantial reward offered for information leading to Dr Bhatt's location.'

'Missing out on the payment is certainly regrettable,' admitted Puri. 'But on balance I would prefer my wife not come to know about my work on the case. We have a saying in India: "Wife is strife".'

'Don't I know it,' said Bromley with an ironic smile.

He called for the bill and insisted on paying.

'My way of saying thank you,' he said. 'We both know who cracked the case, and don't think for a moment I won't remember it.'

Except the case wasn't 'cracked', Puri reflected, as he sat on his own and tucked into a couple of gulab jamams. It was part cracked, only. Chhota Balu had been hired *after* Shrivastava had met with him in the Gymkhana. The mango had been poisoned by someone else entirely, *weeks earlier*, either by whoever had cooked for Dr Bhatt, or someone who had intercepted his mango delivery.

Now agreeably sated, and feeling as though he could think clearly again (it felt as if the green chillies had jump-started his metabolism), Puri began to review the case. He found that he could now visualize the clues like pieces of a jigsaw puzzle laid out before him.

The image of Dr Bhatt lay at the centre of this mental collage. Next to it, he pictured the poisoned mango. The spices in the Regent's Park apartment. The back of Chhota Balu's hairy neck. The image of the faceless woman from Neasden Temple. Nikesh Narayan's grinning portrait in the Centurion Labs brochure. Shweta Bhatt's booking for Grand Cayman.

He moved the pieces around, fitting some together, considering where others belonged.

Bromley's words from earlier came back to him: '*I'd imagine he wasn't alone in wanting revenge. Bombay Duck was directly responsible for at least three hundred deaths, from what I understand.*'

Puri froze suddenly – a last spoonful of sticky, dripping gulab jamun millimetres from his waiting, open mouth.

'By God, you pagal,' he murmured, and slowly lowered the spoon back into the bowl. 'Where's your brain been these past days? Just idling all this time! How you did not see this thing staring you directly in the face?'

Puri reached for his phone to call Tubelight.

He had put the device on silent during lunch, and now found that he had received two new messages.

The first was from Jags. The second, from Flush, read, 'CODE 10', the highest possible.

TWENTY-TWO

'You had better be right about this, Vish, it's my neck on the line,' said Bromley as he pressed the call button for the lift in the lobby of The Shard. 'Let me do the talking, I don't want anyone making any out-and-out accusations. So far, you've got nothing concrete – and you're the first to warn about the dangers of conjecture.'

'I'm not one to go off half-cocked, Inspector-sahib, but if we don't act now, there is every chance they will both slip through the net, so to speak,' said Puri. 'We must delay her departure by fifteen minutes, give or take.'

The doors opened and the two men, accompanied by a concierge from the Shangri-La Hotel, stepped into the empty car. The lift's upward motion was barely perceptible.

'The maid in Delhi, the one working for Shweta Bhatt,' said Bromley, musing over the details Puri had shared with him as they had driven at high speed over to The Shard, 'you reckon she was in on it? She had to be, surely?'

'Time will tell, only, Inspector-sahib,' said Puri. 'Possibly the wool was pulled down over her eyes. I've appraised Inspector Singh of Delhi Police of the situation, and he is standing by, awaiting word my end before taking her and the other staff members for questioning.'

Puri's phone buzzed in his pocket with a new message. 'Some heavy traffic is there,' he sighed as he read it. 'Jags will take at least twenty-five minutes, give or take.'

'That's cutting it fine,' sighed Bromley. 'I'll do my best to stall her, but if she insists on leaving, there's bugger-all I can do about it. This all hangs on your nephew.'

From the windows of the fiftieth floor, London stretched out below like a miniature version of itself. Tower Bridge and the Tower of London were like cardboard pop-ups, the traffic on the Thames mere bath toys. Off to the east, the Canary Wharf skyline appeared an irresistible target for attack by marbles.

The concierge led the way to Room 5014 and knocked on the

door. Shweta Bhatt answered and, giving him little more than a passing glance, turned back into the room, without noticing Bromley – or indeed Puri – hanging further back in the corridor.

'Take my bags and I'll follow you down in a minute.'

She was packing some last things. A zip whizzed; luggage clasps snapped together.

'Has my car come? I've got to be at the heliport in thirty minutes. I'm cutting it fine.'

The concierge politely explained that the bellboy would be along momentarily and that, yes, her car was waiting at the front of the hotel.

'In the meantime, madam, the police are here to speak with you,' he told her.

'What? Again?' She sounded tired rather than alarmed. 'Whatever it is, it's going to have to wait.'

Bromley took this as his cue and, as the concierge stepped to one side, took hold of the open door with one hand. 'My apologies for the intrusion, madam,' he said, introducing himself. 'You may remember we met yesterday. I need a few more minutes of your time.'

Shweta Bhatt had moved into the bathroom and was collecting up her toiletries. 'I'm sorry, I've booked a helicopter to get me out to Heathrow,' she called out.

'I'm sure you're as keen as I am to get to the bottom of who was responsible for your husband's murder,' pressed Bromley, polite but firm. 'This is in connection with your late husband's contacts during the months he was here in London.'

Shweta Bhatt came to the door, holding a bulging wash bag. Puri, who stood back in the shadow cast by the overhead spotlights, had a clear view of her now. Even in a simple frock and leggings, and wearing a minimum of makeup, she was stunning, one of the most beautiful women he had ever laid eyes on. Was it any surprise that Flush had fallen for her?

'I told you, yesterday, Inspector, Harilal called me a few times from London, but that's the only communication I had with him after he left India. There's really nothing more I can add.'

'A suggestion has been made that you may have found a way to travel to London and spend some time with your deceased husband in a luxury apartment adjacent to Regent's Park,' said Bromley.

'What? That's impossible,' she said, derisively. 'I've been at home in Delhi for months. My sister, my staff, the neighbours, they'll all tell you that.'

'It has been suggested you travelled to the UK on another individual's passport, a doppelgänger, possibly a member of your staff who posed as you while you were away.'

'Suggested by who?' her tone sharp, her eyes narrowed.

'I'm not at liberty to say, madam, but the information comes from a reliable source,' said Bromley.

'This is insane!' Shweta Bhatt had shifted her weight on to one leg and was glaring at Bromley like he was the one who needed to be locked up. 'When does this source of yours say that I travelled to London?'

'A few weeks ago, when your husband was staying off Regent's Park – and then again two days ago,' he answered.

'Two days ago I was in Delhi, and went shopping in Connaught Place. I bought some luggage and perfume – paid for on my card. Afterwards I had lunch with my sister at our favourite Italian restaurant in Sundar Nagar!'

'We have been led to believe that the doppelgänger took your place, madam.'

'You think my own sister doesn't know me?'

Bromley deflected the question with another of his own. 'Might I ask why you were buying new luggage, madam?'

'I was planning to finally get away for a while – to Grand Cayman, if you must know. I had hoped to be reunited with my husba . . .'

The words caught in her throat and she paused, her eyes cast down on the floor.

'I just don't believe this,' she said, her voice now brittle and charged with emotion. 'Have you no shame? Harilal has been murdered. I've had to fly here to identify his body. The media is picking my life apart like vultures. And now. And now . . .' Shweta Bhatt gave a sob. Tears were trickling down her face. '. . . I have to fly home to make arrangements for my husband's funeral. And you come here accusing me of I don't know what. I have nothing more to say to you.'

She addressed the concierge. 'Help with my bags, please. I don't want to miss my plane.'

Dealing with luggage was evidently well beyond the man's pay grade, and he hesitated – but was saved by the approach of a bellboy pushing a brass trolley with squeaking wheels.

Bromley had to step aside for the young man, who quickly went about his work, loading up the Louis Vuitton cases.

Shweta Bhatt, for her part, wasted no time in grabbing the last of her possessions and, having donned a Burberry raincoat, swept past Bromley and followed the bellboy down the corridor.

Puri went and stood next to her as she waited in front of the lifts in silence, staring intensely at the up and down arrows, her jaw clenched tight.

'It is my first time in London,' he said in an easy, familiar tone. 'The city is greener than I expected, but the taxis are quite costly. I was invited to collect a major award – from the International Federation of Private Detectives, no less. By chance I got involved in searching for your elusive husband, also. It was not on my original agenda, so to speak. And some challenges have been there, not knowing the UK and all. The lack of quality food being another.'

Shweta Bhatt threw him a derisory, sideways glance. 'Who are you?' she asked with barely concealed contempt.

'Vish Puri, Most Private Investigators Ltd., at your service,' he answered. 'Our offices are above Bahri Sons books, Khan Market. No doubt you've heard of me? Some time back, I was featured on the cover of *India Today*.'

'Mr Puri has been helping us with our enquiries,' said Bromley. 'He's of the opinion that we've charged the wrong man with your husband's murder.'

'You really need to make up your mind, Inspector,' said Shweta Bhatt. 'Just last night you told me the hitman was there at the temple, that you believe he was contracted to murder my husband.'

'Chhota Balu was hired by a certain individual who sought revenge for the death of his father after taking Dia-Beat, but he was beaten to the post, so to speak, by another individual altogether, her motive being precisely the same,' explained Puri.

'And you can prove that?'

'The murderer was extremely cunning, actually,' conceded Puri. 'The plan was conceived and executed in the most masterly way. Rarely during my long and illustrious career have I investigated a murder that has come so close to deserving the title "perfect". That having been said, as in life in general, perfection is not attainable by we mere mortals. Some flaws were there, and Vish Puri did not fail in his duty to recognize them. For one, the extensive collection of spices left at the Regent's Park apartment. Dr Bhatt was no cook, meaning that for some time at least, another individual prepared his khana. Must be this was a trusted person. Someone who could wipe down the entire apartment, erasing all traces of fingerprints, without raising suspicion on *his* part. Someone, also, who bought him a box of his favourite Vanraj mangoes.'

Shweta Bhatt reached out and pressed the down button three times, murmuring under her breath, 'What's taking so long?' Almost instantly the down arrow lit up. It would only be a matter of seconds before a lift arrived.

'Naturally, right from the start, I considered if you his wife had been the one to travel in secret to London,' Puri continued, regardless. 'You are known for your cooking, after all. One *Hello!* interview is there in which Dr Bhatt spoke of his love for your dhokla. But how? You are not a yogi to be able to transport yourself instantly from one place to another, no? Also, you were very much there in Delhi, albeit cloistered at home, avoiding limelight, appearing on your balcony smoking, walking the dog once in a while and so forth. But after spotting on the footage from Neasden Temple a woman taking pains to hide her face from each and every camera, I reconsidered. And at lunch today, I managed to eat a good butter chicken accompanied by some green chillies. Finally the pieces started to fall into place. After making some calls and all, I came to know your dear beloved father suffered from Type One diabetes and was one of dozens who fell victim to Dia-Beat. Naturally you refrained from making this information public as you and your sister were planning your revenge, but the hospital records are there.'

A 'ping' announced the arrival of the lift.

The doors opened and the bellboy pushed his trolley inside. Shweta Bhatt entered quickly behind him, turned and held up a hand to prevent anyone else from joining them.

Just as the doors came together, however, Puri stepped inside – and the lift began its descent.

Furious, Shweta Bhatt started searching in her handbag, frowning in frustration as she moved the contents around.

'You're looking for your pepper spray to use again, madam, as you did on the bus to Old Delhi?' he asked with a knowing smile.

She stopped what she was doing and turned cold, granite-hard eyes on Puri, perhaps for the first time recognizing him as a genuine threat.

'Believe me, I've come to know everything, madam,' he said. 'You've no secrets from me. I know about Savita, how for weeks you posed as her, coming and going from your home while, all the time, she remained inside. This enabled you to slip away, posing as her, and come to London, travelling on her passport. All the while you were playing a double role with your husband also. Naturally, he was aware that, when you came the first time, you did so incognito. He did not question why you took every precaution not to leave any trace in the apartment, save the spices you left behind. But all the while you were planning to murder him.'

Until now the bellboy hadn't appeared to show any interest in the conversation, but at the mention of murder, his eyes darted momentarily at Puri before he adopted again an expression of professional inscrutability.

'Your attempt the first time – you gifted him a poisoned mango in the fridge – failed owing to unforeseen circumstances. Dr Bhatt was forced to leave the apartment before consuming the fruit,' Puri continued. 'So you returned to London a second time, though without his knowledge, and murdered him in Neasden Temple. Afterward, you flew directly to Delhi and arrived back in Shanti Niketan in the guise of Savita, walking directly past all the media persons without raising any suspicion whatsoever. Some hours later, you then reappeared as yourself, now the grieving widow. It was perfect. More or less.'

The lift slowed as it reached the ground floor. Shweta Bhatt had listened to Puri in silence and was preparing now for a quick exit; content, it seemed, to remain silent in the face of his allegations.

'One more thing is there,' said Puri. 'The mehndi is still showing, especially around the knuckles.' Faint traces of henna patterns, typical of those drawn during wedding celebrations, were indeed visible. 'Must be you did the work yourself on the plane while travelling back from London so as to complete the impression that, as Savita, you attended a wedding. Since then, naturally, you've attempted to erase all traces but not succeeded entirely.'

The doors opened and the sound of the busy lobby spilled into the car, overcoming the muzak playing on the speakers in the lift.

Shweta Bhatt allowed the bellboy to leave first and started to follow, but then stopped short of the door, holding it open with her hand.

'You are right about one thing,' she said, with a faint smile that struck a discordant note. 'I loved my father; no one in the world mattered to me more. He was my rock, my everything. And he was taken from me, just as hundreds of others had their loves taken from them. And Harilal knew there was a risk. He knew. But he went ahead and released his so-called miracle drug anyhow. Do you really think he was ever going to face justice for what he did? But I'll tell you this: right now, his victims' loved ones have some form of closure knowing that he's paid a price. And believe me, none of them will be shedding any tears for him.'

With that, Shweta Bhatt strode purposefully out into the lobby and made directly for the hotel's front desk.

Puri exited the lift to find Bromley stepping quickly from the adjacent one.

'There you are! I warned you not to go accusing her of anything and you come straight out with it!' he said. 'Never mind, you've tipped her off that we're on to her. We could have bided our time, gathered evidence from airport security and had her brought back from India. What's to stop her flying off to Grand Cayman now?'

'I took a risk, Inspector, to delay her departure, hoping she would rise to the bait and provide a confession,' said Puri. 'All the while I was recording on my phone, actually. But she is too smart for that. I should have known. That one has beauty and brains. Her husband never so much as suspected.'

They watched from a distance as Shweta Bhatt finished paying her bill and started across the lobby, her car waiting beyond the glass doors.

'Another six or seven minutes, Inspector-sahib; that is all we required,' said Puri.

'We gave it our best, Vish. How do you put it? "Don't do tension",' said Bromley.

In spite of his frustration, Puri could not help but smile at the inspector's impression of him. But it was gone in a moment, his gaze suddenly fixed with surprise and anticipation on the hotel's front doors.

Earlier than anticipated, Jags had reached the hotel and entered the lobby. With him was security guard, Rakesh Sharma.

They could not have timed their arrival better.

Shweta Bhatt was now practically face to face with the pair. And Sharma's reaction to her was unmistakable. His whole face slackened in surprise, his mouth fell slightly agape; and, as she walked briskly past him, his head turned 180 degrees, while his body remained facing forward so that he almost toppled over.

Grabbing Jags urgently by the arm, Sharma started pointing excitedly at Shweta Bhatt's departing figure. For a moment, he couldn't get out the words. And then he found his voice and it carried clear across the lobby.

'That's 'er, blud! She's the one. Innit!'

Bromley, as alert to what had just occurred as Puri, took off after her. His running action was somewhat ungainly, the upper part of his body remaining perfectly perpendicular, but he covered the distance quickly enough, and intercepted Shweta Bhatt as she reached her car.

At the sight of her being read her rights, Jags gave a celebratory 'whoop' and raised one hand, offering Puri a high five.

'Get some, Uncle-gee! We slayed it! What a rush!'

Puri was grinning as he slapped Jags's hand. 'Honestly speaking, it was touch and go,' he said. 'One more minute and she'd have got clean away.'

'The driver knew like a short cut – and we was lucky it was clear sailing down Oxford Street,' said Jags.

'And fortunate, also, Mr Sharma here recognized Shweta Bhatt straight off.'

'Yeah, blud, but she's like well fit,' said the security guard. 'I got eyes on 'er that one time I took up a delivery to the top floor. She was like wearing this little skimpy number. Oh, man, I tell you, she was *blindin'*.'

'Yes, that was her downfall in fact,' said Puri.

They watched through the glass doors as Shweta Bhatt was led away to a waiting police car and put on the back seat.

'Tell me you're gonna take the credit, Uncle-gee,' he said. 'This'll be massive. I mean, you're the man.'

'I would not be much of a man should Rumpi find out what all we've been up to,' Puri lamented.

'Come on, Auntie'll understand. You've just done your job, what you're cut out for. You deserve the recognition.'

'If I've inspired you to continue with your studies and make something of yourself, that is reward enough,' said Puri.

'The past few days have definitely got me thinking 'bout my priori-ties,' acknowledged Jags.

'Then my work is truly done,' said Puri. 'Now, we had better get a move on. It is coming up to six o'clock actually, and I've an award to accept. Not to mention a speech to deliver.'

TWENTY-THREE

ndia's news channels were having a field day. The Bhatt murder was proving the most sensational story of the year – and with almost each hour came another major development.

First, late the previous night, Bromley had held a sensational press conference – sensational in terms of the content, if not the delivery. Mrs Shweta Bhatt, he had announced in his usual dry, matter-of-fact style – his statement carried live to an audience numbering in the hundreds of millions – had been charged with her husband's murder. She had travelled to London disguised as her maid and poisoned Dr Bhatt inside Neasden Temple.

As if this were not salacious enough for the ever-ravenous pack of hacks, Scotland Yard's man had then gone on to announce that the notorious Indian contract killer known as Chhota Balu was facing prosecution for conspiracy to murder and intent to kill following his knife attack on an arresting officer.

Bromley had not forgotten to mention, also, the lesser charge of urinating in public, an act of 'unseemly public indecency'.

The press conference had been timed to allow Puri's erstwhile confederate, Inspector Singh, to make arrangements for the detention of all of Shweta Bhatt's staff, including her gardener and beautician, and to arrest Shweta Bhatt's sister, Nidhi, who had, Scotland Yard believed, collaborated in her brother-in-law's murder.

The Delhi Police had also arrested Puri's former client, Dilip Shrivastava, and the property broker, Veer Sindhu, aka 'Chaddi'.

In the morning, Bromley had appeared before the cameras again to tell the world that the young CEO of Centurion Labs (India) Ltd., Nikesh Narayan, was being questioned regarding his possible involvement in Dr Bhatt's murder. The police had sufficient proof meanwhile to charge Narayan with harbouring the wanted man at two known addresses in London. They were also investigating his alleged illegal acquisition of Bio Solutions' Dia-Beat research.

Flush sat in Indian Coffee House near to Delhi Police HQ, watching Action News! and wondering if the anchor was going to burst a blood vessel live as he and his rent-a-pundits raked feverishly over the details.

'The big question I want to know is what did Shweta Bhatt's maid know? Was she just a puppet on a string?' one of them asked.

'That's what the police should focus on!' agreed another doyen. 'Did she participate in the elaborate deception ignorant that Shweta Bhatt planned to murder her husband?'

'Consider this: she could have lost a loved one, too, and been hell-bent on revenge,' said one contributor. 'In my opinion it's hard to see that she *couldn't* have known.'

Flush was in no doubt as to her part in it all, however. The young woman he had seen yesterday in the market walking Muttu the dog was simply too innocent to have helped plan a murder. She had agreed to play her part, had even posed as Shweta Bhatt and, to provide her with an alibi and maintain the impression she was in Delhi, gone shopping for luggage and perfume and lunched with her sister. But she had not acted out of malice. More likely she had done it for financial gain or perhaps even sympathy: to help a mistress separated from her husband who wanted to see him, yet feared leading the authorities to his door.

Flush knew full well, too, that in India's brutish, unforgiving justice system, Savita was unlikely to get a fair trial – and so last night, despite Tubelight's warning that he was a sucker for a pretty face, he had retained a criminal lawyer on her behalf.

In the past hour, the application for her bail had been approved – and Puri had spoken with Inspector Singh and asked that Savita not be served up to the press pack waiting outside Police HQ for her release.

Having finished his sada dosa and Rooh Afza milkshake at Indian Coffee House, Flush travelled the short distance to the galli behind the back of the imposing building and waited for the gate to open.

When Savita appeared, looking frightened and lost, a picture of young innocence, any lingering doubts Tubelight had planted in his head were dispelled, and he knew that, this time, he could trust his own judgement.

Though she was beautiful (the similarity to Shweta Bhatt minus her finery and makeup was truly striking), he nevertheless approached her and introduced himself as the person who had hired the lawyer on her behalf, free of his usual nerves or apprehension.

Naturally, Savita wanted to know who he was and why he was helping her, and Flush explained that he was part of a team that had been searching for Dr Bhatt and believed she was innocent.

'I *am* innocent, I swear I didn't know what Ma'am was planning,' she told him. 'I've been told not to leave the city, but I've got nowhere to go. There's no way I can go back to the house.'

'You've any family here in Delhi?' he asked.

'Some cousins. I called them but they won't come.'

'I live with my mother in Baparpur, across the Yamuna. We have a spare room. You can stay with us for some days,' Flush suggested.

'I don't know you,' she said, uncertain.

'Nothing will happen, my mother is harmless,' he said. 'She spends most of her time on TikTok and Tinder. She's trying to find me a wife.'

Savita smiled at this.

'Listen, I know what it is to be alone in the city,' Flush went on. 'Before my mother came to stay with me from the village, I had no one.'

A figure appeared at the end of the galli, very possibly a photographer.

'We need to get out of here, they'll come after you,' he warned, and mounted his scootie, quickly starting the engine.

Savita slipped on to the seat behind him and pulled away, escaping the photographer who had broken into a run.

Flush took a quick right and then headed down Tolstoy Marg. Savita slipped her arms around his waist, linking her fingers together, and held on.

Mummy awoke early and took her usual glass of water with lemon. She made her ablutions, spent the best part of an hour reading her Gita and went for a walk. At ten a.m., she dressed in one of her favourite saris, a luxuriant cream-coloured affair with a gold border, a favourite for very special occasions.

She had a cab coming at eleven thirty, having established that the journey to the address in SW1 would take around an hour. Though she was invited for one o'clock, this allowed an extra thirty minutes in case the taxi driver proved to be unreliable and lost his way, or took an indirect route as their counterparts so often did in Delhi.

Once ready, she went downstairs and found Rumpi and Nina in the kitchen drinking chai, still giggling about how Puri, at the awards event the night before, had dropped his speech on the floor, and in bending down to pick it up, split his trousers. This had necessitated him walking sideways across the stage to reach the podium when he'd gone to collect his award.

'He looked a bit like a crab,' joked Rumpi. 'I warned him that he would need a fitting. God knows what he's been getting up to. Working a case behind my back if I know him.'

'We've been keeping secrets of our own, na?' said Mummy.

On that score, Pooja had been released on bail the previous afternoon. Mrs Dhillon's lawyer had sent Nina a confidential agreement for her to sign, meantime.

'Basically the witch is agreeing to drop criminal charges if Pooja signs away any claims against the family,' she explained.

Mummy sighed with regret. 'All night I've been thinking: what to do?' she said. 'But no answer has come. Mrs Dhillon is holding a royal flush, na.'

'I hate to see her get away with it,' grumbled Nina. 'How I'd love to see that smug smile wiped from her face.'

'I feel sorry for the other family,' said Rumpi. 'The Dhillons are using that other girl, just like they were going to use Amber, I know it.'

'Let's face it, the Kitchloo family isn't our concern,' said Nina. 'It's Pooja's interests we need to look out for. I think it's time to face facts: she's going to have to sign the agreement. That way at least she's not going to be branded a criminal and sent to prison. And we will have helped her escape a life with that terrible family. So it's not all bad.'

*   *   *

Puri soon appeared in the kitchen door, on the lookout for a late breakfast – and soon they were all talking about the event last night and looking over Rumpi's photos.

There were plenty from dinner – of the Puris all raising their glasses of bubbly and toasting Chubby's success; of Rinku in his black leather dinner jacket on his sixth or seventh glass, seated next to the date he had brought along, who looked not a day over twenty and whose dress rivalled even Puri's trousers in the tightness department; of Inspector Bromley who had stopped by to say a quick congratulations, staring sternly at the camera as he shook his Indian colleague formally by the hand; and some lovely ones of Jags grinning from ear to ear with his arms around Puri and a proud-looking Joni, who had worn a clip-on red bow tie for the occasion.

Rumpi had got Puri to pose for a number of shots with other famous detectives from around the world, including none other than China's Wendy Qiang and Australia's Ben 'Smithy' Smith. And she had gone up to the front of the stage and taken a well-framed shot of her husband starting his acceptance speech.

There was another wide one taken about ten minutes later from her seat back at the table.

Rumpi swiped through the next, taken at the twenty-minute mark. Then another thirty minutes in. And a final one as Puri had made his way off the stage amidst polite applause following the IFPD President Charles Harding's deftly handled intervention to thank him for providing a fascinating insight into the centuries-long development of investigation in India and to encourage everyone to raise a glass one final time to this year's winner.

'Good you kept it short, Uncle-gee,' said Jags, straight-faced, when he joined the family in the kitchen. 'I think we can all agree we learnt a lot.'

'I suggested to Charles Harding they might wish to publish the speech in its entirety in the next edition of their quarterly magazine, and he sounded most enthusiastic I must say,' said Puri.

'Such a nice time we all had,' smiled Mummy. 'Good memories.'

'And now you are off for your mystery lunch, is it?' asked Puri. 'Must be a special occasion,' he added, knowing that she wore that particular sari but rarely. 'Last time I saw you such attired, we were at the Wankaner Palace for the coronation.'

But Mummy still gave nothing more away. 'Just I'm visiting an old friend, someone I met long-time back. Her home is a grand affair, well-to-do she is, so just I wanted to go in my best,' she said.

It was around twenty minutes past eleven, and Mummy was in the front room, keeping an eye out for her taxi in case it arrived early, when her phone rang. It was Amber in Delhi.

'I know why Sanjiv wanted to marry me; I've figured it out!' she declared as soon as the call connected.

Amber didn't require any encouragement to elaborate.

'You remember I told you I met him on a flight? I was on my way back from Jammu, after visiting my Chacha.'

'Yes, beti.'

'He told me then that he'd been on a work trip with his mother, who had flown back to the UK ahead of him. He even told me they had run into an issue with a new project for the family's manufacturing company. After you told me the name of the other girl's family, I got to thinking. Kitchloo's a typical Jammu name, they're pandits. So I started calling around, to try and find out what I could about them.'

Mummy thought she knew where Amber was going with this but didn't interrupt.

'Jammu's a small place, everyone knows everyone. And it turns out Chacha's cousin sister is good friends with the Kitchloos. Her daughter went to school with Shriya Kitchloo, the girl Sanjiv's got engaged to. So Chacha's cousin sister spoke with Shriya's massi and she told her that the Dhillons are wanting to put up a new factory in a prime location on the edge of Jammu. They've been offered the land for a really good price. Only they've run into one issue. They can't buy it because—'

Mummy finished the sentence for her: 'They're not state-born subjects.'

'Right. I tick that box and so does Shriya Kitchloo,' said Amber. 'So Sanjiv's plan all along was to marry one of us, purchase the land and get one of us to sign the deeds, then after a year he'd transfer ownership to his name.'

'So Shriya Kitchloo was plan B in case you didn't go through with marriage.'

'Or it could have been the other way round. Who knows?'

Mummy didn't have time to console Amber. Her cab had arrived – and she needed to act quickly if she stood any chance of saving Shriya Kitchloo, and getting her own back at Mrs Dhillon.

She hung up, called Rumpi from the kitchen and, having explained what she had just learned from Amber, asked her to delay her plans again for Windsor Castle and come to the Royal Lancaster Hotel.

'How about your lunch, Mummy-ji? You don't want to miss it. Can't we just call the Kitchloos?'

'It has to be done in person, na, otherwise they won't believe.'

An hour later, when she and Rumpi asked in person for the Kitchloos at reception, they were informed that the family had left the hotel.

'Let us go direct to the Dhillon residence,' said Mummy. 'We will confront the family with what we know.'

Rumpi was not prepared to take it any further, however.

'We've done all we can; you've done all you can, Mummy-ji,' she said. 'Sometimes you have to just let things go. Now you've got your lunch to go to. You've got just twenty minutes to get there.'

Mummy knew she was right. There was nothing more to be done. But she hated to admit defeat. 'I should have seen the Jammu connection,' she said. 'Mrs Dhillon mentioned building a factory when we went for tea.'

They left the hotel and stood on the pavement, trying to hail a cab, but those that went past were all occupied.

The sun had come out and – beyond the black railings that ran along Bayswater Road – Hyde Park looked green and inviting. Mothers pushed prams beneath rows of London planes. The paths were busy with dog walkers, joggers and bicyclists. Children waded through piles of autumn leaves.

'Such a green city, so many parks dotted around,' said Mummy.

'I don't see why we all have to rush back to Delhi,' said Rumpi. 'We could easily extend our tickets. Chubby's just all work, work, work. And don't think I don't know he's been involved in something while we've been here. I've kept my mouth shut to keep the peace, but it hurts to know that I always come second.'

Mummy's attention had drifted; she was trying to make out something in the park with one hand held up over her eyes to keep out the sun.

Rumpi followed her line of sight – to a bench about a hundred metres away, where a couple, he in a suit, she wearing a sari, were sitting close together, holding hands.

'Is that Sanjiv Dhillon?' she asked.

'And the Kitchloo girl, na!' said Mummy.

They set off for the nearest crossing over the road, Mummy going as quickly as she could manage in heels and sari.

They entered the park to find the couple now some way off, walking hand in hand along a path that cut through the long grass towards the boating pond.

By the time Rumpi and Mummy caught up with them, they were both out of breath.

'What are you doing here?' asked Sanjiv, more perplexed than concerned.

'We need to speak to Shriya in private,' gasped Rumpi.

The young woman, looking confused, asked who they were.

'My friend's daughter, Amber, was engaged to this one and he called the whole thing off,' said Mummy, gesturing at Sanjiv derisively.

'Auntie-ji, I think you should know that Sanjiv has explained to me what happened,' said Shriya, her voice gentle, respectful.

'He's not telling you everything, believe me,' said Rumpi. 'If we could just have a word in private?'

'If you're referring to my mother's plans, then Shriya knows everything.'

'Including your motivation for marrying a state-born girl from Jammu?' asked Rumpi.

'Yes, she knows,' answered Sanjiv. 'I admit, I wasn't truthful with her at first. But while Shriya's been in London, we've been seeing a lot of each other, without our parents' knowledge, and we love one another and want to be together.'

The two were staring into one another's eyes, clearly besotted.

'Sanjiv told his mother last night that he's marrying me on his terms – and he's not having me sign any land deal on her behalf,' Shriya explained.

'She can't have liked that,' said Rumpi.

'She didn't, but I'm tired of all her manipulation,' he said. 'From now on, I'm going to do things on my terms. Oh, and by the way, I've told mother to drop the charges against Pooja or I won't speak to her again. It's terrible the way she's treated her. That poor girl didn't steal anything.'

Satisfied that he was telling the truth and that Shriya was doing the right thing, Mummy and Rumpi wished them both well and hurried back to the Bayswater Road.

'Where to?' asked the driver of the first available black cab.

Mummy passed him her invitation through the window in the taxi's divider.

He studied it and his rear-view mirror captured his smile.

'I'll get you there as fast as I can, luv. Shouldn't be more than five, six minutes,' he said before returning the invitation.

Mummy held the card in her lap, watching out the window as the taxi passed Marble Arch.

'You know I'm going to see where you get down, so you might as well tell me who your mystery hostess is,' said Rumpi.

Mummy considered for a moment and then said, 'Fine. But you're not to tell anyone. You have to swear it.'

'Not a soul. You have my word.'

Mummy handed her the invitation and Rumpi gave a gasp.

'I don't believe it,' she said, staring at the words and embossed crest in astonishment.

'Like I told you, na, we met in 1961 when she was in India.'

'But how, where?'

'That I swore myself never to reveal.'

Rumpi sat back in her seat with a big, marvelling smile. 'You never cease to amaze me, Mummy-ji,' she said. 'No wonder you were able to get a British visa at short notice.'

The driver took them down Park Lane, around Hyde Park Corner and along Constitution Hill.

'You had better hurry, you're ten minutes late,' said Rumpi as the taxi came to a stop.

'She will understand,' said Mummy. 'Like me, her life has been dedicated to duty.'

Gathering up the hem of her sari, she stepped out of the vehicle, waved goodbye with a smile that denoted a thrill of anticipation on her part; and with her invitation in one hand

and her reliable handbag in the other, approached the side entrance to Buckingham Palace.

Rumpi's eyes filled with tears of pride as she watched Mummy present the invitation to the officer on duty and was invited inside.

Too late, she realized that she should have lent Mummy her smartphone.

'It would have been nice to have a selfie,' she said before asking the driver to take her to the nearest Underground station.

EPILOGUE

Iqbal, the carpenter, had started work in the galli that ran through the middle of Khan Market behind the offices of Most Private Investigators Ltd. Puri had commissioned the softly spoken craftsman to create a bespoke cabinet that would, once finished, display his shiny, big trophy so visitors and prospective clients could not miss it.

The detective watched from the window as Iqbal carefully shaved a length of sheesham wood with an antique plane that had, no doubt, been passed from father to son for several generations. Iqbal's family had maintained a carpentry business in Old Delhi since early Mughal times (though these days he was without a premises and worked on-site). The tool looked as rudimentary and outdated as the others in Iqbal's kit, which he carried around with him from job to job in a simple jute tote bag. Despite the simplicity of his tools, Puri did not doubt for a minute that the end result would be beautifully executed – the product of a master craftsman whose skills had been imparted to him from an early age and who had, in honing his own natural talent, established an exemplary reputation.

'Only a fool believes that success comes from one's own efforts alone, Madam Rani,' commented Puri, as he returned to his desk and retook his place in his comfortable executive swivel chair. 'Those who succeed in life are nurtured by others and must also learn to grasp opportunities when they come.'

It had been ten days since Shweta Bhatt's arrest and this was Puri's first day back at work, he and Rumpi having remained in London for a week longer than originally planned to take some proper meter down. As was customary at the conclusion of any of his cases, big or small, Puri had been dictating to Elizabeth Rani an account of events between his meeting with (disgraced) Additional Secretary Dilip Shrivastava at the Gymkhana Club, through to the arrest of the Bio Solutions CEO, Nikesh Narayan, on a host of charges; and Chhota Balu's dramatic escape from police custody just three days previously.

'In London, I was a fish out of water, so to speak, and required assistance from Jags,' continued Puri who, along with the facts of any major case, liked to add to the file some reflections of his own, much in the way the hero in some of his favourite classic Bollywood films provided a soliloquy at the conclusion of the plot. 'My progress would have proceeded at a slower pace had he not obliged, given his local knowledge and all. But I'm pleased to report that – thanks to my influence – he was able to learn a valuable life lesson, also. Elders, in fact, provide something valuable called experience – and thus they should be listened to. I am proud to say that, as of now, he has quit the Deliveroo and enrolled to study for a degree in criminal psychology, no less.'

'That is wonderful news, sir, congratulations,' said Madam Rani, who sat in front of Puri's desk, the pages of her notebook by now filled with shorthand.

'Who knows, perhaps one fine day he will visit Delhi and then we can teach him to speak proper English, also,' said Puri with a mischievous smile.

'And it seems Mummy-ji's assistance was invaluable as well,' commented Elizabeth Rani, ever a fan of Puri's mother. 'She is a wonder, I must say.'

'Fortunately, she was sitting in close proximity to Chhota Balu on the flight from Dilli and observed unusual behaviour on his part,' said Puri, who felt he had provided a fair and honest record of his mother's contribution to the case, though he was loath to give too much emphasis to her role. She had not solved the case, after all.

'And it was lucky, also, she spotted the hitman in the selfie outside Buckingham Palace,' gushed Elizabeth Rani. 'It never ceases to amaze me how quickly her mind works. I can only hope to be half as sharp when I reach her age.'

'Most certainly she remains an active person,' said Puri, diplomatically. 'Now Madam Rani, I believe that concludes our work here. I've some catching up to do, to say the least.'

'There were one or two details that I hoped to clarify before I type up my notes, sir,' she said as she flicked back through the pages of her notebook. 'After you reached the Centurion Labs offices, you left Jags to make contact with the security guard, Rakesh Sharma. It was he who identified Shweta Bhatt . . . He had spotted her on one of the occasions she visited Dr Bhatt during the first secret trip she made to London . . .'

'You wish me to explain again why exactly Sharma failed to inform Inspector Brom-ley that he had recognized Dr Bhatt, is it?'

'No, sir, that I understood: he was concerned that he might be implicated in the conspiracy to help Dr Bhatt evade the police.'

'That . . . and Nikesh Narayan gifted him £500 to keep quiet about his own visits to the apartment to meet Dr Bhatt and Shweta Bhatt, also,' said Puri.

'I see, sir; that I missed somehow, my apologies. But then how did Jags persuade Sharma to break his silence?'

'The two hit it off, actually. They shared the same interests and spoke the same language. It was as simple as that. Once Jags confided in him that Shweta Bhatt was the culprit, then he did the right thing.' Puri paused for a beat. 'Anything else is there, Madam Rani?' he asked.

'Regarding the maid, Savita, sir. My understanding is that she was hired on the basis that she looked somewhat similar to Mrs Bhatt.'

'Correct, some resemblance between the two is there,' said Puri. 'But it was *after* Savita was hired, only, that she was offered so much of money to remain inside the house. Knowing she was being watched, Shweta Bhatt then played the role of the maid herself each and every day, wearing glasses and cheap plastic sandals and all. Thus everyone in the neighbourhood got used to seeing her and came to believe *she* was Savita.'

'But was it Savita who appeared on the balcony in the evening, smoking and looking sad and nervous?' asked Elizabeth Rani.

'Savita made appearances when Shweta Bhatt was in London,' said Puri. 'Also, like I told you previously, no, Savita played a further role by going shopping and meeting with the sister for lunch that one time. Inspector Singh is satisfied she did so out of sympathy for her mistress wanting to visit her husband in secret in London. For Savita, being so young and all, it was something of a game, and she was paid handsomely for playing her part, also. As for the cook and driver and all, they also were unaware of Shweta Bhatt's true intentions. The mali, though, was a different story, he being the one to supply the high-potency aconite.'

Elizabeth Rani's last question concerned Shweta Bhatt and Nikesh Narayan's relationship: 'Did they get involved before or after Dr Bhatt fled India?'

'From what we have learned, Narayan and the Bhatts met socially twice or thrice prior to the scandal,' answered Puri. 'When Dr Bhatt became an absconder, Narayan made contact and offered him sanctuary in the apartment. Also, he made an offer for the illegal purchase of the Dia-Beat research. It would seem he transferred several millions of dollars to an account in Grand Cayman in the Bhatts' names. Then, when Shweta Bhatt was in London, they started up a sex affair. When Dr Bhatt required cash to purchase a new passport through Amul Joshi, The Nexus's man in London, Narayan provided the cash, also, but did not risk going to the Abbey Road house. Instead, he took a room at the Savoy hotel.'

Madam Rani shook her head slowly from side to side, indicating disillusionment on her part. 'How people carry on in this way, I will never know,' she said.

'The worst of human nature on display, we can say, Madam Rani.'

'Had you not been there in London, sir, there can be no doubt Shweta Bhatt would have got away with her husband's murder. It is remarkable how you saw through her deception.'

'You are too kind, Madam Rani,' said Puri, ever appreciative of the praise. 'Truly it was a brilliant plan on her part. Genius, we can say. To pretend to be here in Delhi while murdering her husband in Neasden, London – who could have imagined such a thing in our lifetime?'

Elizabeth Rani returned to her desk in Reception as the market chai wallah arrived with a cutting glass for Puri. He took it to the window to resume watching Iqbal at work. The carpenter was now sitting on his haunches, his elegant face lost in thought as he pondered the design he was to execute. As Puri savoured the perfect blend of cardamon, clove and cinnamon in his chai, as well as the familiar sounds of home – the cawing of crows, the buzz of scooters on the road, devotional songs coming from a distant Gurdwara – he was in no doubt where he belonged and was grateful for it.

Before tackling the pile of messages waiting for him, he decided to put away some of his mementos from London, including the hat box from Bates for his new Sandown, and his gift from Jags.

He had presented it at Heathrow where Puri had found himself in unusually high spirits, despite his fear of flying, even going so far as to hug the young man in thanks before boarding the plane.

Now, Puri picked up the vintage wooden yo-yo, pulled the loop of string over his middle finger and, with a snappy wrist action, spun the toy down towards the floor.

The yo-yo bounced back hard into his hand, and he repeated the action three or four times, smiling with satisfaction.

'Old is gold,' he murmured, borrowing his mother's phrase, before slipping the gift into his pocket for later.

GLOSSARY

AARTI	a Hindu religious ritual of worship; a part of PUJA in which light is offered to one or more deities.
ACHAAR	a pickle; most commonly made of carrot, lime, garlic, cauliflower, chilli or unripe mango, cooked in mustard oil and spices.
ALOO	'potato' in Hindi.
AMBASSADOR	a car that was manufactured by Hindustan Motors from 1957 to 2014, the design based on the old British Morris Oxford.
ARREY	an exclamation of mild irritation, Hindi for 'come on!'
ATTA	wholemeal wheat flour used to make flatbreads.
AUTO	a common abbreviation of auto-rickshaw, a motorized version of the traditional pulled or bicycle rickshaw.
BAJAJ	an Indian multinational conglomerate; its flagship company, Bajaj Auto, is ranked as the world's fourth largest two- and three-wheeler manufacturer.
BARFI	a sweetmeat made from condensed milk and sugar.
BARSATI	from barsaat, meaning rain; a room at the top of the house used for storage or servant quarters.
BETA/BETI	'son', 'daughter' or 'child'.

BHAGWAN OSHO	the late Indian godman and philosopher.
BHOJPURI	an Indo-European language spoken mostly in parts of northern India.
BHUJUDI	shawls woven in the Kutch region of the Indian state of Gujarat.
BIRYANI	a rice-based dish made with spices and meat, fish, eggs or vegetables.
BOMBAY DUCK	a species of lizardfish. When the railways began their journey in India, this fish was transported from Bombay to Calcutta by mail train and became known locally as 'Bombay Mail Fish' or 'Bombay Daak' – Daak meaning mail in Bengali. The term Bombay Duck was later popularized amongst the British public after its appearance in Indian restaurants in the UK.
BRAHMIN	a caste within Hindu society.
CARROM BOARD	a tabletop game of Indian origin in which players flick discs, attempting to knock them to the corners of the flat board.
CHAAT	a mixture of potato pieces, crisp fried bread, gram or chickpeas and tangy-salty spices, with sour Indian chillies and saunth (dried ginger and tamarind sauce), fresh green coriander leaves and yogurt.
CHACHA	a term in the Indian family system for a father's younger brother.
'CHALO'	'let's go' in Hindi.
CHAPPALS	Indian sandals, usually made of leather or rubber.
CHIC	a bamboo blind.

CHICKEN FRANKIE a popular street food that originated in Kolkata, basically a wrap.

CHINAAL a derogatory term in Hindi meaning an immoral or loose woman.

CHOLE BHATURE a dish of spicy chickpeas served with a soft, fluffy deep-fried white bread.

CHOWKIDAAR a watchman.

CHUNNI Punjabi word for a long scarf worn by South Asian women; 'dupatta' in Hindi.

CHURIDAR a style of leg-hugging drawstring PYJAMA with folds that fall around the ankles like a stack of churis, or bracelets.

CHUTNEY a spread made in a wide variety of forms, such as a tomato relish, a ground peanut garnish, spicy coconut, spicy onion, or mint dipping sauce, etc.

'CRIB' Indian English: verb, to complain or grumble.

CRORE a unit in the Indian numbering system, equal to ten million.

CUTTING a small or half glass of chai.

DAAL spiced lentils.

DALIT a caste within Hindu society; once known as 'untouchables', the word means 'suppressed' or 'crushed'.

DESI a loose term that refers to the people, cultures and products of the Indian subcontinent.

DHABA a roadside eatery.

DHARMA a Sanskrit term that refers to a person's righteous duty or any virtuous path.

DHOBI WALLAH	a man or woman who does the laundry.
DHOKLA	a fast food from the western state of Gujarat made with a fermented batter of chickpeas.
DILLI	local parlance for Delhi.
DILRUBAA	'sweetheart' in Hindi.
DIYA	an oil lamp, usually made from clay, with a cotton wick dipped in ghee or vegetable oil.
DOUBLE ROTI	sliced white bread.
DUPATTA	a shawl-like scarf, traditionally worn around the shoulders and head.
FILMI	of or relating to the Indian film industry or Indian films.
GALI	Indian English for a narrow alley.
GILLI DANDA	an ancient sport originating in South Asia. It is played with two sticks – a large one which is used to hit a smaller one. Bears many similarities to cricket and baseball.
GOBI ALOO	a popular potato and cauliflower spiced dish.
GOLGAPPA	a thin fried shell used to hold spicy tamarind water; a very popular street snack.
GOONDA	a hired thug or miscreant.
GOPURAM	a monumental entrance tower, usually ornate, at the entrance of a Hindu temple.
GORA/GORI	a white person.
GOTRA	a term that broadly refers to people who are descendants in an unbroken male line from a common male ancestor.

GUJARATI	a person from the north-western state of Gujarat.
GULAB JAMUN	a dessert made of dough, consisting mainly of milk solids in a sugar syrup; usually flavoured with cardamom seeds and rosewater or saffron.
GURDWARA	in Sikhism, a place of worship.
GUTKA	a preparation of mostly crushed betel nut, tobacco, slaked lime and sweet or savoury flavourings; a milk stimulant.
'HA'	a Hindi exclamation of surprise, joy or grief; the emotions expressed are determined by context.
HALDI	turmeric.
HARYANVI	an Indo-Aryan language spoken primarily in the Indian state of Haryana and the territory of Delhi.
HING	asafoetida.
IDLI	a South Indian savoury cake, consisting of fermented black lentils and rice.
INCHARGE	Indian English for the person in charge, the boss.
JAIN	a small but influential and generally wealthy religious minority with at least ten million followers.
JALDI	Hindi for 'fast'.
JALEBI	a sweet made from batter fried in swirls and then soaked in sugar syrup.
JAMMU	a city in northern India.

'-JI'	a gender-neutral honorific used as a suffix in many languages of the Indian subcontinent, including Hindi and Punjabi; commonly used to show respect.
KABARI	recyclable junk.
KAJAL	kohl or eye liner, originated in India.
KAKORI	a type of very soft Seekh kebab.
KARELA	bitter gourd.
KATHI ROLL	a type of street food similar to a wrap, usually a roti or paratha stuffed with chicken tikka or lamb, onion and green chutney. Originated in Kolkata (Calcutta).
KHANNA	'food' in Hindi.
'KIDDAN?'	'How are you?' in Punjabi.
KIRANA STORE	a small neighbourhood retail store, selling household essentials.
KRISHNA	a Hindu god.
KULFI	milky ice cream, usually flavoured with cardamon and pistachio.
KUMKUMA	a powder used for social and religious markings in India. It is usually made from turmeric, which is dried and powdered with slaked lime, which turns the rich yellow powder red.
KUNDUN	a style of jewellery that can be traced back some 2,500 years.
KURTA	a long collarless shirt, usually worn with PYJAMA.
'KUTTIYA KI AULAD'	'Son of a bitch' in Hindi.

LADOO	flour balls cooked in sugar syrup, often prepared to celebrate festivals or household events such as weddings.
LAKH	a unit of the Indian numbering system equal to 100,000.
LATHI	length of bamboo or cane.
LAXMI	the Hindu goddess of wealth, fortune, prosperity, beauty, fertility, royal power and abundance.
LIZER	Indian English, derived from 'to liaise'.
MAHARASHTRIAN	a person from the Indian western state of Maharashtra.
MALAI	a thick, yellowish, clotted cream; a key ingredient in Indian cooking.
MALI	gardener.
MANDIR	a Hindu temple.
MASALA	any blended mix of spices or herbs.
MASJID	a mosque.
MASSI	a term in the Indian family system for a mother's sister.
MATAR KULCHA	a spicy CHAAT prepared with white peas and topped with chopped onions, tomatoes and tangy chutneys.
MATKA POT	an earthen pot used to store and cool water. It's not unknown to find them outside people's homes for use by strangers.
MEGAHIT	a box-office hit.
MEHNDI	a form of temporary skin decoration using paste created with henna.

'METER DOWN'	Indian English for 'taking a break'.
METRO	Indian English for a city or town.
MIRCHI	chillies or 'spicy'.
MITHAI	confectionery and desserts of the Indian subcontinent.
MOULI	radish.
MULETHI	liquorice.
MUMBAI	the capital city of the state of Maharashtra in western India, formerly known as Bombay.
'NA'	'no?' Or 'isn't it?'
NAAN	a leavened, oven-baked flatbread.
'NAHI'	'no' in Hindi.
NAMASTE	a customary Hindu form of greeting and leave-taking.
NANI	maternal grandmother.
NEHRU JACKET	a hip-length tailored coat for men or women, with a mandarin collar, and with its front modelled on the Indian achkan or sherwani, a garment worn by Jawaharlal Nehru, India's first prime minister.
NETA	a politician.
NEXUS	the term Vish Puri uses for what he cites as a loose network of politicians, bureaucrats, business interests and national and local crime syndicates who look to their own interests and stifle economic and social development.
NIMBOO MIRCHI	a string of lemon and chillies; an evil-eye averter.

ODISHA	a state in south-eastern India.
PAALAK PANEER	spinach with Indian cottage cheese.
PAAN	a betel leaf, stuffed with betel nut, lime and other condiments; used as a stimulant.
PAAPRI CHAAT	a North Indian fast food. 'Chaat' means lick; 'paapri' refers to crispy fried dough wafers made from refined white flour. The paapris are served with boiled potatoes, boiled chickpeas, chillies, yogurt, tamarind chutney and CHAAT MASALA.
PAGAL	'crazy' in Hindi.
PAGE THREE PEOPLE	Indian English for the glamorous 'in-crowd'.
PAGRI	a turban.
PAISA	one hundredth of a rupee.
PAKORAS	a deep fried snack made with vegetables dipped in a gram flour batter.
PANDIT	a Pundit is a Brahmin scholar or teacher in any field of knowledge in Hinduism. The term Pandit is used to refer to the (Brahmin) Hindus from the Indian state of Jammu and Kashmir. Most of those from the Kashmir Valley fled in the 1990s owing to the growth of Islamic militancy.
PANI	water.
PARATHAS	a flat, pan-fried wheat bread, often stuffed with spiced potato, cauliflower or cottage cheese and eaten at breakfast.
PEG	a measure of liquor.

PEON	a low-ranking worker such as an attendant, orderly, or assistant.
PHAL	'flower' in Hindi.
PORTABLE	a mobile or cell phone.
PUJA	an act of worship.
'PUKKA'	a Hindi word meaning 'solid', 'well made'. Also used to mean 'definitely' or 'absolutely'.
PUNKA	a fan that hangs from the ceiling.
PYJAMA	lightweight trousers fitted with a drawstring waistband.
RANGOLI	patterns created using materials such as dry rice flour, coloured sand and flower petals, etc. Commonly made on the threshold of the main entrance to a house to welcome Lakshmi, the goddess of wealth and good luck.
ROGAN JOSH	a Kashmiri dish made with lamb or goat and a rich gravy flavoured with garlic, ginger and various spices.
ROTI	an unleavened bread made from ATTA – stone-ground wholemeal flour. A ROOMALI roti is wafer thin.
RUMBLE TUMBLE EGGS	Indian English for scrambled eggs.
SAALA KUTTA	a common insult taken to mean 'damn dog' or 'lowdown dog'.
'SAALE'	a derogatory term, expression of disgust.
'SAB CHANGA'	Punjabi for 'all is well?'
SABZI	vegetables.

SAFARI SUIT	a lightweight safari jacket, usually khaki in colour, with a self-belt, epaulettes, four or more expandable bellows pockets and sometimes cartridge loops; worn with paired trousers.
SAHIB	an Urdu honorific now used across South Asia as a term of respect, equivalent to the English 'sir'.
SALAA	a term in Hindi for a wife's brother, but also a common insult.
SAMBAR	a South Indian spicy and sour lentil dish.
SARDAAR-JI JOKES	Sardaar is a term used to refer to male Sikhs. Sardaar jokes are a class of jokes based on stereotypes of Sikhs.
'SAT SRI AKAL'	a Punjabi salutation, meaning 'God is the ultimate truth'.
SATTE PE SATTA	a popular Indian card game.
SCOOTIE	Indian English for a scooter or motorbike.
SEPOY	the lowest enlisted rank in the Indian infantry.
SHIKHARA	a Sanskrit word translating literally as 'mountain peak'; it refers to the rising tower in the Hindu temple architecture of north India.
SHIVA	a Hindu god.
SHRI	Mr in many Indian languages, a polite form of address.
SIGRI	a rudimentary stove or barbecue.
SONF	fennel seeds.
SUPARI	slang for 'contract killer' or 'hitman'; also refers to the payment made for a contract killing.

'SUWAR KI AULAD'	'son of a hog' in Hindi.
'TEEK HOON'	'I'm fine' in Hindi.
TEMPO	a generic term for a van or small vehicle used to transport general goods.
THALI	a round platter for serving food; also a meal made up of a selection of dishes served on a platter.
TILAKA	a symbol or mark applied to the forehead by Hindus.
'TIMEPASS'	Indian English for spending time doing something that does not require effort, like watching TV.
TOPI	a hat.
TOPPER	Indian English for a student who gets the highest grades.
UTTAR PRADESH	a state in north India, the most populous in the country.
VEDIC MANTRA	a sacred utterance (syllable, word, or verse) that is considered to possess mystical or spiritual efficacy and features in the Vedas.
WALLAH	a generic term for a person concerned or involved with a specified activity or business, i.e. a sabzi wallah sells vegetables, a pressing wallah irons clothes.
'YAAR'	equivalent to 'pal', 'mate' or 'dude'.